His American Detective

Summer Devon

2017

Dedication

For Gillian, because she's a good egg.

Prologue
1874

Young Edmund overheard the murmurs from adults. He caught his old name: *Poor Little Ned...the only survivor...that hideous murder*. But then someone would immediately shush the conversation—usually Papa Sloan.

Only once during those early years did someone come right out and ask. In the school's refectory, a new student slid onto the polished bench next to Edmund and, after prayers, introduced himself as Wensler. He picked up his spoon and, between bites of soupy porridge asked, "You're truly Lawton? My mum told me you would be in my year. She said what happened to your family was in all the papers. Even though it was ages and ages ago."

Edmund's stomach squeezed tight. "Years ago."

"Want to hear what my mother told me?"

Edmund didn't want to know. He needed to know. He couldn't help himself—he nodded.

Wensler spoke with relish. "It all happened in the dining room, she told me."

Edmund waited, unable to eat another bite of lukewarm mush. He always had trouble eating at these long tables amongst the crowds of boys, in the air that smelled of burnt toast and sweat, but now his throat closed entirely. The students hadn't been dismissed from breakfast, so he couldn't run away from this conversation.

"The papers said the whole room was all over blood." Wensler, pale and skinny, had a wide mouth and restless hands that he used to build the scene in the air in front of him. "The bodies were on chairs pushed into the table. A grand table in a huge grand dining room. All set up like they were eating, but it was bits of their body they were eating. The eyes were all out."

Edmund couldn't move or speak. After a moment, Wensler went on. "I wager the article didn't say what parts they were eating. Do you know?"

Edmund shook his head.

"I suppose hands or feet?" Wensler gestured to his face and his too-wide mouth. "Shoved right down their throats."

Edmund had a fleeting glimpse of something even worse, so much worse, and he punched the boy hard on the shoulder to keep him from saying another word.

"Ow, hey," Wensler yelped. Up and down the table, chatter stopped and boys watched, amazed, for Edmund was the best-behaved boy in the school. Despite the attack, Wensler didn't lunge at Edmund. No teachers had seen the incident, and Wensler didn't report Edmund.

That was the end of the matter.

Except not entirely, for during his next holiday, Edmund made the mistake of going to the library and asking Papa Sloan about the bodies posed at the table. Papa Sloan carefully lowered the book he held. He stood and motioned to the door. "It's nothing for little boys to think of. You should go to your room now."

That cold disapproval added fuel to Edmund's bad dreams. He woke sweating and whimpering he'd lost another home. Never mind that he'd tried to be a perfect student, a perfect foster son—he'd failed. They would take him away, and he'd lose everything again.

That same holiday, on his last full day, he listened to another conversation—he had become adept at creeping about the house and eavesdropping—between Mother Sloan and her bosom friend. "One shall miss him when he returns to school. He is a quiet, agreeable child," she told her friend.

With that, Edmund became nearly happy. After he returned to school, he even sought out Wensler to beg his pardon for hitting him.

"But you don't want to tell me about the Dreadful Scene of the Terrible Murder?" Wensler asked, obviously disappointed.

A wave of nausea shook Edmund so he had trouble speaking. He forgot his agreeable nature. "If you talk about it again, I'll beat you senseless."

Within weeks, his lost family sank back into the past where it belonged, though several years later, he wondered if that event in his past had turned him into a deviant. But by then Edmund knew better than to express such troublesome thoughts to anyone, even his now-close friend, Wensler. He remained silent as the Lawtons' tomb.

Chapter One

Ten years later, London

The source of information in London had clammed up entirely, not even returning wire messages, so Patrick persuaded his boss at the inquiry agency to let him go find answers in person. The similarities in the murders had to be worth a trip overseas, he told Mr. Greene, and the agency's New York clients agreed.

If he were right, he'd prove himself to Mr. Greene. And maybe he'd get a chance to thumb his nose at the cops. Past time to put out the small fire of rage still burning inside him after his abridged career with the New York Police Department.

He got off the train from Liverpool and made his way to the London inquiry office without taking the time to look around the city. The British agent, a gray-haired man whose walrus-mustache ends dangled past his chin, sat behind his desk and didn't budge from the position he'd stated in his letter. "I have nothing more to report. The gentlemen in question refuse to see us."

"You won't even go to the house to request an interview from Edmund Lawton?" Patrick almost slipped and called him Poor Little Ned.

The ends of the man's mustache quivered and his round face flushed. "He is Mr. Sloan. He hasn't used that other name since he was a small child. And no, we sent a note and were refused. We will not take steps that'll seriously annoy him. Our company's standing is at risk. He or his foster father could persuade our clients we're unethical."

"God save you from the wrath of an irked wealthy man," Patrick said. "He won't invite you to his next dinner party."

Patrick said good-bye and left before the man had an apoplectic fit.

Since he didn't have any appointments until the next day, Patrick went to a library to discover more about the horrible murders from the past—stories from this side of the ocean. And he was direly curious why the two Mr. Sloans wielded so much power in society. He didn't find anything new. The foster father, a lawyer, had appeared in newspaper stories and society columns, attending all sorts of highfalutin events until he'd grown ill a year ago.

The younger Sloan had always been a recluse and was rarely mentioned in those endless lists of party-goers. Lawton/Sloan apparently belonged to a number of clubs and was on all sorts of committees. Neither seemed the kind of men to break legs if things didn't go their way. But what did Patrick know of wealthy men?

Maybe they dispatched their enemies as often as dockworkers, but with more finesse and discretion.

The next morning, he took the time to be a tourist only long enough to walk several miles from his hotel to the home of Mr. Edmund Sloan, born Ned Lawton, a man only two years Patrick's senior, who had spent more money on just this one London address than Patrick would earn in his lifetime. And, ha, the man had another house in the country.

Sloan had lived through hell but now lived in paradise, if a looming townhouse in London fit anyone's version of heaven.

Every inch of Lawton/Sloan's small corner of the city seemed to have been scrubbed clean by an army of servants. Even the potted topiary trees out front of the carved granite steps didn't have a polished leaf out of place.

Poor little rich boy, Patrick thought as he slapped the gleaming brass knocker against the sky-blue door. A guy in tails answered the door. Patrick's very first real English butler. He snapped the man a salute. "I'm here to see Mr. Sloan."

The butler didn't look him up and down, nothing so vulgar. His gaze flickered, though. "What name shall I give?"

"I'm Mr. Kelly, late of New York, on an official investigation." In his old life, he would have pulled out his badge, but he worked for Mr. Greene's private company now and had nothing to show other than a commanding air, which he hoped he could still manage.

"If you would leave your card, sir?"

"No, don't have one," he lied. "And tell him I can wait as long as it takes. I need to see him."

The butler led him into a huge room, all marble, dark wood, and a roaring fire. "Please wait here."

Alone, Patrick pulled off his hat and threw it on a chair. Why would he be allowed run of the house? And then he noticed a burly man standing in the corner, his feet shoulder width apart, his hands behind his back. He had the blank face of a cop or a vagrant, only with a better haircut.

Patrick wandered over. "My guess is you're a footman."

Still staring into the distance, the man gave a tiny nod.

"Ha! Wonderful. What's your name?"

"Liam, sir."

"Irish?"

Liam's mouth went thin, and for a moment, his eyes shifted to Patrick. "No sir."

Apparently even the question was an insult. Patrick's mother might give the man a good talking-to. As it was, Patrick felt the need to prod more, just for the sake of entertainment. He already knew that Mr. Sloan was a well-liked young man with many friends and no enemies, other than anyone who tried to talk to him about his past.

He gazed around at all the knickknacks and statues and thought about the man with no enemies. How had a man as rich as Sloan managed that?

Mr. Edmund Sloan gave to charity. He attended the opera, plays, musical fetes, dances, but he didn't sit down to dine with anyone, not even at his two clubs. Before they'd clammed up, the British inquiry agency had reported that Sloan must live on air.

Patrick asked Liam, "How do you like working for Mr. Sloan?"

"Fine, sir." Liam's gaze shifted to the door. He obviously longed for the butler to return and rescue him. Which, of course, made Patrick all the more interested in quizzing him.

"Have you been here long?"

"Three years, sir."

"Mr. Sloan is a good employer?"

"None better, sir."

"And the pay is good?"

Again the mouth went thin and the eyes grew cold. Patrick had been warned that talk of money was uncultured. "There are no positions open at the time," Liam said, showing real emotion at last. "And if you wanted to work for Mr. Sloan, you would apply to Mr. Becker, the butler, and enter through the side door, the servants' entrance."

That explained the sudden hostility. "Whoops. I'm here for Sloan, not Becker. But I'll keep your advice in mind." He wandered over to an ornate display case and examined the pottery behind the glass. It looked ugly to him, all giant blue and red and green Chinese things. On the mantel, a gold-and-china clock ticked, and a bulging-eyed silver cow stood next to that. Sloan might be wealthy, but his taste ran to froufrou junk.

He grabbed one of the heavier sculptures of a mother and child.

"This one is a tad nicer," he remarked to the footman. "Even though they look feeble-minded, the way they're goggling at each other."

Liam actually took a step forward. "Sir. That's a very valuable piece."

"Really." Patrick turned it over to examine its base. "Looks like something that I could win on the boardwalk at Coney Island."

"I have a Dalou, if you prefer something more modern." The cultured voice came from a man standing in the doorway. He and Patrick might be about the same age, but this man had scads more sophistication, which made him seem ancient in a way—timeless. Wealth at a glance at forty paces. The impression came from all the details added up: a fine gray suit, elegant hands, glossy dark hair, and a patronizing smirk.

"Please put that down," Mr. Supercilious said.

Patrick took another second to look at the sculpture—just to show he wasn't about to take orders. He needed this guy, though, and when he put the thing back on the mantel, he did so with care. He went to Sloan and stuck out his hand.

"Patrick Kelly from New York."

Sloan stared at his outstretched hand before at last giving it a short, firm shake. The strength in his fingers surprised Patrick. Then Sloan took a step away and put his hands at his back. Did he avoid touch, or had he been trained to use parade rest?

"Why are you here in London, Mr. Kelly?" Mr. Sloan's directness suited Patrick just fine.

"To see you, Mr. Sloan," he said. He dropped his voice. "Or, I should say, Mr. Lawton."

Patrick appreciated the way the man fought surprise and nearly won—a fast pucker of eyebrows, a mouth squeezed tight. Sloan had nothing on the butler when it came to hiding emotion.

Sloan must have sent some signal behind his back, because the footman crossed the room and left, closing the door silently behind him.

Patrick tensed when the expression on Sloan's face shifted to something more vivid—the dark eyes filled with anger. The illustrations Patrick had seen of Poor Ned Lawton from years ago had caught the shape of those eyes, rimmed by lashes almost as extravagant as the boy had had. That must have been a nuisance for him with other boys.

"How much do you want?" Sloan asked.

"Huh?"

"To keep your mouth closed. How many pounds? No doubt some dreadful publication has set you on my trail, but I'll pay more to kill the story. What's your price? And I'll add a bonus if you give me your publisher's name."

"Didn't your butler tell you? I'm an investigator from New York. We sent someone from London around to talk to you, but you refused to see him. And apparently he's too frightened of you and your foster father to be pushy. I'm not afraid."

Sloan raised his chin and narrowed his eyes. He still looked handsome rather than threatening. "I am not an idiot, sir. How much will it take? Is that why you were examining the Terrinoni sculpture? Will that suffice to keep you quiet? Take it and go away."

"Mr. Lawton—"

"I am *Sloan*." He snarled the words.

"And I am not lying. I really am an investigator. I'm looking into some murders in New York."

"You're already facing difficulties," Sloan snapped.

"What do you mean?"

"You apparently don't realize New York is in the United States, not Great Britain."

Patrick laughed at the unexpected flash of humor from this man, even if the joke was stupid.

Lawton said, "I'm serious. I've never been to New York and have nothing to offer. The person who was responsible for the Lawton affair died years ago in prison. He admitted to committing the crimes. Why would any investigator wish to unearth the matter now?"

Good. Lawton/Sloan seemed more curious than outraged now. Patrick reached for the papers he'd put in his inside jacket pocket. "We have a theory now that Weller, the man who died in prison, did not work alone. I need to see if any details of the murder scenes I'm investigating match the scene of your family's death."

Sloan took a step back, almost stumbling over a large chair near the fire. "No. The killer is dead and buried. You don't need me. If you're so fascinated by the details, read the newspaper accounts from that time."

"Not every detail showed up in the papers. I just need a quick comparison. I've read the public records and the official reports, and here's the thing. The similarities between that murder and the more recent ones are pretty compelling."

"Weller must have been alone." He pinched the bridge of his nose hard. "If you want to pursue this nonsense, feel free to waste your time. Look at the police reports. You need *nothing* from me."

It finally dawned on Patrick that fear rather than anger propelled this Lawton. Poor Edmund Lawton had been about five the night his family died.

Just like that, Patrick abandoned his hostility for the man, despite Lawton's wealth and sneering. Patrick suddenly wanted to pull the pale creature into a comforting hug.

Patrick knew his world could be simplistic, the way it often divided into two easy-to-spot camps: oppressors and victims. He was firmly on the side of the victims, of course, and handsome, wealthy Mr. Lawton/Sloan had stepped over the line to huddle with the masses.

"Of course a man wouldn't want to revisit the worst nightmare of his life. I wouldn't ask if I could find someone else"—*Oh, very clever, Patrick, remind him he's the sole survivor. That should soothe him*—"but if I'm right and one of the people who did this is still killing people, I need all the help I can find."

"You must look elsewhere for your help." Lawton/Sloan walked over to the door and opened it. "Please leave now."

"Mr. Sloan. No one has asked you for any details in the past, at least not on any official records. No one. Yet you must have seen something."

"Nonsense." But Sloan's voice quavered, and his already pale skin went whiter. "Nothing. They caught the man, and they didn't need me. I wasn't there."

Patrick riffled the papers in his hand. "I've read the inspector's report. You had blood on you, sir. No one could accuse a small five-year-old child of setting that stage. But you wandered onto it at some point."

"No." The man lunged away. Patrick thought he was running from the room, but he grabbed a chair and eased onto it.

"Are you going to faint, Mr. Sloan?"

*

It had been so long since he'd had to fight off the ridiculous cowardice.

"I'm not going to swoon," Edmund said peevishly.

He felt sick but even more disturbing was the rage coursing through him. He longed to rip this man to shreds. *Pieces. Of bodies.*

He imagined plowing a fist into Kelly's face. The last time he'd hit someone had been more than ten years earlier.

He and Wensler had become best of friends after that, but Edmund would never be friendly with this idiot American.

"Mr. Sloan?" Patrick Kelly stood too near him. "Here, let me show you this."

Oh Lord, no. Could this Patrick Kelly have found the other culprit? No, no, there wasn't another.

"Mr. Sloan?"

"I am not going to look at your blasted papers. Reporter or investigator, whatever you may be."

"It's not a report. It's a letter from my boss."

Rather than open his mouth and risk screaming or worse, Edmund took the paper and scanned the words. The bearer of this paper, Patrick Kelly, had been dispatched on behalf of Greene Investigations. Edmund swallowed and managed to speak. "You're not from the police, then?"

"A family of one set of victims hired us."

The faintness and nausea had passed, and Edmund straightened in the chair. He didn't rise to his feet, though—he'd be nearly chest to chest with Kelly if he did. "Could you move, Mr. Kelly? You're crowding me."

"Sure. If you're fine?"

"My health is not your concern." He folded up the paper and handed it back.

"You believe I'm not a newspaper reporter?"

"Yes, but that doesn't change my answer to you."

Kelly walked away. For a happy second, he appeared to be heading out the door. No, he grabbed a chair—a heavy wood-and-padded chair he carried as if it weighed next to nothing. He plonked it next to Edmund's and sat as if settling in for a cozy chat.

"Mr. Sloan, you hide yourself well."

"Apparently not well enough."

Kelly reacted as if Edmund had made a joke. He had one of those smiles that brought laugh lines into sharp relief and lifted his face into magnificence. He'd been too good-looking already, blue eyes, dark hair, pale skin, a round chin, and a full lower lip. That expression made Patrick Kelly into something Edmund thoroughly resented—and he couldn't look away.

"I found you, but others might not. Greene Investigations has resources," Kelly said. "My point is I understand how much you value your privacy and that you don't want to be associated with what happened to your parents and sisters."

Was the bastard threatening him with blackmail? Edmund pulled in a long breath and shifted his gaze to the fire. "My parents are Mr. and Mrs. Sloan. I have no sisters."

Absurd to give this automatic response to a man who knew his secret. Edmund waited for Kelly's ridicule or the threat.

Instead, Kelly only nodded. "Edmund Lawton died that night, then? In a manner of speaking?"

No, he survived, the little rotter. "Yes, that's right," Edmund said cautiously. Yet the investigator's statement had a ring of truth after all. Edmund, once known as Ned Lawton, hadn't died that night, but soon after—when Mr. Sloan had taken him in.

Several days after his family died came a far smaller loss, one he barely noticed. Ned became Edmund. Mr. Sloan had insisted the name didn't fit. Strangers might call him Poor Little Ned, but nobody who actually knew him called him by that nickname again. Mr. Sloan, always formal and kind and always calm...except perhaps that one time.

The investigator's presence brought back too much. Papa Sloan's expression of horror as he reached to pick up Edmund—had that been to haul him up from the bloody table? That came from a dream. Papa Sloan hadn't been at the scene—neither he nor Edmund had been...

Edmund wet his lips. Another person had been there? When Kelly had said there had been two perpetrators, the expression *the other shoe has dropped* came into his mind. He hadn't been as shocked as he should have been.

Weller hadn't been alone. This man had come to his house now to find another killer.

Now Edmund felt as frozen and compelled as he'd been that morning with Wensler in the school's refectory. "Where was the blood?"

Kelly's dark brows went up. He leafed through the papers on his lap. "Everywhere. Some had been put in teacups and—"

"No! No." Edmund lowered his voice. "I mean where was the blood on young Lawton?"

"On his nightshirt and his foot. And a few small footprints."

He used third person for Lawton. Mr. Kelly wasn't as much of a brute as he'd first seemed.

Still, Edmund could not, would not, open that box in his mind any wider. He'd lose everything. "I can't help you."

"I could give you some descriptions, see if you find anything familiar in the other homicide scenes."

More than the man's obnoxious persistence, that last word seemed to punch Edmund in the chest. Because he'd said *scenes*, plural—more than one horrific incident had taken place. More people had died, and his nightmares might be coming to life.

He didn't want to hear any sort of description of murders. The thought nauseated him. But killing had happened again, and he couldn't ignore Kelly now, no matter how much he longed to, no matter how insufferably pushy the man might be. "How many times?"

"Three. Two in New York, one in Boston. A total of seven victims. We've been hired by one of the New York families. You haven't heard of these murders? They've made it into the British press. Our local agent sent us the clippings. The man you refused to see?"

Edmund shook his head. "I had no idea. I have an assistant to deal with any inquiries." And curse the man for going out of town for a wedding.

"Of course you would," the detective muttered.

Edmund didn't know what that meant, so he went on. "I avoid even glancing at articles with headlines with words such as 'gruesome' or 'murder' or 'hideous deaths.'"

The detective nodded. "That makes sense."

Edmund could breathe easily again. He still resented this man's intrusion, but the past was slinking back into the shadows. "I find it hard to believe there's any connection to the Lawton family. That event occurred more than a dozen years ago and outside of London."

Kelly leaned forward, elbows on knees, an informal hunch. "I have read the reports from the authorities, Mr. Sloan. Parts of the reports were secret. Details were not repeated in the press because they were so…offensive."

"What body parts do you suppose they ate?" Wensler had asked

Kelly went on, "But those same specific details were repeated in the American murders. Do you see? Someone who had firsthand knowledge of the Lawton event is now killing people in the US. Or maybe it's one of the investigators or a witness. We need all the help we can get to find the killer."

The Lawton deaths were very old news, Edmund reminded himself. Never mind that after all these years, simple talk could send him careening into a near swoon. Never mind that there could be another perpetrator.

What more embarrassing thing could happen if he explored the forbidden past? It wasn't as if he'd die. He wouldn't be dragged to the table and slaughtered.

Edmund felt a kick of frustration. Come, frustration must be an improvement—it might drive out the terror.

Papa Sloan had said don't talk about it. *Don't think about it.* All these years, Edmund had stayed true to his promise he wouldn't. But that vow had been made before someone asked for help…Kelly asked not out of morbid curiosity but because he required assistance.

"Mr. Sloan?" Kelly's voice broke into his peculiar, disjointed thoughts. "Is that some kind of whisky or something in that decanter? Do you need something to drink? You're awfully pale."

"No." He shook his head.

"Should I come back another day?"

"I will try to help you if I can. Now." He wanted this man gone.

"That's the boy!" Kelly said enthusiastically.

Edmund concentrated on Kelly's smile, until he realized he was staring at the other man's lips.

"You sure you don't want something to drink?" Kelly asked.

For the first time since he'd entered the room, Edmund felt like laughing. "Good heavens. I've just realized that ought to be my question. Would you care for some tea?"

No, that was a mistake. He shouldn't treat an investigator as a guest. The man would be more at home eating with the servants in the kitchens.

"Sure, thanks," Kelly said, so Edmund had to rise to his feet and walk to the bell. At least he felt as steady as usual now.

Now that he'd offered Mr. Kelly food and drink, Edmund would be stuck with him for at least another half hour. They'd talk about the day the Lawtons had died. Another wave of dizziness hit him, but Edmund would be damned if his body's strange response would control him.

When Becker appeared almost at once, Edmund considered requesting hot food for Kelly—a laborer might enjoy the fare of high tea—but that would take more time. The less time the man remained, the better. "Also a selection of cakes and perhaps a few sandwiches. Nothing elaborate."

"Yes, sir." Becker took a second to examine the visitor. No one else would have noticed the pause, but Edmund knew his butler—and he could tell by the quirk of his mouth that Becker strongly disapproved of Patrick Kelly. Too rough? Too loud? Was the disapproval simply because Edmund entertained him like a gentleman? Edmund wished he could simply ask, but he knew better than to gossip with the servants.

Mr. Kelly's dark blue suit and frock coat couldn't be called elegant and had probably not been made for him, yet he presented a reasonably sober and businesslike appearance. If it weren't for his size and breezy manner, and accent, he could be mistaken for a professor over from Trinity College in Dublin. Once he walked or opened his mouth or slouched in a chair, however, that impression was lost.

The trays of food were soon delivered. Edmund dismissed Liam, Becker, and Joseph as soon as they set the small table for tea. He held a cup and saucer and didn't even pretend to eat.

Mr. Kelly ate enough for two of them.

"This is excellent, thank you," Mr. Kelly said after he'd consumed nearly all the sandwiches and cakes. "Are you sure you don't want anything? Oh, wait! I recall you don't eat in strange company, and I guess I count as a stranger."

Edmund drank his tea and didn't answer. What else did the intrusive stranger know about him?

"From what I understand, that and your reclusive nature are your only eccentricities. Pretty good, considering your past. And avoiding dining with others makes sense too."

And, for the first time, the pieces fell into place. Edmund understood as well. How ridiculously simple the explanation. Why had he never seen it for himself? The dining room. That night and food, a link he hadn't seen, despite the obvious truth.

A link had been formed—very well, he would break it. For a moment, his throat closed again. He coughed.

"It is a choice," he lied to Kelly, his unwelcome guest. "Nothing to do with my past."

He didn't even bother with a plate but simply plucked a small sandwich from the pile and put it in his mouth. It tasted of dust and cement, but he chewed, swallowed, and said, "See?"

A sense of pure triumph chased away nausea. The next time his parents invited him to dine with strangers, he would do more than simply cut and mangle the food on his plate. They'd be astonished, and their one complaint about their foster son would be silenced.

A grown man needn't woo his family, he reminded himself. An adult could be less eager to please.

The private inquiry agent watched him intently, like a cat taking position outside a mouse's nest. That hungry gleam irritated Edmund.

He said, "Surely you didn't sail all the way across the ocean just to talk to me."

"I want to check all possible details of the Lawton case, and some of the police reports and other material can only be examined here in London. I'd hoped you'd be able to come with me."

"Never. Not if my life depended on it."

Kelly chuckled as if he'd said something funny. "All right, all right, Mr. Sloan. I won't force you. And no one else will either. Apparently, the police are scared of you."

"I beg your pardon?"

"Part of the reason I'm here today is that I couldn't get anyone in the whole blasted country of England to come to your house and talk to you about your past." Kelly put his empty plate on the table. "I'm not sure who you paid off or threatened, but I'll bet it must have been some tidy payment to shut them all down."

Edmund's palms had grown damp, and he rubbed them over his thighs. He hadn't spoken to any representative of the law about Ned Lawton for years. Not since he was a child. Papa Sloan... But why would he go through so much effort to protect Edmund now that he was an adult?

"You exaggerate," Edmund said.

"Probably a little." Kelly leaned forward and held Edmund's attention. His hunter's gaze would see far too much, yet Edmund couldn't look away. Kelly said, "But I'm not lying. I wrote to the metropolitan police and two private agencies, and they refused to contact you. They said you threatened them."

Edmund shook his head.

"No? You're still not going to cooperate?"

He had to speak. More people had died, and he must answer this man's questions. He had to clear his throat again. "No, that's not it. I have never instructed the police or anyone other than the press to leave me alone. And I've never threatened anyone with more than expulsion from my home."

Kelly's eyes sparkled with obvious amusement. "Well, well. Isn't that interesting. The one person who was willing to write to me seemed to think the prohibition and bullying came from you."

"What did he say?"

Kelly opened the packet and rummaged around. He pulled out a grubby bit of paper and handed it over. "A police constable. You'll forgive me if I don't show you his name and address." The page, part of a letter, had been written in a rounded hand.

I showed your missive to several of my superiors. The detective I talked to was told we should not bother the gentleman named Mr. Sloan, who you say is poor Little Ned Lawton. We are not to open the case despite the information you shared with us. I am curious, as you can imagine. I must believe money has changed hands, tho I dare not say more. If you find out anything, I hope you will send a note. Best to send it to my home address.

Edmund read and quickly put down the paper so Kelly wouldn't notice the faint tremor in his hand. "Likely this man imagines conspiracies behind every potted palm." He was about to say something about those who resent the wealthier members of society, but he suspected Mr. Kelly might also be one of those.

Mr. Kelly ignored his remark. "If you didn't stamp your foot and demand silence, then who did on your behalf?"

He wasn't ready to answer that question, not yet. Not until he'd had a chance to speak to his father.

Chapter Two

Patrick had been prepared to dislike the wealthy Mr. Edmund Sloan, but he couldn't hate him despite his best effort. The heir's entitled manner seemed more like a dread of the past than snobbery. Patrick couldn't even loathe him for his good looks—they didn't have that exaggerated winsomeness of the old etchings of Poor Little Ned Lawton. This adult version of Ned/Edmund had grown into those eyelashes and large dark eyes all those drawings had shown. The rounded cheeks had given way to hard angles in a thin face, though the Cupid's bow mouth still had a strong indentation on the upper lip.

Despite his confident and well-groomed exterior, the gentleman's hands trembled with any mention of the Lawton case. Ned Sloan was frightened, and that intrigued Patrick. More than just fear of the past, he likely had a secret—probably the identity of the person who'd forced law enforcement to stay away from Edmund Sloan.

Patrick would put his money on the lawyer who'd taken in the boy after the murder. "Say, I know you took his name, but how come Lawyer Sloan didn't formally adopt you?"

The way Sloan started, Patrick knew he'd hit on the truth of who Sloan might be thinking about.

"That's quite a personal question," he sputtered.

"Yep." Patrick waited.

"It has nothing to do with your investigation."

"I'm a curious person."

"An intrusive one."

"Of course. I'd be a rotten investigator if I wasn't."

The hint of a smile flashed across Mr. Sloan's face. "There is a good reason he did not formally adopt me."

He told Patrick some peculiar story about the Lawton inheritance and Sloan's unwillingness to touch it. "He is my father," Sloan finished. "There might not be legal papers to prove it, but he has always been my father."

"No, not always," Patrick said.

"Nearly as long as I can remember."

"Nearly, you say? That must mean you do have some memories of life before that night."

Sloan scowled. His shoulders-back, chin-high gentleman's posture seemed to melt a little, as if he slid into himself.

No one should hide from memories the way this Sloan did. But it wasn't Patrick's job to drag the poor man to the truth. He only needed some details of that day, but that would be kicking a puppy at this point.

Patrick sighed and gave up. "If you want to toss me out on my ear now, I won't protest. I guess I'll look for answers elsewhere."

"I said..." Sloan stopped and drew in a breath. "More people have died. I must help. If there was some connection...and I ran away—that would be selfish."

Patrick reached over and put a consoling hand on Sloan's arm. Bad idea. Under his palm lay surprisingly firm muscle and heat—and all sorts of images and ideas flooded his mind. *Pull him over onto your lap. A long embrace will help you both.*

He'd long ago shut away that nonsense and spent very little time regretting his misdirected instincts. Life was too short and interesting to moan about such things. But sometimes when lust woke up and picked out a particular fellow, his mind got clouded. Patrick didn't want that now, and not with this man.

"Right, good." What were they talking about again? He shifted away and became the awkward one in the room—unusual for him. "Thank you for helping. Um… You don't need to see the illustrations. All thirdhand drawings, at any rate. No artists or photographers visited the scene."

Sloan folded his arms over his chest. "Perhaps the reports are exaggerated."

"Sorry, no. Not from what I've read and heard. Many of the same descriptions come up in the reports." He didn't look down at the paper. He didn't need to. Instead, he watched Sloan's pale face. "In the attack on the Americans, all of their faces were mutilated…"

"The eyes were gouged and laid out," Sloan whispered. He closed his own eyes for a long moment. "That was from my…past. I'm not sure where I heard that detail. I must have gotten it from Wensler."

"Who's that? An officer who'd been on the case?"

"No. A boy I was at school with. He insisted on approaching me and talking about the Lawtons. I didn't even know him then."

"Was his father a police officer or inspector?"

Another ghost of a smile touched the corners of his full mouth. It took a sharp eye to see emotion on Edmund Sloan's face. "The school I attended had no sons of police officers or even inspectors. His father was a wealthy merchant, I believe. Wensler was considered highly vulgar by my classmates."

"Ah. So no one you associated with."

"He eventually became my best friend."

"Interesting that the one pushing person would end up your friend. But here's something even more interesting. That detail about the eyes being laid out in a row was not mentioned in any newspaper stories. If you know it, you probably didn't learn it from your boyhood friend." Patrick waited, but the man only stared at him. In a soft voice, Patrick said, "I suspect you saw it, sir."

"Dear God," Sloan whispered. He rose to his feet. No more subtle emotion—his face had gone pale as milk. Patrick sprang up, ready to grab him should he fall.

Sloan managed to steady himself—but a tear ran down from the corner of his eye. Patrick silently cursed. He'd hurt someone who'd done nothing to deserve it. Never mind the fact that Patrick had to gain information—or perhaps the man's pain wasn't real—he fought the urge to say *never mind all this; I'll go now.* Being a tender-heart could be a nuisance sometimes.

"Aw hell," he said. "I'm sorry you have to face that night again."

That stiffened the gentleman's backbone. "There is absolutely nothing wrong," he said stiff and correct. "You have no reason to worry about me."

31

Patrick reached over and touched the trace of a tear with his forefinger. "It's fine," he said. "I won't tell anyone."

And he did the one thing he'd already dismissed as lunatic. He pulled Mr. Edmund Sloan into a hug—not the hail-fellow-well-met sort of hearty embrace, but something far more gentle, without so much as a slap on the back.

"Mr. Kelly, you are absurd. You forget yourself." Yet Sloan didn't push away. All right, Patrick liked the feel of the man, just a bit taller but more slender than himself, skinny, even. For a moment, Sloan rested against him, only a second and his breath came faster.

He held on through several heartbeats, only dropping his arms when Sloan pushed against him.

"Sorry," Patrick said, without feeling a bit of remorse. But seeing the stricken look in Sloan's eyes, he did feel a bit sorry after all. "Aw, no, don't tell me my poor attempt to offer comfort has made the whole thing worse."

"No, no." Sloan backed away and put a chair between them. He glared.

Patrick raised his hands, palms out. "I won't assault you again, I promise."

"That is correct. You won't."

"At least you're not sad or afraid anymore. You're just angry."

Sloan shook his head. He did that a lot. A few seconds passed, marked by the tick of a clock somewhere in the room. "You are one of the strangest men I've ever met." Sloan sounded nearly steady again, though hardly friendly.

"Ill-bred, I'll bet you'd say," Patrick said.

Sloan only raised his eyebrows.

"Just occurred to me. You liked that Wenceslaus character you went to school with, so I must be the sort you're attracted to for friendship."

"Mr. Kelly, you have no right to…" he began, then blinked a few times. "You've distracted me."

"That's a good thing," Patrick pointed out. "You were upset by what I was saying, so I kinda stomped on your toe, so to speak, and sidetracked you." He gave Sloan a big grin.

Sloan put his face in his hands. For a moment, Patrick worried he'd broken down entirely, but no, he just gave his face a brisk rub and looked up again. "What an interesting method. I'm not sure I understand what you intend with that particular 'sidetrack.'" His voice had gone even colder.

"Sure you do."

Sloan's attention dropped to the empty platter that had held the sandwiches. Maybe he was hungry. Patrick shouldn't have wolfed down all the food.

"I don't know where you received your information about me." Sloan spoke to the crumbs on the plate, it seemed. "But I won't admit to anything. You're wasting your time if you think I'll pay to keep silent about that." He looked up and met Patrick's eyes. "If I'm wrong and you're not trying to entrap me, I apologize for the insult."

Understanding finally dawned, and Patrick began to laugh. "I must be tired or something. I didn't catch on."

"I beg your pardon?"

"I didn't understand—now I do. You think I'm going to extort money from you because you...ah..." Words failed him. He wasn't sure what men who desired men would be called here in England. Sodomite was an ugly word, and Sloan was already on edge, poor bastard. "Because you got more than comfort from the hug."

The skin around Sloan's mouth went white.

"I can see you're pressing your lips together so tight you're liable to hurt yourself. Go on and tell me what you're thinking."

"I don't wish to continue this sort of conversation with you. I don't know you. I don't know if you're honest or a schemer. You walk into my house and upset my...my plans."

"You have something to do this afternoon?" He really was curious but that question came out all sneering. It didn't help when he explained, "What does a gent like you do all day? I couldn't figure it out from the report."

"Never mind." He began to pace. "I can't stand this," he muttered.

"What's the problem?"

"I'm not allowed to leave that goddamned night behind. You're..." He shook his head and didn't continue.

He remained too pale, with spots of color on his cheeks, and his eyes seemed haunted, little lost Ned Lawton once more.

"All right. Let me try again," Patrick spoke too heartily. "Say, I'll bet being cooped up in this house while we talk isn't a good plan. How about we go for a walk or something. I can walk and take notes—a peculiar skill of mine. The air outside helps to settle jangled nerves."

"My nerves are fine. And they're not your concern."

Yes, they were his concern, at least until he got what he needed from Sloan. And the poor man vibrated with suppressed emotion. Maybe Patrick could help alleviate the tension.

He allowed himself the sort of grin he only used on occasion, usually late at night in very particular company. It had been a long time too since he'd indulged in visits to a private club's smoky back room.

"But *my* nerves are shot." Patrick lowered his voice. This was a dumb risk, but he did enjoy watching the man's eyes widen. "That hug we shared? It might not be something you enjoyed, but I did. Yes, indeed. Enjoying male companionship? I'm not sure what that kind of thing does to a man here, but back home, it would earn me five to twenty years." He leaned close enough so he could smell the scent of expensive cologne and warm male and see the rapid rise and fall of Sloan's chest under the elegant suit. "Do you ever risk time in prison?"

He came closer still. Sloan didn't move, and Patrick actually brushed his cheek with his fingers. He felt warm flesh and a wash of air from an astonished gasp. Just a bit of a lean and he could feel that roughened skin under his lips. Not that he'd indulge with Sloan, but he could contemplate the idea—and see what such a suggestion did to the man.

"No." Sloan drew away from Patrick. "I do not do such things." Hallelujah, he didn't scream for the constable—or deny such impulses ever came to him.

Patrick rubbed his fingers over his mouth to wipe the start of desire. Hell, he'd touched other people, even his own mother in such a way, but this moment held far more power. Who was he fooling? It had been an intimate touch and he shouldn't have done it. It had been a sort of taunt—to them both, really.

Sloan was speaking, understandably furious under his calm tones. "The only reason I will deal with you, Mr. Kelly, is because you've convinced me that, if I can, I must help catch a criminal. I pray you're not a criminal as well. Let me assure you once again that I am *not* going to break any laws."

His voice might be even and quiet, but he did an awful lot of protesting—Patrick was smart enough not to point that out. He was too busy yelling silently at himself for being an idiot.

Sloan strode toward the door, though at least he stopped to look back and jerk his head at Kelly to follow. In the grand foyer, Sloan tugged on gloves, grabbed a swell-looking hat from his butler, and slammed it on his head, all without looking at Patrick. The butler handed him a silver-topped walking stick. And sure enough, Sloan had a narrow-eyed expression, as if he wished he could thump the cane over Patrick's head.

Fine. Sloan had shaken himself out of that strange state. And good thing he hadn't said yes to Patrick's baser desires, because maybe they could get back to business. The thought of Sloan's body, those dark eyes glittering with excitement, oh, and that warm body against his— he'd contemplate that image later. Now he'd return to the details of murder.

*

Edmund did not care for strong feelings—and that meant he was a hypocrite, because he had some very strong emotions about change and mayhem. He loathed them. Patrick Kelly appeared and offered him both with a twanging accent and a big, white-toothed grin.

The American should have behaved as a professional, not treated Edmund like a casual acquaintance, pushing him every which way, offering sympathy and then offering pure temptation. He'd never seen such a jolly, easygoing attempt at sodomy, and had rarely been so tempted to break the promise he'd made to himself.

Utter nonsense. They should both be more concerned by the fact that the Lawtons' killer might still be alive.

That chilling thought would be enough to draw any man out of the confusion of desire.

Edmund stood indecisively on his own doorstep, unwilling to walk one of his usual routes. They would not go west toward Hyde Park or east in the direction of the British Museum. He didn't want to have to explain Kelly to anyone he knew.

He set off in the direction of Regent's Park. If they walked far enough, they might see the ladies of Bedford College, and he could and *would* admire their figures and fresh faces.

Kelly walked with a small leather-bound book in one hand and a pencil in the other. His fingers were long, and a bit of hair showed at his cuffs. Those hands and roughly cut short nails drew Edmund's attention too thoroughly but Kelly apparently didn't notice as he flipped through the book and didn't turn those annoyingly blue eyes in Edmund's direction. He stopped and looked up from the book briefly, but didn't meet Edmund's gaze. "Let's start with what you do recall." He spoke briskly, as if he hadn't embraced Edmund or made outrageous suggestions. "You don't have memories of that night."

"No, I don't." Edmund walked a few more steps. The words stuck, and he forced them out. "I have had dreams about it, though."

"Oh?"

Before he could continue, someone called out, "Sloan, it *is* you. How d'you do?" A familiar man walked quickly toward them, holding out a hand ready to shake in greeting. He had reddish hair and large teeth, and was probably on some board or another. The orphanage? Edmund's skill at recalling names and faces abandoned him.

The man grasped Edmund's hand and pumped it. "I'm Dawlish, and of course you wouldn't recall me. I was two years behind you at university."

Dawlish turned his attention to Kelly. "How do you do, sir?" A prompt for an introduction that Edmund did not want to perform.

"Dawlish, yes, of course. You read history I believe? We shall have to meet and discuss the old days. Another time." Edmund wasn't usually so clumsy, but he wanted to get Kelly on his way. That outspoken man would announce the American investigation to the world. Poor Ned Lawton would rise up again.

"I'm Patrick Kelly, visiting from the US." Kelly shook Dawlish's hand.

"Are you enjoying your stay?" Dawlish asked.

Kelly glanced sideways at Edmund, and his eyes glittered with amusement or mischief. The bastard. "Yes indeed, London's a lovely city. I'm here on business, but I hope I'll get a chance to see all the sights."

Edmund began to breathe easily again.

"Ah, wonderful. What sort of business brings you here?"

Hadn't this prying Dawlish ever paid any attention to the rules of society? Why couldn't he discuss the unseasonably warm weather like an ordinary gentleman?

"I'm investigating possibilities for my company," Kelly said. And even Dawlish, pushy though he was, wouldn't try for more information after that ambiguous response.

They exchanged a few more phrases—agreeing that the weather was indeed fine—before Dawlish continued on his way in the other direction.

Edmund felt as if he had successfully clambered to safety. He relaxed as much as he could in Kelly's presence.

Chapter Three

"Thank you for not telling Dawlish about your purpose here," Edmund muttered.

"I'm not going to drag your old life into your new one, Mr. Sloan. I think I've already made that promise. If I hadn't, I will now. Anything we say will be confidential."

"In exchange for my cooperation, of course."

"Sure," Kelly agreed. "Now that Mr. Dawlish is out of earshot—"

"Lord Dawlish, actually."

Kelly stopped walking, and a delighted smile lit his face. "You're kidding. My first British lord, and I didn't even know. I'm collecting these things."

"I beg your pardon? What are you collecting?"

"I've met up with my first butler and footman. And now a lord? This is a rich day for me."

"And what, pray tell, will you win when you have collected a full set?"

"Bragging rights? What do you get when you collect all that sculpture in your house?"

"Many of the pieces of art came to me from my…past." He hadn't told anyone. Only Papa Sloan knew that, as an adult, Edmund had taken many of the Lawton family's items from a warehouse where they had been stored.

"Interesting."

What the devil did that mean? Interesting how? Why? Edmund increased his pace to stop himself asking. Kelly kept up easily. Edmund asked, "What else is on your list for this visit?"

"If I have the time, Madame Tussaud's, of course."

"I'm not surprised," said Edmund.

"Hey? I'll just bet you hate the place."

Edmund, who'd heard there was a wax figure of the Lawtons' murderer with red fingers, would rather go blind than set foot in it. He said, "I've never visited. Any other objects or people you need to meet for your list?"

"None I can think of. But I'll know what I should check off my list after I see it."

The conversation had lapsed into something almost normal, nearly the sort of talk Edmund would have with any friend—and that was strange enough. Kelly's intimate way of holding his gaze added a surreal quality to their walk together.

Those glittering eyes, that admission that he liked men. Gracious Lord, why would someone admit such a thing to a near stranger? A fool—that would be the answer. Only a fool would say such things out loud.

But perhaps Kelly had been showing a peculiar sort of humor as he sat in Edmund's house, because now he changed and became an investigator, brisk and businesslike. He held his pencil above his pad. "You don't have memories. Very well, tell me about the dreams."

Edmund had spent so much effort trying to drive the nightmares from his mind that they had burnt themselves into his brain. Those perverse images lingered, though they were considerably less enjoyable than his usual form of perversion. The one doctor he'd consulted had surmised his desire for men arose from the trauma of the past.

He'd have no trouble seeing the images, but describing them, saying them out loud with real words… He had not done so before.

His throat spasmed and clicked as if it would close up and not give him the air he needed to speak. He wet his lips, tried to swallow. Start with the easy part, he told himself.

"Go on, Mr. Sloan." The voice was soft, coaxing, but not allowing him to escape.

Edmund stared at the pavement just in front of his shoes as he walked and spoke in a low voice, dragging up the dreams. "I'm under the table. I was not a well-behaved boy. I was…willful." He had nearly forgotten how headstrong he'd been—a spoiled little boy used to getting his way. That might have been in the dreams, but hadn't it been true as well? No one talked about his life before that day.

"In the dreams, I'd been given a chance to eat with the others, and I was ruining it for myself. Once they dragged me out, I'd have to go back upstairs with Nanny. But not then, because there were no servants? Sometimes I think the servants are dead in the dream, all of them."

"Only the serving maid was killed at the Lawton residence. And the nanny was drugged. The rest had the night off for a dance."

"Look, these are dreams, bringing in reality makes it go blurry. I have trouble enough sorting them out. I'm not mentioning the dreams with packs of wild dogs or a battalion of soldiers." Or hordes of naked men, he didn't add. "So I shall tell you what I recall and let you pick through it all."

Kelly nodded and touched his fingers to his lips, indicating he would be silent. He ruined it by saying, "Sorry. You take your time, Mr. Sloan. No more interruptions from me."

Edmund pulled in a long deep breath he felt all the way to his belly. An easy inhalation, because he was alive and healthy and strong enough to take on an attacker. He looked too thin, but he was very strong. This reminder usually proved enough to calm himself. Walking faster helped. Kelly broke into a trot to catch up. Once Kelly strode next to him again, Edmund began to speak.

"The dream I have most often... I'm under the table, and sometimes there are screams and sometimes shouts. Mr. Lawton's voice sounds nothing like him. That is a consistent feature of many dreams. Funny, I can't remember how Mr. Lawton actually sounded— except that voice in the dreams. His voice is too high-pitched. Wails and cursing, a deep man's voice curses. Just one I think. Just once, and not every time. The worst ones are the dreams when there is only silence except for a drip, drip, drip, and I know it's blood or tears."

He slowed a little. The telling wasn't as terrible as he'd expected. The dreams always created dreadful images that lingered after he woke from a nightmare. Saying the words, describing the pictures, didn't seem to increase the terror they conjured.

"In the dream"—and after—"I'm very quiet because I'd been too loud. That was one of my sins, talking far too much for a small boy. I am the favorite child because, after the girls, a boy at last. So I remain silent for once, because I don't want to be punished again. I'd be sent to the nursery alone, without Nanny there. And blood on the floor there…" He cut a glance sideways at Kelly who wrote in his notebook without looking down at his hands doing the writing. The tall, broad figure in the ill-fitting suit seemed to be a guardian, keeping him safe even as he forced Edmund to watch this scene. Safe enough so Edmund could say, "I suspect there wasn't blood in the nursery, but these are dreams."

He waited. Kelly remained silent. And for the first time in his own memory, Edmund asked a question about the Lawtons. "Was there? Blood in the nursery?"

"Only a small boy's bloody footsteps around the house. The remainder stayed in the dining room."

Remainder—such a genteel way of describing the cups and puddles of blood. Edmund felt yet another strange stab of gratitude to the blunt Kelly for the moment of tact. He cleared his throat and went on. "So young Lawton wandered after the—after the fact. That doesn't come up in my dreams." Memories, he reminded himself, despite the fact that they'd been polluted by years of silence and nightmares.

He remained calm even after asking about the actual murder scene—though perhaps that was not surprising. Reality couldn't be worse than some of his dreams.

Now that words came more easily, Edmund described other details. He didn't remember how he got out from under the table, but now it occurred to him he might have slipped away while the monster did his postmortem work.

"If the boy left footprints, the monster could have easily followed. But he didn't." Edmund concentrated on the part of the dreams where he escaped, but he couldn't remember any details.

"I recall scrabbling claws, but that can't be right," he said. "Sometimes I see him and the...the murderer has bright red skin and horns."

"Could it have been a mask? Was there a dog?"

His skin prickled as a chill ran through him. "No dog but...otherwise, I don't know. Usually I see bare feet. Sometimes when I'm under the table, I see a pair of shoes. Well-polished. Other times, they're workman's boots." He paused. "Did they find any footprints to match those?" Asking questions about that night felt almost normal now.

"No, which was quite odd considering how much..." Kelly trailed off. He looked at Edmund with narrowed eyes. *How much blood there was*, he didn't finish saying.

Edmund nodded his understanding. "You don't need to use delicate language with me. Not anymore," he added. "If there is another man out there, doing those things, you need to catch him at once. I must help you." He wasn't sure why he'd avoided vivid words. Some nightmares remained powerful no matter how you describe them.

Something deep inside him relaxed and unfurled. He was reminded of a snake he'd seen once that choked its victims to death. The snake of his past still lay ready to tighten again, but he wasn't on the edge of being choked any longer.

Even if he should come face-to-face with the man who'd killed the Lawtons, the fear wouldn't—couldn't—reach the heights it had in his past.

He nearly stumbled over his own feet when he understood that Patrick Kelly had done him a favor.

*

Sloan came to a stop, half turned, and gazed at Patrick as if he were some kind of angel. Kelly backed away. This couldn't be good. But Sloan's handsome face showed nothing more than pleased astonishment.

"Thank you." Sloan practically whispered the words.

"For what?"

"For trusting that I could say those things."

"I didn't…" He stopped—he'd been about to say *I didn't have any choice*. "I didn't have any doubts."

"Hmm." Sloan sounded dubious.

Best to turn both of their thoughts back to the murders. Patrick recalled something else that Edmund Sloan might not have heard.

"There is one difference between the Lafayette Street murders and what happened to the Lawtons. The people in New York weren't killed right away. That is, the New York murderer did some of those, ah, things to them while they still lived."

Sloan put his hand to his throat as if he'd swallowed something sharp. "Do you mean..." He stopped, blinked, and then began again. "What do you mean?"

"No one told you? Have you ever listened to any talk about what happened?"

"I was never told and I don't want to hear details. I didn't." He stopped and shook his head hard. "What are you saying to me?"

"The Lawton family was killed quickly, soon after they'd been tied up. The uh..." Patrick had been about to say *gruesome dismemberments* but decided to use neutral words. "The other things happened to them after death."

Sloan's eyes went round. He did an about-face and began to walk away quickly. Patrick cursed, shoved his pencil and notebook into a pocket, and took off after him.

Sloan had begun to run, not a sprint but a fast jog. They raced along the crowded streets. Sloan didn't seem to notice the stares that followed him. The gentleman had some good wind, and Patrick, who fancied himself in fine shape, panted along behind him and felt relief as Sloan finally slowed and walked into a small graveyard next to a church. For a moment, Patrick wondered if they were going to visit the Lawton family grave but, no, the family crypt lay off in some northern part of England. It had to be locked up, or tourists and other ghouls would visit.

Sloan dropped onto a stone bench. He gulped and seemed to have trouble breathing as he hunched forward. His elbows rested on his thighs, and he buried his face in his hands. Patrick had forced Sloan's impressive façade to crumble. And wasn't that something to be proud of, taking away a bit of a gentleman's dignity.

"Are you all right?" Patrick sat next to him, though not so close their bodies touched. He didn't want to put those ideas back into either of their heads. "Is there anything I can do to help you?"

Sloan mumbled something.

"What'd you say?"

Sloan lifted his head, and his back straightened again, thank goodness. He still appeared pale, but his eyes were dry and his gaze was steady. "You have, rather. Helped me. Thank you for telling me about the Lawtons. I hadn't known."

"You thought they suffered longer?"

Sloan nodded and rubbed the back of his gloved hand over his mouth.

"Doesn't sound like you know much of anything," Kelly said. "Even facts that might have been a comfort." Not that he could come up with anything else.

"Hmm." A grunt of agreement, or just a noise to put him off? Sloan did seem to employ a number of sounds rather than conversation.

"Anytime you want to know more, I can show you the reports."

Sloan interrupted with a snort of incredulous laughter. "Anything to get me to read those miserable papers, eh?"

Kelly retorted, "Not my intention, this time, at any rate."

"Why did you mention it?"

"You're in pain. I can see that."

Sloan opened his mouth as if to argue. He shook his head. "It is temporary, I assure you. One occasionally overreacts."

Kelly examined Sloan's eyes which had lost the brilliance of strong emotion. He should let the man retreat, but the words came out anyway. "I've met the people who lost family members in the manner you lost yours. They are bereft, confused, angry, prone to outbursts of all sorts. Even the gentlemen I've met cried hysterically when talking of their lost loved ones. You are hardly overreacting."

"Time heals everything, Mr. Kelly. I've had a number of years to recover."

Patrick doubted it. "Did you attend a funeral and mourn?"

"I was a small child. They didn't believe I should indulge in morbid reflections."

Patrick only nodded. In his small family, wrongs and tragedies were discussed until they became memorized stories. He supposed the Sloan family's method had its advantages.

"What did you say to those other survivors and those families?" Sloan's voice was strong again. "Did you make them see illustrations or read descriptions of their loved ones' deaths?"

"No. Now why are you turning prickly again? I didn't show them a thing. They'd probably already seen, and what would have been the point? They weren't witnesses."

Sloan pushed back his shoulders and raised his chin so his back was as poker straight as a military man's. No doubt that was his usual posture. "No, of course not. They would not have been able to contribute anything to your investigation. I fear I am still resentful."

"Don't worry about it. You have the right to be angry at me. I expected it."

Sloan pressed his lips tight, yet another of his signals of strong emotion suppressed. Less than an hour in the man's presence and Patrick felt as if he could read him very well indeed. But then Sloan surprised him. "You are a most peculiar man," he said calm as could be, perhaps for the first time.

"Oh? I guess I've heard that before."

"You are simultaneously aggressive and kind, attacking and comforting."

Patrick grinned. "Makes me sound like a boxer, jabbing, falling back."

"Do you box?"

"Not me. I had my fill of fighting when I was a kid." Damn him for reminding this guy about their differences.

"Did you win your battles?"

"Sometimes."

Kelly tucked away his book and pencil and pulled out the envelope. "If we talk now, get this done, plus one more interview, I'll go away and only bother you again when we find the murderer. We'll find him, I promise you." He tapped the folder.

"Another interview?"

"With the other Mr. Sloan."

"Why on earth do you need to bother him? He's quite ill—surely you don't suspect he has anything to do with this."

"No. But perhaps you talked to him years ago, and you made some confessions about what you'd seen. We forget what we said as children, but the adults in our lives don't forget."

Sloan shook his head. "You think I am recalcitrant, but he is far more unwilling to discuss the murders."

"Why is that, do you suppose?" Kelly had some suspicions and wondered if they'd ever occurred to this Mr. Sloan.

But Ned Sloan answered without any hesitation. "For my sake, I believe."

"If he thinks it'll cause you pain, I'll speak to him when you're not there, see if you said anything about any sort of description. Hair color, age, something that young Ned Lawton might have said. And he could have something to say. After all, he's the one who found, um, the boy."

"Found the boy." The man surely did a lot of echoing of Patrick's words.

"Yes, the report I read said that the lawyer discovered you on the scene." At Sloan's stricken look, he hastily corrected, "Discovered Ned Lawton, I mean."

Sloan didn't speak.

"Do you have any memory of that?" Kelly prodded but without a lot of hope. Sloan had gone pale again. Damn. When Sloan remained silent, Kelly rose from the bench and started walking again, figuring he'd give the guy some room to think. When he looked back, Sloan was staring off into space.

*

A chilly breeze brushed Edmund's neck, but that wasn't the reason he shuddered. He saw Papa Sloan's worried face staring down at him. The first to find him in the house of blood. Why had he never asked about that fact? Papa Sloan had been there. *After*, Edmund reminded himself.

The detective had walked away but waited for him now.

Edmund reluctantly got up from the bench and strolled toward him, determined to remain calm. He said, "I do think it is one of my memories."

"Oh? Can you tell me…was Mr. Sloan alone that day?"

"Are you implying he was part of the murder?" Edmund's laugh wasn't forced.

"Just trying to connect that one memory to another. And another. A chain of them, maybe."

He sounded so innocuous, but Edmund suspected Mr. Kelly was anything but.

"My foster father is ailing, and if you would speak to him, I will be present. I don't trust you to leave an issue alone even if it disturbs him."

"All right. I'll go to my hotel to wash up and meet you at his house."

Edmund made a decision then. "A hotel? No. You should come and stay with me."

"What on earth?"

"I have plenty of rooms, eight bedrooms, which is quite a few for a London house. You won't notice me at all."

"Why are you inviting me?"

A good question, and he wasn't sure he trusted his own mind. That peculiar moment when they embraced and that confession of enjoying men should make Edmund stay far away.

But the urge to keep him close surely had to do with the case—to stop him talking to anyone without Edmund's knowledge.

Why should he care what this man did?

An answer might be *to protect my father.* But of course his father was innocent of murder. Very well then, he wished to protect Papa Sloan from the onslaught of this persistent investigator.

Mr. Kelly said, "You're hesitating. It won't bother me if you change your mind."

"No. I won't. I want to know what happened to my—the Lawton family, and you are the best way for me to learn the truth. It makes sense that I'd wish to help you." Edmund's own emotions had become so muddled, he wasn't sure he spoke the truth or not, but his answer seemed to satisfy Mr. Kelly.

The investigator shoved his hands deep in his pockets, pushing the dark blue, ill-fitting jacket out of shape. "Truth is, the hotel I got is beyond what my employers will pay. I don't want to take the time to find something less swank."

"You are in a hurry, then."

"Sure. I expect our guy in the States will strike again soon."

Relief filled Edmund, because Mr. Kelly obviously couldn't suspect Papa Sloan of the murders. His relief was immediately followed by horror. "Good Lord. You sound as if you're certain there will be other murders."

"Don't let my confidence kid you—I have no idea. But best we can figure, the first attack in the US happened a couple of years ago, then one last year, and the third six months ago. So seems like it could happen again."

Edmund managed, "Awful."

"That's the word for it."

"And it couldn't be my foster father. He grew ill several years ago and has had relapses several times."

"So I understand. Sooner I get the answers I need from you and others, the faster I can get back to New York and hand over the details." Kelly smiled. "I'll stop cluttering up your spare room."

He sounded amused—almost brutally casual about murder—but of course he spoke of his work. He would not be haunted by old dreams...memories...whatever they were.

"I guess I should talk to the other Mr. Sloan as soon as possible."

Edmund said, "Ah. Would you like to see more of the city? Peters, my secretary, can arrange a tour. He should return from out of town today and might show you the sights himself."

That would kill two birds with one stone. Get his infernal hovering secretary out of his hair and keep watch over Kelly without having to take on the duty himself.

The breezy manner vanished. "I'm here for one reason. When the villain is seized, sure, I'd love to see the place. I'd enjoy seeing it with you." He held up a hand. "Not a flirty thing to say, Mr. Sloan. I figure you'd be a good guide to your city, and you could use some time relaxing."

Flirty? And the way he said the last bit seemed so outrageously seductive, Edmund had trouble getting his breath to stop stuttering. He would take this moment to clear up the issue. "You do understand that I offer you the hospitality of my London residence to help you with your goal of finding the murderer. If you attempt anything else...any..." He stopped and waved a hand.

"Intimacy?" Kelly supplied with the earnest air of a man only wishing to help.

"If you attempt anything like that, I will be obliged to turn you out." He considered adding *and I will not help you find your killer*, but that wouldn't be true. No matter what, he must try to help if it meant stopping another murderer.

"Understood," Kelly said cheerfully. He raised a shoulder in a half shrug. "I guess I should apologize for what I said, and maybe for the hug, but it would be a false apology. Do those count?"

Edmund didn't bother offering a reply. He wished he could forget the potency of that damned kiss. It had lasted only a second but seemed to still tingle.

"This afternoon, I should visit the police investigators I corresponded with for a couple of months, and then later, your father later."

Edmund donned his best aloof and chilly manner. "Naturally, I shall accompany you to visit my father."

Apparently, Mr. Kelly had no notion of being repressed. He squinted at Edmund as if weighing the possibility. "We'll see. Thank you for your time but I'd better get to work."

Edmund realized he was being dismissed. He'd recited his account of his nightmares until he fairly shook with awful memories...and now Patrick Kelly was finished with him.

He tried to think of a way to trail along after Kelly, but Edmund had no interest in visiting the police.

He wanted to keep as close an eye as he could on the man. "If you tell me the direction of your hotel, I'll send a man to fetch your things."

"Oh no, no. I'll do that myself. That counts as putting you and your staff to extra trouble. And, truth be told, I don't want anyone fiddling with my collars and notebooks." Kelly pulled an ornate watch from his waistcoat and clicked it open. The thing was flashy, cheap, and attractive enough to catch the eye, perhaps a reflection of its owner. "Wow. Look at the time. I better hurry. Thanks for the invitation. Before I come to your house, I'll feed myself. That's easier, eh? And if I'm later than seven, I'll find way to let your butler know." He shook his head, a big grin on his face.

"What's amusing?"

"Becker the butler. A frosty old guy who's a real live *butler*. We have some butlers back home—I've met a couple. Even had drinks with one who works on Fifth Avenue. But they don't seem as real, even though they had the right accent." He must have seen how nettled

Edmund felt, because Kelly grew serious and said, "Don't mind me, I can talk all day. Thanks for everything, Mr. Sloan. You're generous with your time and your resources. A true gent, and I am sorry for disturbing your peace."

Edmund opened his mouth to say something, but Mr. Kelly raised his hat, turned, and walked away.

He realized his mouth still hung open and snapped it shut. Edmund Sloan, wealthy, influential, and above all polite, was not used to being treated without a modicum of respect.

He began to walk slowly toward his home, wondering at his own indignation. Informality was not a crime, and he had not been injured.

That embrace, though. It had been a spontaneous act of comfort but then something more happened. With a stranger. Such a simple and outrageous act and Patrick Kelly acted as if he hugged men every day of his life. And why didn't he offer an apology for his unprofessional and unwelcome attentions?

Outrageous.

Although, to be fair, Kelly *did* say he would apologize. Was such a thing really polite once he'd added that it wouldn't be a genuine apology? And did that comment qualify as more annoying or amusing? As Edmund walked, someone said his name twice, the second time almost pleadingly. Edmund realized that he had almost cut a gentleman he knew, because his brain was preoccupied by the strange Patrick Kelly.

"I beg your pardon," he told the gentleman, a member of his club, who was very glad to see him and shook his hand heartily.

They discussed the weather, a popular horse's chances at Goodwood Races, and several other subjects. The polite conversation flowed smoothly. After he said his farewell and walked away, Edmund had to search his brain hard to recall what they'd said to each other.

He dithered as he walked around his library. He wished to call on his parents to tell them about Kelly's possible visit, but he should wait in his own house for the annoying man. Perhaps the best solution would be to ignore the peculiar excitement aroused by Kelly. Yes, ignore him and go about his daily business… "I have things to do," he indignantly informed the absent Mr. Kelly. "And they aren't all trivial."

He returned to his home and ordered a carriage. He would visit his father and mother. His father's illness had grown worse, and Edmund didn't want anyone disturbing them, especially a slippery cove like Kelly.

Casille, the butler, greeted him with a solemn "Master Edmund" and led him straight to his mother's favorite drawing room.

Their townhouse smelled of leather because of Papa Sloan's law volumes. The floral note came from Mother Sloan's passion for flower arrangement. His foster parents' interests hadn't changed in all the years he'd known them, and their ambitions had remained modest.

More than once, they had refused his offers to buy them a grander home or new furnishings. He'd browbeaten them to allow him to pay their servants' wages and upkeep for the house, but they wouldn't allow him to give them more. They were steady, predictable people who wanted no reward for raising him. Papa Sloan was austere with his praise and he disliked humorous comments, but he was as honest as any English gentleman.

Edmund had been raised to be polite, so he managed to hide his shock at the sight of the change in his foster father, whose cheekbones and prominent nose seemed to take up more of his face as his waxy flesh receded. The shocking lumps on his face seemed to have grown larger and multiplied since they'd met a week earlier.

Seeing him and listening to his conversation silenced any doubts for Edmund. Mr. Sloan was not the sort of man who'd harbor horrible secrets, much less create them in the first place.

Pale and angry, Papa Sloan loomed over Edmund, coaxing him up and out. His big hands shook. "My dear boy, my dear boy." Did he sob?

He spoke to Edmund of a Labour candidate he didn't trust and of rising interest rates. Edmund listened with affection, though not with much interest. He'd listened to so much trivia today. He did every day, but only the contrast of his encounters with Kelly told him as much.

And that dream or memory of Papa Sloan seemed more shocking than the drip of blood and dead, staring eyes, perhaps because Edmund had rarely recalled it.

After a few minutes, Papa Sloan excused himself to prepare for dinner. Of course. No matter if they had guests or dined alone, they would change for dinner. The fact that Papa Sloan was donning more formal eveningwear did not tell Edmund if his father was well or not. Even if Mr. Sloan perched at the edge of death, he'd dress for dinner.

The butler returned with tea for Edmund. "Mrs. Sloan wished me to inform you she'll be with you in a few minutes, sir."

Edmund thanked Casille and dismissed him. He stared into the fire, trying not to think about anything other than the heat of the tea on his tongue.

Days, weeks had gone by without him thinking about that cursed past. Now he couldn't banish it. "Devil plague you, Patrick Kelly."

"I beg your pardon?" Mother Sloan had entered the room, and he hadn't even noticed.

He rose to his feet and went to kiss her hand. "I was talking to myself."

"Such an odd boy," she said fondly. "Will you join us to dine?" She gave him a conspiratorial smile. "Since it's only family, we won't tell that you're not properly attired."

He felt glad for another sign that she'd grown less rigid with the passing years. There'd been a time when she wouldn't have tolerated a man underdressed at her table.

Edmund planned to be at his own home when the interloper returned, but what if Kelly came here? Edmund wanted to be a shield between that annoyance and his foster parents. "Yes, thank you."

They spoke of nothing in particular. An exhibition, the weather in France, and a pattern for drapes she wanted to purchase. Comforting, easy conversation that soothed him.

When the soft bell chimed to announce dinner, he escorted his mother to the table. Papa Sloan waited for them. In the stronger light of the chandelier, his skin's yellow tinge was more evident, the sign of liver failure. Once a handsome man, now the odd bulges on Papa Sloan's face made him appear to be a distorted death's head.

Edmund shook hands again and wished he could force his own warmth into those icy fingers. And oh God, one of those lumps had formed there too.

Edmund didn't know what was wrong with his father. Mr. Sloan refused to discuss his illness, and when Edmund had made polite inquiries of his doctor, the doctor had apologized but said he couldn't speak of the matter. He was blunt enough to tell Edmund that Papa Sloan did not have very much time left and that he wished to keep other details private. That seemed very in character, and Edmund felt his eyes sting at the thought of the dignity his father required—and would lose—as he slipped away.

At least he knew Papa Sloan was receiving the best care available.

They sat and ate. The lack of company meant Edmund could eat without too much trouble, but he found he had little appetite. His foster father had been sick for several years, but his waxy appearance disturbed Edmund. The fact that the comforting conversation continued—a long lecture from Papa Sloan about safe investments, one of his favorite topics—didn't allay Edmund's alarm.

After dinner, Mother Sloan withdrew to leave the men to their alcohol and tobacco, as if they were a real party and not just the three of them.

Edmund decided he should warn his father. "A man named Patrick Kelly came to see me earlier."

"An Irishman?" Papa Sloan looked mildly disgusted.

"American. He is investigating several deaths in the States. And they are…they resemble… He's looking into murders."

Papa Sloan carefully placed the snifter in his hand on the white tablecloth. "Why did he want to talk to you?"

Edmund considered saying it wasn't all talk, there was a peculiar tension between them, but he'd never so much as hinted at his deviant interest in men. Now was hardly the time to begin. He regretted even bringing up the topic of Kelly. "He wanted me to describe my memories."

"He sounds like the worst sort of swine, one of the men I have spent years repressing." Papa Sloan didn't sound upset, of course. He never did—yet his hands trembled. Those large hands had once held such strength...

My dear boy. He'd cried out those alarmed words in the past, not just in Edmund's nightmares.

Edmund had to look away. He'd lost track of the conversation.

Then he recalled how Kelly had told him how his foster father had worked hard to keep Edmund sheltered. He ventured, "He told me you'd threatened some people who'd attempted to approach me. I hadn't understood the extent to which you kept the journalists and curiosity seekers at bay."

"Of course. I considered that my first duty to you, Edmund. You must not be drawn into that morbid interest. It is unhealthy, and, worse, that sort of interest perverts all it touches." His bony fingers rested on the snifter, but he didn't lift it.

"I know, Papa Sloan," Edmund said then stopped. He'd heard it often enough before.

"And I know I repeat myself because I'm an old man and I wish to drive home the lesson. After all, I shan't be with you much longer."

He seemed entirely calm and matter-of-fact—though he didn't look Edmund in the face and instead stared at the brown liquid in his glass. "I hope you will protect yourself and my widow."

Edmund had no idea how to respond to such plain speaking. They didn't mention his illness and certainly didn't chat about his demise. Should he protest Papa Sloan's statement? That seemed disrespectful. "I will protect her always," Edmund said at last.

His foster father raised his gaze to look at Edmund. He even smiled. "I'm reassured. You'll keep away those who would want to shovel up the dead past. Ah, Edmund, I couldn't cherish you more if you were my son."

The rare show of affection warmed Edmund, though he noticed the usual addition at the end. Just as Mr. Sloan would never allow Edmund to address him as plain Papa, he never let Edmund forget the truth of their relationship. Perhaps it was to pay delicate respect to the parents Edmund had lost or to remind him that the Sloans, as they were not his real family, had had no true obligation to take him in.

"Thank you," he said to Papa Sloan. "Shall we join Mother Sloan?"

Edmund swallowed the rest of his port, pushed away from the table, and rose to his feet. Someone knocked, and at Papa Sloan's "Come," Casille entered noiselessly.

"Mrs. Sloan is in the library with a guest." He pressed his full lips together, then admitted in a lower voice, "She didn't ask for you to be informed, sir, but I suspected you'd want to know."

"Who is the visitor?"

"An American gentleman."

"Mr. Kelly," Edmund said, disgusted.

"I'm glad you warned me about this creature," Papa Sloan told him, but Edmund didn't really listen. He'd turned the disgust on himself, for he felt a rising excitement. He might have been a boy hearing about a circus or an explosion in the neighborhood.

Edmund helped Papa Sloan from his chair, and they walked slowly to the drawing room.

Mother Sloan sat on one of the stiff-backed wooden library chairs, and Kelly stood near the fireplace.

She beamed at her husband. "This is Mr. Kelly. He didn't wish to disturb you."

"How did this man enter the house without my knowledge?" Papa Sloan sounded as reasonable as ever, but Edmund knew that the more evenhanded he sounded, the more inflexible he could be.

"Why, he's a friend of Edmund. They share an interest in art."

Edmund's astonished laugh came out far too loud.

"No, my dear, He is the worst sort of trickster." Papa Sloan's voice was as quiet as a whisper, which made everything else in the room go silent. He said in an only slightly louder voice, "Why are you bothering my wife, Kelly?"

"Here, now, no need to worry. I'm not a thief or some such scoundrel. Nor a murderer." Kelly looked at Papa Sloan as if he'd just scored some sort of points in a game. "I'd heard you weren't well and wanted to check with the missus before I talked to you. She said it was a good plan to talk to her first."

She murmured something about him being so considerate, and Edmund realized that Kelly's appeal affected her as well. Patrick Kelly must charm everyone he met, except, apparently, Papa Sloan.

"I know your intentions. Edmund told me about you," Papa Sloan said.

"Fast work." Patrick grinned at Edmund, who resented that intimate look.

Thank goodness the effect of that cheeky expression could be dulled by annoyance. "What can you mean?" Edmund asked stiffly.

"Well now, I figure you all finished dinner less'n a half hour ago, right?" No one answered, so he said, "Or was it only fifteen minutes? Half hour?"

"Fifteen minutes," Edmund said, to shut him up.

"And before that, I mean during the meal, I'm sure you didn't mention the main reason I'm here in England, not with a lady present. So there you go. You got the information to him just now when you gents were alone."

Mother Sloan's smile vanished, and now she wore an anxious frown—and Edmund realized fretful was her more normal expression. He grabbed a chair and placed it next to hers. When he sat near her, she reached across, patted his arm, and murmured something apologetic.

"We will not discuss your business in my house," Papa Sloan told Kelly.

"Did you eat?" Kelly asked Edmund. "Can you with them?"

"Go away," Edmund growled.

"Sure. Just a few questions and I'll be gone."

"Go *away*. You sneaked into my family's house. You are an unscrupulous and dishonest devil." Edmund never lost his temper. That hazy thought hit him even as fury filled his throat and he trembled with emotion, stronger than any he recalled. It was as if fire licked through him.

Kelly should have winced or shown some kind of pain with the rage Edmund directed at him. Instead, he only nodded. "You're probably right about all that unscrupulous and whatnot, but I'm also hunting a murderer. That's what's most important."

"I'm so sorry, Edmund," his foster mother whispered. "I had no notion he was not whom he claimed to be."

"It's all right," he murmured to her, ashamed of his show of emotion.

She put her hand on his arm again and once more spoke to Edmund rather than her husband. "Hunting a murderer? Why would he want to speak with us?"

"Dear, perhaps you and Edmund should take some tea in your drawing room?" Papa Sloan said. "I will deal with our unwelcome visitor."

"I'll stay," Edmund said.

"I think not," Papa Sloan said. "Please escort your foster mother."

Edmund rose at once and held out an arm. He'd escort her, yes. But he'd be back as soon as he could.

Chapter Four

Patrick couldn't believe how such a skinny, sick old man could give off an almost palpable sense of power—and Ned Sloan the Polite had his own moment of authority when he'd gotten angry. Too bad for these Sloans Patrick didn't get cowed easily when it came to his job. He really shouldn't have teased poor Edmund, though, nor the sick old gent either. Something about the stuffiness of the place must have awakened that devil in him.

He liked the lady, though. She'd been wildly curious, but far too stiff and polite to ask pointed questions. He hoped she wasn't sick too.

The lady and Edmund left the room. The old man at last eased himself into a chair, slowly and painfully. Patrick only watched. He itched to help but knew he'd be cursed if he tried, or whatever passed for cursing with Mr. Sloan.

"That's some obedience you command there, Mr. Sloan."

"Tell me what you came to say and be gone," Sloan said. "Before you start again, I want to tell you that if you go near my son again, I'll have you arrested."

"For what?"

"I will leave that to the authorities."

"Got them in your pocket, do you?"

"What I have or don't have is none of your business." He waved a skeletal hand, which also had some of those odd lumps on it. "I assume you're looking at some murders in your country, and you're convinced the Lawton murderer is involved?"

That silenced Patrick for almost a quarter of a minute. "Did you have to time to check into me, or am I not the first person to come calling about this?"

"You're not the first to invent a lunatic theory. The murderer is dead. And he did not rise up from the grave to kill again. I suspect you're on the hunt for something else, so I tell you, be gone."

"What else would I want?"

"The only surviving Lawton's autograph in your book of trophies? His story you'll write up for some loathsome publication? A souvenir of the scene?"

"I guess Ned didn't get to the whole story after all. I really am an investigator."

"He is Mr. Sloan. *Edmund* Sloan. Go away, Mr. Whatever-your-name-is. I'm tired of your sort trying to hook your name to the Lawton fame."

Infamy more like, but Patrick didn't say as much. He walked over and took a seat near the table.

"I didn't invite you to remain." Mr. Sloan sounded like a querulous old man. "I shall have you thrown out."

"I don't give a darn about the Lawton murders except how they relate to the Smith, Bergee, and Phelps murders. Those are the people who've been killed in the same manner as the Lawton family."

"Nonsense."

Patrick launched into the explanation about how the murders had similarities. Two spots of red appeared on the old man's cheeks, his yellowing eyes widened, but other than that, he seemed made of stone.

"I have nothing to offer you," Mr. Sloan said. "Nothing."

"Does Edmund know of your connection with the man who died in jail?"

Mr. Sloan's astonishment looked real to Patrick, but he never underestimated anyone's ability to act, particularly people like this guy, who'd spent a life hiding emotion.

Patrick watched carefully as he said, "Today I paid a visit to a friend on the force. The investigators listed everywhere the man had worked. Most of his life, he was a low-paid messenger."

"I recall that from the trial." Mr. Sloan spoke slowly as if truly considering the idea. "And at the time, I hadn't considered it, but he might have delivered some papers for me."

"Maybe. But what didn't come up at the trial was before that, when he was a boy, he was a gardener's assistant. He worked at your family's home in Sussex."

He could have sworn the old man blinked rapidly a few times. But otherwise he seemed calm. "The murderer was almost my age. So if he worked at Moorwill, it would have been decades ago."

"Yes. You were about six years older than he."

"And I was away at school when he worked at Moorwill House."

"Holidays—"

"This is fruitless talk, Mr. Kelly. I didn't know the man. Go away, sir."

"Not yet. I have a few more questions. I want to know what Edmund might have told you about what he saw and what you saw that day."

Now the astonishment was real. "I?"

"You came to fetch Edmund, didn't you?"

"That wasn't in the official record. That has nothing to do with the investigation."

"I have the record. I've studied every bloodthirsty detail in the police record. Your name was mentioned once in those accounts, as the person who was called to fetch the lone survivor."

"Go away."

Patrick leaned close. He didn't feel good about asking, but he'd guessed what ailed the old man and wondered if it could be of use. "Soon enough, I will go, and you'll never see me again. Does your family know what's wrong with you?" he whispered.

"Go away, sir." He looked on the edge of tears, but Patrick knew he wouldn't fight after that veiled threat.

Patrick chewed on his bottom lip, unwilling to push the poor old stick of a man after all.

He sighed and sat back again. "I wanted to figure this out with your help. I think the answers are here in England, and I can't leave until I have them."

"You... You are the worst sort of ghoul."

From the doorway, Ned spoke. "That's what I believed, Papa Sloan, but now I imagine the worst sort of ghoul is one who knows a fact that might help catch a murderer and doesn't speak up."

Patrick didn't dare glance at Ned—he didn't want that too-sharp old man to get even a hint of Patrick's attraction, and looking the handsome form of Ned Sloan did something to Patrick Kelly, giving him a lift of the heart that surely must show on his face.

He watched old Mr. Sloan, waiting for him to consider Ned's words. Best not to interrupt.

Mr. Sloan closed his eyes and breathed audibly for several seconds. Had they managed to give the sick guy a heart attack? Patrick leaned forward, his own heart going pretty darned fast.

"I...I don't feel well," old Mr. Sloan murmured. For a second, his bright, unfogged gaze locked on to Patrick's. The crafty old gaffer was obviously faking.

"I say, sir," Ned started forward from the door. He seemed devastated.

No doubt the obviously suffering idiot never admitted weakness. The old man seemed the stoic sort who'd describe a lopped-off arm as just a scratch.

Ned put his hand on Mr. Sloan's shoulder. "Shall I send for the doctor?"

"No, no. I think I shall retire."

Within a minute, a stout butler and footman—far less impressive than Ned's own Becker and Liam—had come to help the old man leave.

The servants exchanged wide-eyed glances. Yep, the son-of-a-whatnot had them in a real stew about his health, so this wasn't his standard ploy to get out of talking. Ned followed the old man and his parade out of the room.

Everyone seemed to forget about Patrick, which was fine with him. He rubbed his hands together and looked around. The desk seemed the ideal spot to start.

He wouldn't find any evidence about the murders, of course, but he might find something about Mr. Sloan the barrister, who had secrets and more secrets. The old man had changed the moment Patrick mentioned Moorwill House, the Sloan family's old pile. The big stone house was impressive enough to be included in the Great Halls of England collection Patrick had found in a stereoscopic display during that afternoon's research.

Settling behind the desk in a leather chair with wheels, Patrick got to work.

The papers on the desktop revealed nothing more than other people's business, and even the locked drawers didn't contain anything more interesting than a copy of Sloan's will. Standard provisions, leaving it all to Ned with notes about the care of his widow and other interests. Other interests…hmmm.

"What the devil are you doing?" Ned strode to the front of the desk. His face was red.

"I'm snooping," Patrick said. He put away the will and slid the drawer shut. He didn't dare use his picks to lock it again, not in front of Ned.

Ned's mouth opened, but he didn't say anything. He snapped it shut with an audible click.

Patrick pushed away from the desk on the rolling chair and held his empty hands high. He opened his jacket and showed the interior of first one side and then the other. "Not robbing him. See?"

"Are you always so brazen?" Ned sounded hoarse, but with amazement, not outrage, not yet.

Might as well tell the truth. "Sometimes at work. I'm a mild sort of guy otherwise."

Ned made a snorting sound that could have been derisive laughter.

Patrick went on. "It depends. You know? Missing pearls, I probably follow all the rules. This case is different, Ned, you know it is."

He took a risk using that first name, but he wanted to appeal to the survivor, not the Mr. Edmund Sloan who'd taken over from the little boy.

"I'm *Mr. Sloan.* And I'm removing you from the premises."

He'd do the same if he were in Ned's shoes, so Patrick decided to skip anger. He asked, "Should I go back to my hotel?"

"Not at all. I'm accompanying you to my home."

Good—but Patrick tried not to show his pleasure. "Keeping an eye on me, eh?"

"Precisely."

The carriage was waiting for them, and the coachman sprang to open the door and shut it behind them. No wonder Ned stood with his hands behind his back so often; he had servants who would take care of any obstacle blocking him. He didn't need to use his hands to so much as open a door.

"What did you do this afternoon?" Still the too-polite gentleman, Ned disguised his inquiry as an innocent social question but he kept his gaze fastened on Patrick as if he wished he could pry him open.

Patrick tended to keep quiet with anyone who wasn't his employer, but why not tell him the truth?

"I visited the police and didn't have a lot of luck." He pulled out his notebook where he tended to keep exact conversations on record. He held it up to catch the last light of the dying day. "The officer who was sent to me, ha, not much use there. 'You're interrupting my busy day to badger me with questions about a murder that took place nearly twenty years ago?'"

He put down the notebook because, really, there was no point in trying to remember that useless conversation.

"What else did he say?" Ned frowned now, apparently lost in new, unpleasant thoughts.

"When I told him I just wanted a bit of information, he said I wouldn't get it from him. He pointed out that he and I were small boys when the murders were committed. And he had a horrible cigar he puffed the whole time.

"I tried to tell him about the murders in the States, and he told me he had enough work and headaches without me adding to them."

"I can sympathize with him," Ned muttered.

Patrick had to smile. "I made enough of a nuisance of myself I nearly got arrested, but he gave me the name of a retired sergeant who lived near the East End. That man was a joy."

He paused.

Ned asked, "Are you being sarcastic?"

"Not at all. He showed me around his small house and garden and gave me tea, chattering away about the most notorious murder of his career. Nothing new there, but he did give me the name of a delivery boy who'd witnessed your—um, Ned Lawton's departure from his family's premises the day of the attack."

He waited but couldn't make out the expression on Sloan's face. The gentleman probably lounged in the dark corner of the carriage on purpose, to hide. He'd spent a lifetime hiding from curious people.

Patrick went on. "So I got the name of the delivery boy, Peter Mason. The story the sergeant told me was Mason hadn't known what he was seeing, but the boy had come forward to the police once news of the murders had hit the popular press. And what's more, the sergeant still knows Mason. He married the sergeant's daughter's husband's cousin. Or was it second cousin? He told me which pub the man frequented."

He fell silent, unsure if he wanted to tell the rest. He'd found the witness in the corner publican's. Mason had grown into a red-haired man with paler red muttonchops, and owned the business he'd done deliveries for all those years ago. Almost as welcoming as the sergeant, Mason had agreed to allow Patrick to buy him a pint.

Patrick had listened to Mason's story, and then, in a moment of what seemed like inspiration, suggested Mason come around to visit him in the grand house where Patrick was staying.

At the time, it seemed a good plan. If Ned Sloan listened to the greengrocer's account, it might somehow loosen more memories of the horrible day.

Too bad he'd pushed Mr. Lawton/Sloan enough already. He'd already barged in and caused trouble at Lawyer Sloan's house, just to see what might happen. He'd operated like that more than once working as a cop and for Greene Investigations. Sometimes something came loose. Just as often, he ended up in a fistfight.

He considered warning Ned about the potential visitor, but Mason had seemed on his way to being drunk and had probably forgotten the address for Ned's house.

Instead, Patrick spoke into the darkness about another topic. "You must not be too concerned about your stepfather's health, or you'd be back there instead of dragging me away."

Ned sighed. "I am worried, but I knew he wanted us to leave. I know him well enough to understand that if he were truly in pain and suffering, he would grow quieter about his condition, not complain."

"So he's fine." Good to know that Ned wasn't taken in by his stepfather's act.

"No, he most certainly isn't. It is a sign of weakness that he'd use that sort of complaint."

Weakness and perhaps desperation. The lawyer was starting to suffer from one of the worst symptoms of his disease. Patrick wondered if Sloan's wife and son family knew what, exactly, was wrong with him. Patrick doubted it. He knew what the old guy had. Syphilis. He'd seen bums on the streets of New York with the same ailment. Had insanity set in yet?

Ned interrupted his thoughts. "I suppose we are all sad to see our parents aging."

It wasn't up to Patrick to point out that Sloan Senior had worse than age eating him up. Ned shifted in his seat, looked at him then licked his lips and looked away.

He asked, "Are your mother and father still alive?"

A mighty personal question from the formal Mr. Sloan. "Just my mother," Patrick said. He didn't bother adding that his father had never been on the scene. When he recalled his relentless pursuit of the truth about his father, his scalp crept. Sometimes he'd been paid back for his relentless pushing. He shifted closer to the carriage window to gaze out at gaslights and carriages and distract himself. "She's got more energy than I'll ever manage," he said.

Ned made one of those snorts, a genteel exhalation of breath that Patrick suspected meant *stuff and nonsense.*

"I beg your pardon?" Patrick tried an imitation of Ned at his most coldly formal.

Ned actually laughed. "Your mother must be formidable indeed."

"That's the word for her." Patrick grinned, gaining too much pleasure from making Ned laugh. Much of the day, he'd enjoyed the secret pleasure of that embrace and light touch he'd taken from Edmund Sloan—when he wasn't reading descriptions of the murder scene and the trial.

Strange that a quick embrace could create such a stir in a busy man like himself. Never mind the fact that his current state of physical tension fit a younger man's mooning—or that his plans didn't include any sort of entanglement.

Of course, as his mam and boss might point out, planning wasn't his strong suit. "Intuitive" was the word his boss used. "Impulsive dafty" was his mother's description.

They fell silent during the ride to Ned's house.

Patrick, who usually didn't give a darn about what other people thought of him, hoped they'd grow comfortable with each other. Not likely he'd relax due to the physical awareness keeping him charged and alert near Ned. He couldn't stop staring at the man and shifted his eyes away quickly when Ned looked back. A game of tennis with his damned eyeballs. It would give him a headache just when he needed to use his noggin.

Something had awakened in Patrick Kelly and he wondered if he could put it back to sleep. Maybe a nice quick encounter with someone. Yes. Something casual would let him think clearly again. Where would he find such a dangerous, illegal encounter in a strange city? Best make an appointment with his own hand. He needed to get his mind off the subject of Ned's slender body, lush mouth, and dark eyes.

He'd been a fool to admit anything to Ned, of course. In the spirit of keeping the man off-balance and thinking outside his usual limits, Patrick had succeeded in pushing himself over. Maybe Ned didn't notice Kelly's attraction seemed to be growing and taking up more room. It damned near filled every inch of the carriage.

Once they'd step outside, the whole thing would dissipate.

He was wrong. Once they stepped into the house, Ned shifted from foot to foot and shoved his hands in his pockets in a most ungentlemanly manner. He didn't even pretend to hide his nervousness.

"A drink?" Ned hesitantly asked. "I mean, would you care for a drink?"

"Sure. A beer would be fine."

Ned led him to a fantastical sort of sitting room, a large space with lavish displays of flowers and plants. It wasn't a greenhouse exactly, but the room smelled of clean, damp earth and the sweetness of too many flowers. Patrick sat on a rattan chair that creaked under his weight.

After he ordered their drinks from the butler, Ned took a chair near Patrick. He looked at a palm, at some flowering thing that overflowed a brass bucket, at the fireplace, everywhere but at Patrick.

"What's the trouble?" Patrick took pity on the man. "I don't need that drink if you'd rather just go about your business. I'm grateful for the place to stay, but I don't want to be a bother—"

Ned's eyes widened with indignation, and he opened his mouth to reply.

"Beyond the investigation," Patrick added hastily.

Ned shook his head slowly, as if with disbelief. He said, "Your presence is disturbing even if you aren't in the room."

Patrick liked the sound of that. "Oh? Do I haunt you?"

"Yes. You do."

The butler sailed into the room. He poured a neat whisky for Ned and, after a tiny pause probably denoting disapproval, handed Patrick the glass of beer he'd requested.

"That will be all," Ned told the butler, who departed more slowly than he'd entered.

Patrick sipped and wondered why the British drank beer that was so strong it could go for a stroll around your gut. He'd already drunk an ale with Mason the greengrocer, and he wanted to stay alert, so he put the lukewarm glass on a lace-covered rattan table with artfully bowed legs. Ugly damned thing alone, but in this strange room, perfect.

"Tell me why I haunt you," he demanded.

The gaslight wasn't strong in this room, just a few sconces on the wall between tall plants, but he could see Ned grow pink and gulp down the whisky in one swallow.

"You know why."

"The way I bring up the past? The way I turned up at your father's house?" He leaned forward, elbows on knees, hands loose. "Or do you mean the way we touch?"

"Everything on that list." Ned rose to his feet and put the glass down hard on the small round table. It clinked against Patrick's as if in some sort of toast. "I'm fed to the teeth with feeling…feeling…" He trailed off.

Patrick stood. "Would it be better or worse if I stayed now?" he asked, impatient as well. "I'm done for the day."

"Good night, then." Ned sounded angry.

"No, I mean I'm done working and done with… Well, tired of not understanding you, what you want." He knew, of course, but he'd be damned if he'd be the aggressor again.

Ned gave another of those breathy snorts. He took two slow steps toward Patrick so they were nearly toe to toe. His chest rose and fell quickly. Patrick longed to grab on and pull him close. He took a page from Ned's book and put his hands behind his back. It proved difficult to stand still as Ned's eyes, wide and bright, examined Patrick up and down. Ned the hidden man at last seemed unwilling or unable to hide naked desire.

"Go on," Patrick said, quiet and encouraging, he hoped. He expected tentative touches—a gentle brush of the hand, a soft kiss on the cheek—and didn't want to frighten Ned away.

What he got was closer to an explosion.

With a hissed curse, Ned came close and kissed Patrick. He put his arms around Patrick, who sighed with pleasure.

Ned let go of him and began to back away. Ned was about to apologize or worse, run away. Patrick must stop that nonsense immediately. He put his hands on Ned's shoulders and squeezed. He leaned back and held Ned away from him. The yearning and misery on that face made Patrick's annoyance melt.

"Here, now, don't stop. We'll take our time."

"No, we can't go slow. We won't. I can't think about this." Ned dropped his hold on Patrick's waist. He raised a hand, and Patrick readied himself for a fight, but Ned only drew his trembling fingers through his hair.

So if he left it to Ned, Patrick would get passion and nothing else. "Ned," he began.

"*Edmund.* Sloan."

"I don't require love with my partners."

That was greeted with the customary snort.

"But a bit of respect and thoughtfulness isn't too much to ask for."

Ned shook his head, and his eyes shone. He gave a small groan of frustration, or desire. Patrick hoped it was the second.

"Yes? You think it is too much?" Patrick probed.

"I don't want to think at all. I don't want any part of thinking," Ned said. "I just want to do this. Get it over with, and maybe my brain will stop pushing me to…" He licked his lips, which must have gone dry from his breath coming fast and hard.

Patrick usually had some sympathy for a man who didn't want to crave other men and who longed to banish that lust as quickly as possible. He'd had moments like that in his own life. Heck, less than hour ago he'd considered seeking out an anonymous encounter. But for some reason, Ned's intention to use him to reach orgasm—and nothing else—annoyed him. It would be a challenge, he decided.

"Ah-ah." He bent forward and pressed his mouth to Ned's jaw. He inhaled the scent of the flowers around them, of the male nearly in his arms, all expensive linen and wool and lust. "If you want this, I'm more than happy to oblige, but only if we go at a slower speed. We talk when I want to talk." He punctuated each word with a tiny kiss or nip. "Or perhaps if and when you want to talk."

"Oh no. No," Ned groaned the words, and he raised his chin like a dog offering its throat. Giving up control. *Oh no, no* was right. Ned obviously didn't want to blame himself for whatever happened.

Patrick cupped Ned's warm face in his palms and leaned forward. A gentle touch, nearly a kiss, their breath mingling until Patrick needed more. He slid into kisses, deeper and deeper, and then he grew as urgent and feverish as Ned.

For a time, he allowed himself to taste, and feel—and he groaned and moved closer, thinking only that he needed a shave and perhaps his beard burned Ned's lips and softer skin. Such soft skin and lips and delicious kisses. He'd pressed Ned to the door, and his hands moved from his cheeks down, down, over his shoulders and then around Ned's body clinching him tight so they again pressed together, hard, moving, panting.

Already too excited, Patrick warned himself. Too fast, too much. He would not allow mindlessness to control either of them. He stopped leaning his weight on Ned and murmured, "Calm down," to both of them.

Ned grunted. Stronger than Patrick had imagined, Ned dropped to the floor, dragging him along. Patrick lowered himself slowly, going without protest. They lay on their sides, entwined and kissing. Soon Patrick lay on his back, the surprisingly solid form of Ned on top of him, straddling him.

Patrick couldn't stop himself from touching Ned, but he also said, "So much passion knotted tight in you." He let his fingers work Ned's flesh, pressing along his back and shoulders.

Ned moved his prick, rubbing and pushing against Patrick's belly, hard and urgent. Patrick sensed the throb and the heat even through the layers of Ned's fine eveningwear and Patrick's rougher trousers—or perhaps he felt his own engorged organ. So close, so fast. He circled his arms around Ned and twisted to dislodge him.

"Sorry." Ned scrambled back, rushing off as full of terror as he'd been when he'd shoved forward.

"'S fine, Ned. Edmund. No need to worry."

Ned sat, knees bent, and rubbed his face with both hands. His fingers trembled, for goodness' sake.

Patrick sat up too. "Touching you, kissing you, is lovely. Don't worry, hmm? I know what you want."

A wisp of a smile or grimace touched Ned's face. "Oh?"

"You want to have it happen without you saying anything about it. No blame on you. You don't want to enjoy it, but you crave it."

"Fool." Ned spoke without heat. "Why do you have to talk? Why?"

"Why do you have to stay silent?"

Ned swallowed and shook out his arms, then brushed the fabric of his jacket. "When you go to the loo, do you discuss the details?"

"This? Is like going to the loo?"

"I don't mean to be insulting, but rather. Yes."

"You have never loved anyone, have you?"

"My family, but I understand what you mean. Physical affection such as between spouses. That's not... No. Have you?"

"I've come closer than you, that's for certain. Have you had some experience with this loo thing of yours? Lain down with another man?"

"I have."

"How often?

"This is none of your affair." He began to rise, wincing. The rise in his trousers was still obvious.

"Calm down," Patrick urged.

"I intend to."

Patrick patted the floor. "Sit again. We'll not talk about your past, I promise."

"I should probably retire," Ned said, even as he slumped back onto his rear, less gracefully this time.

"Then you should relax. When I touched your back, I could feel you were as tight and hard as iron. Take off your jacket and let me help loosen your flesh with a massage."

"What do you mean?"

"Rubbing your muscles."

"I know that, but…"

"A Finnish boxer in the city showed me how." He stopped to remember the pleasant sessions he'd enjoyed in a dingy cellar that held the permanent musk of men and sweat. "*Effleurage*, friction. It'll loosen you a bit." He snapped his fingers. "Coat and vest off."

"Vest?" Ned crossed his arms over his chest.

"Waistcoat. I forgot you call your underwear a vest."

Ned frowned but pulled off his jacket, carefully folded it, and put it on a chair. A man like Ned probably wouldn't even lounge around his own house in shirtsleeves.

"I'm not going to lie down again," he said and sat instead on a rattan chair near his jacket, as if he could grab it up for protection.

"All right, but you'll have to turn around." Patrick made a circle with a finger. "So you're facing the back of a chair. And come to think of it, that thing is too elaborate. Too tall. Funny you having rattan chairs indoors. Doesn't seem very English."

Ned still seemed ill at ease, but at that remark, he brightened. "I know. My parents were horrified when they saw I brought garden furniture indoors."

When he finally got Ned seated, leaning forward, arms resting on the back of the only wooden chair in the room, Patrick managed to calm himself. Good. The strange tension had meant he had less control over his own responses.

But once he'd gotten his hands on Ned's shoulders, desire hit him hard. He spoke to ward off the need to kiss the skin under his fingers. "You're strong for a gentleman."

The already relaxing muscles tensed. "I make certain to stay strong."

"Oh yep. Of course. You'd want to be able to fight back." He probably shouldn't have said anything, because now the muscles under his hands stiffened to iron again, or perhaps only wood. He lightly thumped Ned's shoulder blade with a fist.

"At least try to relax," he coaxed. "I promise not to say anything awkward again."

"I doubt that's a promise you can keep," Ned said, and his shoulders remained hunched to his ears. "I don't know why I'm allowing you to do this insane thing."

"Because you're curious," Patrick said. He considered adding *and you want me almost as much as I want you,* but decided that came under the heading of awkward talk.

He pressed his knuckles in and felt warm flesh under the fine fabric of Ned's shirt. Even such a businesslike move, not even on bare skin, gave him a powerful shiver of arousal. He had gone too long without touch or taste—innocent touches above clothing shouldn't carry such a wallop.

Ned moaned softly as Patrick worked on his neck. The sound went up Patrick's fingers, his arms, into his body. And his erection would become uncomfortable soon.

He moved to Patrick's supple body and worked on his spine without speaking for a few minutes, listening to his own hitching breaths and Ned's groans.

Patrick knelt by the chair to work on Ned's slender waist and glide his fingers along his hips.

"Turn and get comfortable on the chair," he said, "so I can get to your front."

"No." Ned's back stiffened again.

"Because you're aroused?" Patrick guessed.

No answer came. Damn, was he wrong to say such a thing out loud?

"Many gents find massage arousing." He had no idea if he lied or told the truth, but he knew Ned yearned to be a regular gentleman.

Patrick sat back on his heels and waited. Ned gazed at him over his shoulder, then at last moved, sliding around so he sat on the chair. Sprawled, more like.

He closed his eyes, the sacrificial lamb again. Patrick examined the figure in the chair, head rolled up, throat exposed, arms resting at his sides. Ned resembled Saint Sebastian minus the arrows.

Fine, Patrick wouldn't try to make him more active. He'd enjoy coaxing the man back into passion.

He rubbed Ned's hard thighs through his trousers, then moved to unfasten the buttons of his fly. Ned's fingers twitched, but his hands didn't move.

Patrick could take and give, and perhaps he could make the experience so wonderful that Ned wouldn't need to hide from him or pleasure again.

Although that thought stopped his busy hands. Again? He hadn't even finished this encounter and he was already planning his next? Greedy, greedy Patrick. *Take only what you can eat*, he thought, and his mouth watered.

He unpeeled the gift of Ned as much as he could, exposing skin from armpits to knees, and set about worshipping what he'd bared. He rubbed skin and hair and tense muscles, and then licked and sucked at everything but the ruddy prick and balls in the middle of the pretty tableau he'd created. A drop of fluid formed at the tip of Ned's thick cock.

Ned moaned and at last flexed his rear and pushed up. His eyes opened.

"Want something?" Patrick trailed two fingers along the line of Ned's hipbone.

"Please."

Patrick wiped the back of his hand across his mouth and liked the way Ned watched with glazed eyes, and panted.

They'd both had enough of teasing. Patrick rose to his feet for only a second so he could kiss a startled Ned on the mouth, then sank back to his knees and kissed Ned's erection.

Ned bucked up, nearly sliding off the chair. His belly slammed against Patrick's cheek.

"Are you...? Did I hurt you?" Ned asked, voice gruff.

"Fine and dandy." Patrick grinned like a fool. "I am going to enjoy this."

This time he kept one hand on Ned's thigh. The other wrapped around the base of Ned's prick, and Patrick licked and sucked as if his life depended on getting that cock into his mouth and down his throat. Oh, he loved the flavor and smell and texture. His own erection demanded attention, and he freed it awkwardly and one-handed as he attacked Ned's.

His rising orgasm took him by surprise coming so fast and hard—he nearly clenched his teeth—God, no biting down. He pulled off at the last moment. With one hand, he stroked Ned absently as he enjoyed the pulsations spiking through him. He gasped and shuddered.

Patrick studied the man whose cock he held. Ned didn't appear to notice Patrick's distraction, if that amazing release could be called that.

Eyes closed again, lips parted, brows furrowed, Ned looked as if he'd forgotten something. Lost in his own world of pleasure, locked away from Patrick, but that was fine for now.

Patrick wished he could permanently capture the image of Ned pumping into his hand. Memory would have to serve. Ned's head went back, and then he cried out, a sob or shout, and Patrick leaned close to lick and suck again. The cock in his hand hardened.

He suspected once the ease of the release passed, Ned might be filled with regrets and self-recriminations, and he had no interest in watching that dreary battle with guilt. He pulled out his handkerchief and carefully cleaned off Ned and then his own body and hands. "There," he said as he used both hands to button up Ned's trousers. "You have finally relaxed."

Ned's eyes widened, and he gave a crack of laughter, then covered his mouth as if he'd made some sort of faux pas. Patrick didn't point out that his cries as he'd spent were louder than his laughter. Good thing the servants hadn't burst in to see what was wrong with the young master.

"Thank you," Ned said awkwardly. "May I, uh? Should I?"

"No need to reciprocate. I took care of myself." Patrick tucked himself away.

Ned looked worried. "It's not good to do that, you know."

"Bring oneself off?"

Ned nodded. "It can be dangerous."

"Ah, jeez, I doubt it's the health hazard the doctors tell us it is. I don't do it excessively," Patrick added. Not anymore, at any rate. "I think that's where the trouble might lie. Like alcohol. A glass of wine with dinner won't kill a man. Too much and it *will* kill him."

The scowl on Ned's face was fierce. Patrick nudged him. "What's wrong, Ned?"

*

Edmund rose to his feet and hastily adjusted his clothing, embarrassed to even speak of the vile habits of men. "I am Mr. Sloan." He grimaced. "Or Edmund, I suppose, since we must be on a first-name basis now."

Patrick laughed as if he'd made a funny joke, and yes, perhaps it was amusing. Edmund smiled even as he blushed.

"I figured you'd be the sort to look like you'd faced a firing squad after exchanging some pleasure," Patrick said.

Edmund felt nettled, as if shame was something to be ashamed of. And that thought was odd enough to make him smile again.

Patrick licked his lips. "I guess I was wrong? You don't mind what we did after all."

Good Lord, if he agreed he didn't mind their...activity, would Patrick Kelly go after him again? An alarming, arousing thought. "No. I believe that what we did was wrong." What a relief to say things like that and know it wouldn't hurt Patrick, who apparently had the sensibility of a tree stump.

"That's a pity. I had a wonderful time, and it's sad to have that ruined by regrets." Patrick looked so solemn; Edmund must have misjudged the near-stranger's resilience.

"I beg your pardon," he said. "I do not blame you."

"Nope, I don't feel regrets—not a one. But it's too bad you do, because..." Patrick shrugged. "It's sad. Should I leave?"

Edmund realized he didn't need to be alone. In fact, he felt comforted by the presence of the blunt and unapologetic Patrick.

He had trouble looking at Patrick, though. What they'd done remained too vivid, rather like Kelly himself, whose attention seemed to be a tangible object. "No," Edmund said at last. "We might talk. I suppose. You might tell me about your life in America. What is it like, being a private inquiry man?"

"Dull work. I comb through old records for evidence or follow people who lead boring lives. And I could tell you about my time as a cop, but it was mostly dealing with drunks and wife beaters."

Two might play at this game of direct speech. Edmund said, "You wish to avoid the topic."

Patrick's eyes widened. "Damnation. Am I that easy to read? And, ha! You of all people calling me out on it."

"Of all people?" Edmund settled in the wicker chair again, suddenly glad to be here, glad to be talking to Patrick Kelly. "What does that mean?"

"You're so polite, you'd apologize to an empty chair if you bumped into it."

Edmund had begged the pardon of furniture more than once. But he was done with such sharp attention on himself. "Why do you want to avoid talking about your work?"

Patrick adjusted his cuffs and rubbed at a mark on his trousers. "This is going to sound bizarre. No one has asked me, and I haven't said it out loud."

"Go on." Edmund leaned forward, now curious.

"I have what I guess I might call a real hunger for the work."

He had a hunger for other things as well, but Edmund only said, "Yes, one can't help noticing. You are focused."

"And if I talk about it too much, think about it intensely, maybe I'll lose that focus."

"You are a strange fellow," Edmund said. "I'd think what just happened between us would be more distracting."

Patrick began to laugh.

"What is so amusing?"

"The way you said it. 'What just happened between us.' You'd be right, certainly. That does take the sharp edge off a man. But you made it hard to resist that particular challenge, what with those eyes of yours."

Edmund flinched. He'd heard more than enough about his blasted eyeballs all his life.

"And then there's the rest of you." Patrick's voice had dropped to a softer note, and he still hunched over his knees, staring at Edmund, a hunting creature sizing up its prey, nearly ready to spring. "And the way you wanted me too. I suppose you not bringing yourself off means you walk around in a restless state."

Edmund swallowed. He was unused to allowing his thoughts to stray in such a direction. "I have learned to direct any energy into more wholesome matters." Even to himself, he sounded priggish.

Patrick showed that wicked, unwholesome grin of his.

There was a knock at the door, and Edmund jumped to his feet as if he'd been poked. He looked about the room. No sign at all of "what just happened," other than a crumpled handkerchief on the floor and perhaps a scent in the air. He swooped down on the handkerchief, then called, "Enter."

Becker said, "A person named Mason has arrived. When told the hour is late, he announced that he came at the invitation of Mr. Kelly."

Patrick groaned. "Aw, dang it. The greengrocer. And I expect he's more than tipsy."

Greengrocer? Edmund wondered what the devil Patrick was up to now. He turned to his butler. "Well? Is Mr. Mason under the influence?"

"The gentleman is worse for drink."

"Who is he?"

Patrick looked sheepish. Edmund suspected Mr. Mason had to be bad if that brash American could be embarrassed by him. The visit must have to do with the Lawtons' murders, he suddenly understood.

It would do him good to remember why Patrick was here. And it would be best to get this subject covered and over with as soon as possible. Edmund waved a hand. "Never mind, show him in."

As soon as Becker left, the words burst out of Patrick. "Listen, I should have said something. Cripes, I'm sorry I gave him this address."

"Oh?"

"He's someone who saw you, saw Ned Lawton, leaving the house that day."

Edmund sighed. "I suspected it must be something like that."

"But you still didn't send him packing?"

"No." Edmund felt relaxed. His body's tension had been relieved, and, more than that, he'd witnessed an anxious Patrick Kelly—what a pity he couldn't possess a photograph or painting of this event. He rose to his feet, and so did Patrick.

They stood side by side, waiting for the greengrocer. Edmund took a step away from Patrick but he could still sense his heat. He rocked back on his heels. "This has been one of the most interesting days."

Kelly whistled. "I'll say."

The door opened, and a man with astonishingly red hair entered. Mason tugged a forelock when he spotted Edmund. He even ducked a bit of a bow.

"You and your grand house have that effect on people," Patrick muttered.

Edmund spared him a scowl before dismissing the butler.

"Good evening," he said to his visitor.

"Sir, and hallo, it's my new friend Mr. Kelly too." The redhead directed a toothy grin at Patrick.

Had the lusty Patrick invited the greengrocer to talk of murder, or did he have ideas of his personal entertainment? That might form the reason of his embarrassment. Mason had broad shoulders and the smile and gleeful manner of a man who'd had at least two pints, so maybe...

"This is Jimmy Mason," Patrick said.

"How do you do? I'm Mr. Sloan." Edmund didn't offer his hand.

"The words are polite enough, but you could freeze hot tea with that glacial tone," Patrick muttered again.

"Be quiet," Edmund said. He spoke too loudly, but Mason didn't appear to notice.

"Sloan? Sloan! That's the name of the big black bird all those years ago." Jimmy Mason lurched forward. He punched Patrick on the arm. "The lawyer bloke I told you about. The one who flew from the house. Flap." He moved his arms to demonstrate.

"Different man, different spelling, no relation." Apparently, Patrick lied easily. "Mr. Mason here told me a story about the Lawton murders. I thought because you're another *investigator*—" He said the word loudly with a significant glance at Edmund.

"More lies?" Edmund asked quietly. He supposed he should be grateful Patrick was trying to protect his identity, though it seemed absurd to think an investigator would be able to afford a home like this.

Patrick went on as if he hadn't said anything. "—because you're interested in the topic, maybe you'd like to hear his account."

"Is that what you thought?" Edmund said. "You invited a stranger to my house to tell me a story you believed I might want to hear about that night?"

"Perhaps. I mean, yes." He lowered his voice. "I'm sorry about being a nuisance."

Now he apologized? Edmund tried to suppress a smile. He should have been upset, but the absurdity of Mason, of the whole evening, proved too much. "It's kind of you to make express regrets for your behavior, and likely out of character."

Patrick blinked. "By golly, you're teasing me. I think."

"A little, perhaps." He wished Patrick wouldn't stare at him with such open delight.

Edmund moved to the tray of drinks. "Would you care for a drink, Mason?"

"I think he's had enough," Patrick began.

"Yes," Mason spoke loudly over him. "I wants a drink."

Edmund gave Mason whisky and himself one as well. He settled back into his chair and waited for the show to start.

"So, you're not Sloan," Mason declared. He wobbled a bit.

"Please, take a seat if you wish," Edmund said.

Mason lurched to the wooden chair, the one where Edmund had sat during his massage. He nearly overset the chair but managed to plunk down before it tipped. "The Sloan I saw was a big black bird. Like I said. All dark and skinny-like. I only noticed because he had blood on him. He left bloody footprints. His coat or cape must have been what flapped, because he had his arms full. A boy."

Patrick watched Edmund, who decided to ignore him. The lump in Edmund's throat didn't vanish, but neither did it grow. He even managed a sip of the drink. "Did the boy cry?"

"Nosir. Boy was as silent as he. The house was full of people, mostly cops. I wouldn't have noticed those two at all but for the footprints."

"Did you see if there was blood on the boy?"

Mason sniffed the drink, gulped it down. "Can't recall, sir."

"Did he seem awake? Asleep?"

Mason tilted his glass mournfully. Edmund rose, took it from him, and filled it this time.

"Here now," Patrick began, but he stopped when Edmund gave him the look—a stare he'd copied from his old headmaster.

He handed Mason the drink and resumed his seat. "Asleep?" he prompted.

"No, come to think on it, the boy was awake. Big eyes. Everyone knows about those eyes." Mason drank, then squinted at Edmund. "Kind of like yours, sir. Mr. Uh…"

"Was Mr. Sloan speaking to him?"

"It was years ago, sir. I was just a boy." He drank the rest of the whisky. "I think Mr. Sloan's face was all crumpled-like for a moment. Like he was sneezing or crying. I stopped paying him any mind when they dragged out the girl. Older lady to be sure."

"The surviving nanny?" Patrick asked.

"Her, a turtle-faced kind of a woman, blinking like they woke her up." Mason leaned back in the chair. "I'm tired," he announced.

"We shall have to see about getting a hack to take you home," Patrick said.

Less than a minute later, a loud snore rose from Mason.

"Why did you want me to meet him?" Edmund asked, wondering at the ease he felt. He should have been jittery and nauseated after the conversation with Mason.

"I, umm, I wanted to see if he could bring back any memories for you, I guess. Or maybe his story would make it clear your foster father was something of a witness and you'd agree to help me talk to Mr. Sloan—or ask questions of your own. But don't worry. I can see inviting Mason was a bad idea."

"Yes, it didn't do you any good. I don't have any clear memories, and you're a fool if you think my father will speak to either of us."

"That's not why I think it was the wrong thing to do." He got up, went to Mason, and removed the glass he still clutched. He gave Mason a poke, but the sleeping man didn't so much as grunt.

Patrick sat near Edmund in that peculiar, thoroughly informal hunched pose of elbows on thighs.

Edmund said, "I can see you're anxious to explain why you regret the invitation. Go ahead and tell me."

"First let me say how awed I am by the way you managed to ask him good questions, and so calmly too."

Edmund tried not to feel a swell of pride that he'd impressed Patrick, who went on. "But see, you are helping as much as you are able. Inviting drunken greengrocers to your home isn't going to make you like my presence any better."

"Consideration from Mr. Kelly? I am shocked."

Patrick grinned at him. "That's not what you thought a half hour ago."

A vivid picture of Patrick Kelly kneeling, greedy but gentle as he reached...reminded him how considerate the man could be.

Edmund looked away, his glance falling on the greengrocer, whose mouth gaped open and eyes stayed closed.

He went to the bell. Less than a minute later, Becker appeared. He'd probably been listening at the door.

"I think we need to call a cab for Mr. Mason to carry him home."

Patrick had lowered his face into his hands and now said something.

"Beg pardon, Mr. Kelly?"

"I'm not sure where he lives. Not above his shop like a decent shop owner should," Patrick grumbled.

Edmund grimaced. "We'll have to put him to bed here for the night."

"Sir." Becker would never argue with him, but his disgust was apparent.

"Let him sleep with one of the footmen. No, this snoring is too loud. We'll put him in a guest bedroom."

"*Sir.*"

"I know it wounds your sensibilities, but I can't think of another solution."

"A hotel," Patrick said. "I'll pay. Please, let me pay for the hack and the hotel. And I'll drag him out."

Edmund examined him. A bit of embarrassment made Patrick more human. "Very well," he said.

"I'll stay there too," Patrick said.

Wait, that wouldn't work after all. Edmund held up a hand stopping his protest. "In fact, now that I think of the matter, it is silly to take him away from here."

"Sir." Again, Becker managed to express a world of astonishment and displeasure in that single word.

Edmund ignored him. "I have many unused bedrooms." He had to keep Mason so he wouldn't lose track of Patrick. He didn't want to consider why he cared.

He spoke to Becker. "Please summon Liam and Timothy to help this, ah, gentleman up to the smaller room on the north end."

"The blue bedroom, sir?" He'd managed to return to a neutral tone.

"Is the room blue? I never enter it. They should take him to whichever bedroom will mean the least work for them. I suspect they'll have to drag Mr. Mason. He's almost as large as Mr. Kelly here."

The butler bowed and went off to find help.

"You don't know what your guest rooms look like? You never have guests," Patrick guessed.

"Of course I do." Wensler and his new wife had stayed with him only a month earlier. Before that, no, he'd never had guests. "I have two tonight," he reminded Patrick.

"Yes, thanks for that," Patrick said. "At least I won't pass out. The last time I took on that much alcohol was in college."

"You went to college?"

"Now, now, no need to sound so shocked."

"Where did you go?"

"It's a couple of decades old, a small Jesuit institution outside Boston," Patrick said. He stood and walked to Mason. "It's only fair that I help your footmen with this galoot."

"Nonsense. It is a job for the servants."

"My life is more like theirs or Mr. Mason's here than your station."

"You are an educated man," Patrick said. "Despite your demeanor."

Patrick threw his head back and laughed. "That's more like it."

Liam and Timothy entered the room and didn't appear to notice Edmund next to the palm. They glared at Patrick. "What? Why do you need help? We heard you were drooling drunk."

"No, that's the fellow." Patrick pointed at Mason.

When they turned, they saw Edmund. Timothy visibly started. Liam covered his mouth with a hand for a second, his eyes wide. "Sir. I'd supposed you'd retired for the night."

"Go to bed early, do you?" Patrick asked Edmund.

"Mr. Mason is the gentleman who requires your assistance. I believe Mr. Kelly has another, larger room." He waited until they'd hoisted a muttering Mason up, holding him under the arms. "Timothy, Liam, I hope," he said as mildly as he could, "you will treat my guests with respect."

"Sir."

"Of course, sir." The servants scuttled off, escorting a blinking Mason from the room.

"You can hardly blame them for being resentful if this isn't what they're used to," Patrick said.

"They were ill-mannered to you."

"Plenty are, and from all walks of life. Doesn't bother me."

Edmund remembered his own father's response to Patrick. "No, I suppose rudeness directed at you doesn't trouble you at all." He wondered what it would be like to be so unworried about the good opinion of others. Freeing, probably. "However, I expect better behavior from my servants."

"And even more from yourself." Patrick's smile appeared genuine, even warm, and not mocking. Edmund damned himself for caring what that expressive face told him.

"I should hope so. I have had a life of privilege—noblesse oblige." Edmund waited for Patrick to point out that his life wasn't always one of ease, but the other man only nodded.

"I'm not surprised you take that old phrase seriously. When I came here, I expected to find a spoiled, unpleasant gent. You're nothing like that."

His voice was warm and enthusiastic.

Edmund felt his face flush. "You hardly know me."

"Well. Your servants praise you, d'you know? That's always a good sign, or so the novels tell me."

Patrick had no experience with this sort of intimate conversation. Chatting about weather would be ridiculous. Absurd japes or joking, such as Wensler enjoyed, didn't fit either. "Mr. Kelly, ah, would you care for another beer? Although the hour is late."

"Mr. Kelly, is it? When no one else is around? All right, all right, I'll stop trying to force you into friendship." He sounded easy and unoffended. Slightly amused as if he were speaking to a growling puppy. "I shan't push again. But please, if you want more from me, I'll be in London for a while longer. Oh, but if you send round a note telling me to depart these premises, believe me, I'll understand." He laughed. "I think if there's a prize for worst houseguest of the year, I've won it. I'm truly sorry about foisting Mason on you."

Edmund wanted to flee, but a good host wouldn't abandon a guest. As if reading his thoughts, Patrick held out a hand, offering to shake. Edmund shook and refused to notice how large and warm the hand enclosing his felt.

"Well. Good night," Patrick said and left Edmund standing in the plant room, confused and oddly excited.

He woke early, but when he came downstairs before nine, he discovered both of his guests had vanished for the day. Becker reported that the greengrocer had been apologetic in his manner and had already delivered a basket of vegetables to the kitchen.

Edmund paced his house and waited to hear from Patrick Kelly. He gave himself a sound scolding for his preoccupation. At around noon, his secretary reminded him that he had an appointment with a board member of a museum. Anything to take his mind away from the picture of Patrick Kelly kneeling before him, his face filled with heat.

Edmund practically ran from his house. He'd had years of practice avoiding memories, but his thoughts of recent moments full of arousal might be too strong to escape.

Chapter Five

The bright morning seemed to cheer the entire population of London. Patrick hummed to himself as he walked along the platform. A man running in front of him had the same long-legged, well-tailored look as Ned Sloan. Patrick stopped short, ready to call out a greeting. But of course, it wasn't he.

Aw, cripes, now he'd be mistakenly spotting Ned in every crowd or gathering. Patrick had been smitten before and knew that he'd see the man everywhere. Never mind. Passion would be a nuisance, but he'd survive.

He determinedly began to hum again and made his way to the second-class compartment of the train. He was traveling to a small village outside London, one of many that would soon be swallowed by the city. The sergeant had told him the Lawtons' nanny had a cottage near the village church.

The train lurched into motion. After helping a stout and wheezing woman in widow's weeds push a valise up onto a rack, Patrick thumped down onto a comfortable leather bench seat next to her and decided to sleep.

The distraction of Ned Sloan had kept Patrick up much of the night. At around two, he'd grown determined to find Ned to see if he wanted company, or perhaps apologize again. Good thing his better sense had stopped Patrick and kept him in the bed. That and the fact that he didn't know where the gentleman slept.

Twice in his life, he'd bumbled along into infatuation. During both of those episodes, he'd at least retained some dignity—Patrick wasn't used to being an idiot in his personal life.

He shifted on the seat as he recalled the horror of Mason's visit. The only person who apologized more for that scene than Patrick was Mr. Mason, who swore upon his family's bible not to tell anyone of his drunken visit. Naturally, the dratted man had figured out that the house belonged to Mr. Sloan, formerly Lawton. Londoners knew entirely too much about other people's business.

Patrick suspected Mason would be as discreet about his stay under Edmund Sloan's roof as he'd been about the day the Lawton family had died—that is to say, as soon as he drank again, the greengrocer would tell anyone who so much as glanced in his direction.

As the train chugged out of the station, he noticed the sky had turned gray. The pleasant weather hadn't lasted long. His own mood darkened when he thought about his own idiocy with Sloan. He'd been paid back for his intrusion into the gentleman's life with this new unwelcome attraction, apparently accompanied by the need to somehow prove himself to Mr. Ned Sloan.

The best way to get Ned's approval would be to find the other person who'd killed the Lawton family, and Patrick didn't need more fuel for that particular fire in him.

He couldn't sleep because the large woman, whose black bonnet covered most of her face, wanted to talk about his funny American accent and about her sister in Philadelphia. Perhaps Mr. Kelly had met her? She seemed far more cheerful and outgoing than most of the British people he'd met, and he didn't mind talking.

Patrick sadly informed the stout lady he'd never been to the City of Brotherly Love. She then described her sister and her family in case he should ever meet up with them. Patrick considered asking her about the Lawtons' nanny. He only had a name and a nine-year-old address for the old lady.

Mrs. Dalton—Miss Miller when she'd been the nanny—hadn't had to testify. Somehow she'd avoided interviews with the hungry press as well. The only descriptions Patrick had of her came from Mason and the sergeant. She'd been older and homely, they both said, worse than plain, though she'd apparently found a husband, Mr. Dalton, soon after the event.

A fine rain sent drops dotting, then streaking the windows of the train. The compartment filled. The woman turned to another man to discuss the change in the weather. Patrick pressed against the window and gazed out at the lush green countryside, pondering why the nanny had been spared by the killer.

At a rambling house in New York, a nearly bald middle-aged man with a potbelly hadn't been harmed. He had been tied up, blindfolded, and gagged. The homely nanny had been tied up and been knocked unconscious with chloroform.

Maybe it had been a coincidence, but the American families had been very attractive people—as pretty as the Lawtons. Perhaps the killer had targeted only fine-looking people like the Lawtons and their serving maid. The sergeant had laughed at Patrick when he'd pointed out that particular similarity, saying a man practically had to stretch across the ocean to make those pieces fit. Once again, his argument wasn't enough to convince the authorities.

Finding the connections was up to Patrick.

The train pulled into the station, a new building that looked like an architect had gone wild with decorative brickwork and turrets.

Patrick made his way to the plain Norman church that lay not far from the station. He'd already discovered that records of marriages and deaths in churches seemed far more comprehensive than other municipal records.

The vicar, a slender man with a pince-nez, beamed at him. "Welcome, sir. Welcome and good morning!" With his pointed nose and narrow shoulders, the gent resembled an intelligent ferret. "How may I help you?"

He shook Patrick's hand, and Patrick wondered if the clergyman showed so much delight because he was bored, over-friendly, or another sodomite.

The vicar gladly led Patrick to his office and hovered nearby as he looked through the massive leather volumes, looking for records of Miss Miller's marriage to Mr. Dalton, or the man's death. He found nothing.

Patrick asked about Mrs. Dalton, and the vicar immediately volunteered a great wealth of information about the kind lady who sat on many committees and worked with the poor.

When Patrick asked about her husband, the vicar frowned. "She was widowed when I arrived here five years ago. She keeps a bit to herself. Apparently, she worked as a servant but inherited some money a while ago."

About ten years ago, Patrick suspected.

He bade the vicar good-bye and strode down a narrow, twisting road toward the small cluster of new cottages.

Mrs. Dalton had a fine flower garden, red roses clashing with a brighter red door set in the whitewashed building

Patrick paused to focus on the questions he had for Mrs. Dalton. First of all, where was Mr. Dalton? Not on any record he could find in London or in the little village church.

She answered the door wiping her reddened hands on a cloth. She had no actual chin but a series of folds that served as several. Her eyes, of no particular color, were small and set too close together. She had a slight mustache under a big shapeless nose. But her smile seemed genuine and happy, though it showed many missing teeth.

It was the sort of warm expression that made you want to smile back. He said, "Good morning, I'm Mr. Kelly, recently arrived from the United States. I wish to ask you a few questions."

"Oh. I've never been to that country." Her voice was pleasant and calm, yet her hand on the door moved a little as if she wanted to slam it shut.

"The questions I have for you relate to incidents in your past."

Her eyes widened. "You'd best come in."

The scent hit him hard: roses, bread, and some sort of animal musk, something strong. Polecat, perhaps?

"Uh, you have cats?" he asked.

"Foxes." She led him down a dim hall past several vases of roses sitting on tables and a few closed doors. When she opened the last door, she revealed sunlight spilling across a pleasant kitchen with a flag floor. The animal smell was stronger in here. Three cages sat next to each other, and three pairs of bright eyes gazed out with some alarm. Their red fur seemed almost as bright as the vases of roses in the hall.

"I keep 'em locked up when there's a hunt scheduled. There's one in two days."

She nudged something under the table, and another one emerged. It had only three legs but seemed to get around fine.

"Take a seat," she said, looking at the fox. Patrick decided she was speaking to him.

He sat on a solid wooden chair at the small kitchen table and watched her shove a kettle onto the stove. She brushed her hands down the front of a white pinafore over a shapeless gray gown. Still looking at the fox, she said, "I expect you mean to ask about Mr. Dalton."

Best to sound as if he knew what she meant, so he made a noncommittal grunt.

"They told me it wasn't a crime."

"Oh."

"I mean, I changed my name legal and all. Although what that has to do with America, I don't know."

He ventured a guess. "Your husband was fictitious."

She sat down heavily on the matching chair across from him. "I had my reasons for leaving my past in the past."

"Because you worked for the Lawtons," he said softly.

She heaved a sigh that made her large front rise and fall slowly. "Ah, and what do you know about that, eh?"

He folded his hands on the well-scrubbed round table and told her about his mission and about the families he worked for.

She listened without speaking. Only her bright small eyes showed her attention. When he finished, she rose to her feet. "Now then, Mr. Kelly. You think I had something to do with all that slaughter?" She sounded surprisingly belligerent.

He took on soothing tones to calm her down. "No, I don't. Remember what I said about the murders in the US? They're what I'm interested in. I might believe that someone, maybe a British someone, is responsible, but I don't think you had anything to do with their deaths or the Lawton killings."

She seemed to deflate some. "Many did think me guilty. That's why I went along with the idea of changing my name. And even if you did suspect me of that crime, I could barely do anything so active. My heart is all skittery still today because of what chloroform can do to a person."

"The day you were drugged. Can you tell me what you remember?"

She sighed again. "You tell me this, Mr. American Kelly. You're truly not a reporter?"

"No." He pulled out his card stating his employer's name, and it seemed to satisfy her.

She held the card between two fingers for a long time before putting it on the table closer to her side than his. She shuffled to the stove and measured out tea into a flowered pot. "I don't like reporters, not even a bit, and I'm not supposed to speak to them."

He wanted to know who'd issued that order, but remained silent because he could see by her stiffening posture that she was working herself up to speak.

She put down the spoon. "All right, here's what I know. I was in the nursery, dozing in a chair. Next thing I know, someone had dropped something over my face and held that nasty cloth for minutes and minutes." She returned to her seat and sat across from him. "No matter what you've heard, it doesn't happen fast, chloroform. Takes more than a few minutes. That man was strong, but so was I back then."

"Was he taller than you? Shorter than you?"

"They asked me that same question. I said about an inch taller, but they said he was more like three inches taller. And they could have been right. We struggled, and most of the time, I was in the chair. I couldn't see, and I was screaming like a piglet." She looked at a small vase with two roses sitting in the center of the table, glaring as if the flowers had disagreed with her. "I woke up when the police hit me across the face. They thought it was me who let the killer in. They thought he was my lover."

She made a rude sound. "I showed them my hands. They were bloody from the ropes and from him too. Once they caught up with him, they found he had scratches all over his face and neck."

"He came up behind you over the top of the chair? While you were sitting? Did you scratch him while you stood?"

"Can't recall that anymore, now. A lot of details are blurry. That awful drug."

"I know this is a difficult topic for you," he said.

She gave a brisk little sniff. "It shouldn't be. All happened years ago, and I didn't see the bodies. Or if I did, I don't remember."

"Had you worked for the Lawtons long?"

"About six months. I liked the family. The girls were sweet creatures."

"What about the boy?"

"A hellion, a devil." She looked him in the eye for the first time, before dropping her gaze to the flowers again. "Ah, sir, I'm too harsh. He was not a bad boy, not at all, but he took risks, climbing bookcases and trees. And he knew how to get his own way. Even with me. He called me his Neenah, and it does me good to remember that, the sweetness of him. And to think that he mightn't have had to see what happened to his family if he'd stayed in the nursery. Though I hear he hid, so maybe he wouldn't have been safe if he'd been with me the way he was supposed to be." She pursed her lips, released them, then pursed them again as if fighting back a smile or a whimper.

He gave an encouraging "Hm?"

"The meal that night was planned to allow the girls to dine with their parents. They were older than Ned and needed to practice their manners with company. Usually the children would eat in the nursery, you see. Neddy was supposed to stay in with me. Of course he carried on. Instead of ignoring his tantrum the way she should've, Mrs. Lawton scooped him up and took him downstairs as well. I don't believe in striking a child, at least not often. That boy was too lively and could have used a spank or two."

She stared at the roses hard now, as if she would set them on fire. "He most certainly did not deserve to lose his family, poor lad."

Edmund Sloan? High spirited and naughty? Patrick's heart hurt to think of the active boy's fire quenched that day, all that energy leashed up tight inside. And wasn't that a poetic turn, his mother would say— then again, if she heard Ned's story, she'd be weeping uncontrollably. Maybe if Patrick could bring this story to a real close, he'd help Edmund regain his confidence of that brash little boy.

"Mrs. Dalton—"

"You might as well call me Miss Miller. I haven't heard the name in years." She rose to her feet and poured water from the kettle into a teapot. Another cup of tea, Patrick thought morosely. But chances were she'd kick him out after the next set of questions.

"You're pretty comfortable out here in this village. If you didn't marry to get the money to retire at a young age, can you tell me how you managed?"

"You don't hold back, do you?" She stirred the water in the flowered teapot.

"You didn't answer my question."

"No, and I shan't." She ambled over with two cups and two saucers then brought the teapot, a plate of sugar lumps, and a pitcher of milk over too. Several of the foxes wagged their tails and made a small yipping sound.

Patrick leaned forward. "Can you tell me why you don't want to talk about how you got your money?"

"It doesn't relate to your case, my boy. I think you're prying for no good reason." She poured out the tea and stared into her cup. "The tea is too strong."

He liked this woman's straightforward manner and her refusal to be offended. "I'll tell you, Mrs.—I mean Miss Miller, I think it might relate to my case. My guess is that the Lawton estate paid for your cottage and maybe an annuity."

She picked up her tea and drank. "Perhaps."

"But I think the whole thing might have been arranged by Mr. Sloan the lawyer."

She started at the name and then added a shrug, perhaps to cover her surprise. "Could be." She drank more tea. "I suppose it doesn't hurt to say yes. After all, the lawyer arranged everything once the Lawtons were gone. I liked that gentleman. He'd already helped my brother Kenneth by getting him a job. But I admit I wasn't sure I agreed with everything he did. I mean, I told him I'd be glad to go with the boy into his house. I did have a care for little Ned. He was sweet under the wildness. And I thought it would be good for him to have a familiar face."

"Mr. Sloan refused?"

"Yes. He said the boy needed to start fresh, no reminders of that awful time. I could see why that would be best. I was in a dreadful state myself. I wanted to run away and never talk to anyone again once the police started in with me. And then with Kenneth going away for his new job, I had no one…not that he and I were ever close. He was a difficult, angry sort of a person. But then I felt all alone, and those horrible police were going after me."

Patrick thought about his own time with the police. To get to the truth, cops regularly used their fists, rubber truncheons, and straps, and they'd never let a suspect sleep. Women got less roughed up—unless they were attractive.

"Their suspicions lasted only a day but..." Miss Miller shook her head. "That whole family. Such grand people gone in such an awful way. When Mr. Sloan told me about little Ned starting fresh, I supposed he wasn't wrong."

"Has anyone come to bother you about the story?"

She poured herself more tea. "I hid myself well enough. The press talked to the other servants, you know. The ones who wanted to make some pennies by telling their stories. Some of them saw the scene. I didn't, and I wanted nothing to do with the day or talk of it."

"The man who attacked you said nothing during the attack?"

"Not a word. And the rest of the house was silent too. So I supposed he'd finished his...what he did to the family." She covered her mouth with a ruddy hand. "Or if what you said is true? There was another man. Oh, my gracious. You think those poor Lawtons could still have been alive downstairs? Those lovely girls."

She picked up her cup and put it down again without drinking. "But if there were two men, the other must have been the one with the family, because I scratched the villain who attacked me, that Weller person they hanged. Oh, Mr. Kelly, I almost wish you hadn't said anything, because now it's coming back to me."

She reached down and hauled the three-legged fox onto her lap. It rolled onto its back and made an odd sound while she stroked its belly.

"I'm sorry," he said.

A tear rolled down her doughy face, and she wiped at it angrily. "You're doing your job. But I think… Yes. I don't have anything else to say to you." With a grunt, she put down the fox and stood.

He was being dismissed, and he decided not to object. He rose to his feet. "You have my card, and I have penciled in my address in New York on back." He pulled some coins from his pocket and put them next to his untouched cup of tea.

"I don't need your money," she said, sounding offended for the first time.

"This is to pay for postage. If you should think of anything else, such as more memories of that day or if you can recall gossip about possible enemies of the family or something odd about them and their acquaintances." He paused, wondering if he should add *especially any information relating to Mr. Sloan the lawyer*, but decided not to. He said, "Please, Miss Miller, if you think of even the smallest detail, I would appreciate a letter—even if it's just rumors you've heard. Send it to me at that address."

She glared down at the money, her cheeks red. A long moment passed, and she blinked several times before speaking in a far milder tone, "A letter? All the way to America? I well know that's expensive."

"You know someone there?"

She folded her arms and didn't answer. "All right. What if I don't think of anything?"

"Buy meat for the foxes, then." He pulled out more coins. "Do both."

Patrick spent the rest of the day in a fruitless search of possible connections between Mr. Sloan the lawyer and Weller, the man who'd been hanged for the murders, and then he looked for something that would link Weller and any notorious criminals in the US. Maybe Patrick was working so hard because he needed to justify this journey to England. More than that, he'd love to punish whoever had stripped Ned of his family and turned him from a happy, noisy boy into a stiff and formal gentleman.

As he put down the scrawled list of known miscreants the sergeant had handed over, he decided that even if he was correct about the British origin of the murderer, the answers probably lay back in New York or Rhode Island, not in the killer's past.

He trudged back toward the house in Mayfair, wondering if he should offer to pay Mr. Greene for most of his own expenses. Patrick hated failure. Of course, he occasionally hated attaining his investigative goals even more.

There was the time he found out that a sweet-faced little girl had killed her own infant brother.

Uncovering the story of his own father was his most miserable success. Patrick's mother, who claimed to be a widow, had always told inconsistent stories about his father, a man she'd met on the ship coming over from Ireland.

One night, Patrick had decided to interrogate her about the facts that were so flimsy they shifted like leaves in a stiff, changeable breeze. He'd sat her down in their kitchen and used the soft cajoling manner he'd learned as a cop. At least he didn't have to be totally ashamed of the memory—he hadn't yelled or pulled out a truncheon.

He'd questioned his mam like a fragile witness, not a suspect. "Tell me about my father. I accept your explanation that he died, Mother, but nothing else holds together."

God, what an ass he'd been. *I accept your explanation*, indeed, as if she'd been filing reports that he'd have to check over.

Patrick had continued, "Was he a member of the crew or a passenger? Was he dark-haired or fair? You know I won't judge you if you admitted you weren't married."

She'd stared at nothing as he spoke. Then silence had filled their small apartment, broken at last by the scrape of her chair over the wood as she pushed it back to rise. "I'll tell you once, and then not again. I do not know, because I never saw your father's face. I was feeling poorly, went out to the deck. He grabbed me from behind and put his hand over my mouth so I couldn't scream or turn around. Then he dragged me into a small room, no windows and dark as pitch. It was done in less than five minutes."

"Mother, *Mam*," he'd begun, but she'd raised her hands.

"I'll finish this now, Patrick. After he left me there, I went to the crew, and they didn't believe me. They didn't care, or maybe they were covering the crime for the sake of one of their own? I don't know. All I know is no one believed it wasn't my choice, not even your late uncle, who met me at the docks."

Patrick understood that had been why she'd fled her relatives after landing in New York. Alone and violated, carrying the child of her rapist, she'd run away.

The night she'd told him the truth, she hadn't wept. He did, though, and as he sobbed, he'd tried to tell her he was sorry that he'd badgered her, and then he begged her forgiveness for his very existence.

"Don't be daft," she'd said. "It's time I told you. And come now, I said I want no more talk of this." She'd walked around to his chair and given him a playful punch on the shoulder. "Although I don't think you can promise to never ask questions. You always were a pest with your curiosity. I doubt that'll change now. As for the last, don't make me box your ears."

He cried for his poor mam, a name for her he hadn't used in years, and of course she comforted him.

"This is a ridiculous reversal of roles." He'd half laughed, half sniffled as she'd hugged him. "I didn't suffer, you did."

"I've had years knowing a story that's brand new for you."

"I'm sorry," he'd said again for the hundredth time. "I'm sorry such an awful thing happened to you."

"Enough. No, I mean it, Patrick. You've always been a strong boy. Stop indulging yourself," she'd snapped, and then she'd smiled. "Weeping is my job, not yours."

He'd choked back the tears and wiped his face. "I wish I could hunt the bastard down and kill him."

At that moment, he'd realized one of his long-time suspicions had been true. He was a bastard—though that was hardly the worst of the story.

His mother had hugged him hard, over and over. "He was the worst sort of villain, but he also gave me the best thing in my life."

After that night, she took to calling him the best, which became bestie. The nickname always reminded him of his guilt for his existence, but he wouldn't admit such a thing to her.

As he walked toward Mr. Sloan's house, Patrick considered the reason he'd been so astonished by his mother's confession of his conception and why he had never guessed the circumstances. She'd always treated him as if he'd been a blessing. He'd seen enough violence in his job. Patrick couldn't imagine loving a baby conceived during rape.

He'd known his mother was overemotional—he'd witnessed her breaking down at the sight of a plucked chicken or at the sound of a hymn. But after that, he knew she was strong as iron as well. The truth she revealed that night confirmed that a sentimental nature didn't mean weakness.

He doubted Mr. Ned Sloan believed that. Strength meant stoicism to the Sloan family and others in their class. It hardly seemed fair to begrudge Ned anything that would lend him strength. Yep, except for the fact that Patrick didn't like anything that let Ned keep him at arm's length. He wanted to be closer, at the very least a friend who could help Edmund Sloan become Ned again.

But Patrick reckoned Ned had already made progress. Coarse and aggressive manners had to shock gentlemen as well, and yet Ned allowed himself to succumb to Patrick...and hadn't that been a wonderful interlude last night. The memory made Patrick walk faster.

As he drew near the large pale house, he realized he hadn't thought of his case for several long minutes. Something had loosened inside him. More than just his focus had shifted from hunting a killer to hunting Ned Sloan. He didn't usually indulge in personal reflection in the heat of the chase, and he'd done practically nothing else since getting off the train at Paddington. Patrick slowed his steps, unsure if he approved of the change.

He'd be silly on his own time, once he'd finished this case. A killer still walked free in the US, and he'd best not forget that.

Chapter Six

Edmund sat, glowering at some sheets of papers his secretary had left on his desk, lists of numbers relating to his investment in a South American port facility. Usually he was scrupulous about adding the numbers and making sure his sums matched those of the reports he read.

Now he found he couldn't give a damn about the numbers, the port he'd never visit, or the money trickling back to his account.

"Sir?" Becker stood before the desk. Behind him, a footman held a tray of food. Edmund glanced at the clock standing in the corner of the library. It was nearly seven p.m., and he hadn't eaten since breakfast.

"I didn't order a meal," Edmund pointed out.

"Yes, sir, I know."

"I don't require a nursemaid, Becker."

"No, sir. We shall just leave this tray here, then?"

Edmund's stomach growled, and he gave up. "Thank you."

He waited for Becker and Liam to leave before standing to examine the tray's contents: a plate of sandwiches, stewed fruit, and roly-poly pudding. Standard fare for a schoolboy, and more than good enough for him in this uncharacteristically sour mood.

Damn Patrick Kelly. Damn him to hell and back, and just where in hell was he? Had Patrick gone blithely off to seduce his next man or woman in order to get the information he needed?

Edmund sat down with the plate of sandwiches and gloomily ate them while imagining the letter he might compose to Mr. Greene. *Your employee burst into my home and my life. He intruded on my well-ordered, peaceful existence and insisted I help him in the most personally painful manner by delving into best-forgotten memories, which did not appear to be of any use to either of us. And then, far worse, he left again without so much as a formal farewell.*

He reached for the pudding and ignored the stewed plums.

Edmund had never before indulged in so much shockingly immature sulking. Luckily, no one else appeared to notice his childishness, except perhaps Becker. Hence the roly-poly pudding, which tasted better than Edmund had recalled. Once he finished eating, he felt more himself and reached for the papers again, although why he needed more money added to the fortune he already had... He sighed and began to total columns of numbers. When Becker and Liam came in again to collect the tray, Edmund took a moment to look up. "You were right, of course," he said. "I was hungry. Thank you."

The faint sound of the front doorbell jangled at eight p.m. He heard the sound of voices. Edmund put down the papers and waited but didn't rise to his feet.

Becker came into the library. "Mr. Kelly's arrived, sir. He says he will retire if you are uninterested in entertaining him."

"Tell him he can do what he likes." That sounded far surlier than he felt. Edmund tried again. "That is, if he cares to join me here, I'll be glad of his company."

Less than a minute later, the cheerful and loud "Good evening!" made his heart beat harder and faster. It was as if someone had opened a window on a bright day and a breeze blew into the dusty corners. Did Patrick's presence always change a room? And did his smile show a kind of raucous brilliance? A silly question to ask, because two days ago—in fact, just yesterday morning—he hadn't known Patrick Kelly existed.

He knew so little of him. A few minutes ago, Edmund had felt certain Patrick was off charming another person to advance his investigation. The encounter of their bodies had to be what changed Edmund from a man who valued thoughtful evaluation into some kind of eager animal.

That helped Edmund feel sober, and he greeted the exuberant Patrick with a more level, "Please take a seat. I hope you had a productive day?"

Patrick sat and perched his hat, a dusty bowler, on his knee. The thought of those long, powerful legs jolted Edmund's desire awake.

Edmund waved a hand. "Why didn't you give that hat to Becker?"

"I was in a hurry and wanted to see you."

The simple answer threatened to shove Edmund toward rapaciousness. He pushed back his desk chair, ready to pounce or flee, he hadn't decided which.

Patrick's sharp gaze moved around the room. "This looks like the Astor Library."

"Beg pardon?"

"The Astor Library in New York. Floor-to-ceiling books, and lots of them."

"You like to read?"

"Sure. Are you surprised? Or did you think I'd only like penny dreadfuls?" He grinned. "No, don't look so worried. I'm not offended. I was teasing you a little."

"I forgot you went to college."

"Yes. And where I come from, people don't usually stay in school past fifth grade."

"Were you so very exceptional? I'm rather surprised."

Patrick looked delighted by the insult. "Not at all. But I had a couple of teachers and a mother determined to keep me in school. I couldn't fight that stern army, or rather I didn't want to. And then I got a scholarship, so it seemed a waste to let it go."

"You had more education than most policemen."

"Yes, and it didn't do me any good in that profession. The regulars on the beat thought I was too snobbish for them, and the higher-ups didn't like my background."

"I thought many of them were Irish."

"Sure, sure." Patrick waved a hand as if to dismiss the topic of his background. Edmund suspected he hid something. With anyone else, he'd be far too circumspect to tread on an obviously sensitive subject. But the fact that Patrick, who delved and dug like a badger, might be hiding something of his own proved irresistible to Edmund.

"What didn't they like about you, Mr. Kelly?" He added a "Hmm?" The same sound Patrick made to add emphasis to a question.

"I'm a bastard," Patrick sounded entirely unconcerned. "Illegitimate, I mean."

"I'm sorry," Edmund said and wondered if that was the wrong response.

He'd met a few illegitimate people, of course. But he'd never met one who'd so easily admit to being born on the wrong side of the blanket or use that crude word.

"It was no reflection of my mother," Patrick said emphatically, and Edmund nodded, though he wondered how that could be true. Patrick went on. "I didn't mean to shock you, for once. I figured I know your secrets; it's only fair you know some of mine. Some, anyway."

Edmund wished again for the tray containing brandy. He sat back in his chair and folded his arms. "Very well, I'll ask some other questions. Are you married?"

"Me? Of course not!"

"Now it's your turn to sound unreasonably astonished." Edmund tried to sound jaunty, but his voice faltered as Patrick held his gaze. Edmund was glad for the desk that lay between them.

"You know exactly why I'm not married. You know what I like. What I want." Patrick's voice was something between a growl and whisper.

"One supposes such…but for a lifetime…" He swallowed, unsure what he meant, because his thoughts had grown disordered and now followed a dark path, one filled with delicious ideas and images. He wanted to look away, didn't he? Edmund must not allow himself to fall into this sort of desire again. His prick had other opinions and pressed against his smalls, aroused not by touch but by a simple phrase, that heavy gaze and Edmund's own vivid imagination.

Patrick's smile was knowing, and his eyes shifted down, as if he could see through the cherrywood desk onto Edmund's lap.

"That shan't happen again." Edmund spoke sharply, admonishing himself as much as Patrick.

"Certainly," Patrick agreed.

"I mean it." Edmund felt foolish, though he couldn't entirely recall why he was so determined to keep Patrick at a distance.

"Yes, I know. You've said as much." The man sounded unruffled, much as Becker had when offering the sandwiches.

Desperate to find a neutral topic, Edmund tried, "Was your day successful? Did you hunt down any answers?"

Patrick studied him for a long moment before answering. "I met someone from your vanished past. Would you like to hear about it?"

"I suppose so," Edmund said, and his haze of desire dissipated as he braced himself against history dredged from that nauseating well of memory. "Yes, please," he added.

Patrick kept close watch on him, but Edmund refused to blink or look away. "Miss Miller," Patrick said slowly. "Now she's Mrs. Dalton, though Mr. Dalton is imaginary."

A knot that had drawn tight inside Edmund eased. "The name is not familiar."

"She was your nanny."

"Oh?"

"She said you called her Nimue... No, that's the lady in the painting with Merlin. You called her Neenah."

"Neenah." The name seemed to come into his head and settle there, oddly familiar yet unidentifiable. Then he remembered. "A great white apron, always starched. Yes. And a gray dress. She vanished too, but I heard from someone, probably Wensler...she went away and didn't die. I was an awful child, you see. That was what—" He stopped abruptly, realizing the ludicrousness of what he'd begun to say. *That was what killed them. They died because of me.*

"What?" Patrick said, leaning forward.

"Something old and silly." And as he realized how absurd that notion was, his breathing seemed to come more easily. He'd put down some idiotic weight, like Atlas throwing down the world and seeing that it didn't crack into pieces. He shook his head. "Neenah. Yes, she was always scolding and didn't like me."

"You're wrong. She did like you."

"But...she didn't come to see me." He pursed his lips. "I beg your pardon. That came out sounding as if I were a child whining after missing a treat."

"No need to beg my pardon. But she did want to see you."

Lost in thought about Neenah's crackling apron and her fondness for clapping her hands, he almost let the words slide past unnoticed. But then Edmund understood, and another world view shifted. "She? What? What do you mean she wanted to?"

"Your foster father decided it would be best to let your old life just vanish."

"But not even to say good-bye? He didn't let her?" He clamped his lips against his plaintive tone.

"I suspect he wasn't thinking very clearly at that time."

Edmund's rising confusion transformed into something less frightening: anger. "What are you implying? You needn't dance around what you believe."

"I didn't mean anything." Patrick tilted his head. "If I'm not implying anything, how's about you tell me what you're inferring?"

"I infer that you are annoying, Mr. Kelly."

Patrick laughed. "Old news, Mr. Sloan. Why does it irritate you when I speak of your foster father?"

"It doesn't!" Damn and blast, he seemed unable to rein in this emotional nonsense.

"Here's my guess. When I said 'he wasn't thinking very clearly,' and the fact that he kept the old nanny from you, you believe I think he was involved in the murder of your family. That's not what I believe. Does that help? Or am I so far wrong?"

Did it help? No. Because the thought had entered Edmund's head on its own, without Patrick's help. He didn't want either one of them to implicate Papa Sloan in the Lawton murders, not in any way, shape, or form.

Edmund pushed from the desk and rose to his feet. No longer any need to worry he'd show signs of arousal now.

"Are you retiring?" Patrick asked as Edmund walked away.

"Getting a drink."

"Not disturbing the staff—that's kind of you."

He didn't bother responding, but he did stop at the door. "Would you care for anything?"

"No. After last night, I've decided to imbibe less."

"Were you the worse for drink last night?"

"I don't want to end up like our friend Mr. Mason."

Edmund left the door open and returned a minute later with a crystal decanter in one hand and two glasses in the other.

"In case you change your mind," he said as he put one of the glasses down in front of Patrick. He filled his own, put the decanter and the other glass near the edge of the desk, and returned to the safety of his seat across from Patrick. He took a sip and only then noticed he'd grabbed the sherry, not the whisky as he'd intended, but he wasn't going back.

Patrick continued as if Edmund hadn't stomped out and back again. "Miss Miller, your Neenah, didn't have much to add to my store of information, but what she said didn't contradict the idea that two people took part in the...event. She's the one who left scratch marks on the one man, the one who was hanged. Key evidence, of course."

"I didn't know."

"You don't know very much about that trial or crime, do you?" He didn't sound in the least judgmental. "That must be by choice, so I won't tell you details unless I think it'll help me, all right?"

Edmund was going to agree, but then he said, "No, please don't protect me. It's unnecessary. I am a man full-grown." Usually.

Patrick's smile was huge. "Well, that's a relief. And not just because it'll make my life easier in that regard. I want to make things easy between us."

"I've already said no about that sort of…about that."

Patrick raised his dark brows in mock surprise. "And once again, you've inferred something. Although this time, yes, I meant to imply it."

Edmund couldn't help it. He laughed. "You are ridiculous."

Patrick leaned forward and poured himself a small portion. "You've wounded me so that now I need a stiff restorative after all."

Edmund swirled the liquid in his glass and drank it down. "What else did Miss Miller say about me?"

"Not much. She called you overindulged."

The usual swirl of black guilt crept in, but…no…wait. Absurd thought. "A spoiled child doesn't destroy anything," he muttered.

Apparently, Patrick had very good hearing. "At worse he'd kick a vase. Besides, your old nanny didn't blame you. She seemed to think it was your mother's fault because she indulged you."

Edmund drew in a long breath and managed to casually ask, "So I was terrible?"

"Naw." Patrick shrugged as if the topic were of no importance, which, Edmund realized, once and for all, was correct. He had been five years old. Nothing he'd done or said or felt could have changed a thing.

Why did his heart race now? Of course he must have known this fact. Hadn't he?

Edmund ventured, "Miss Miller said nothing else?"

"She didn't have an easy time talking about it. She reminded me of you that way, because she seemed to blame herself."

Edmund jolted back in his chair as if he'd been struck. No, this was nonsense. "That's ridiculous." He attempted a laugh.

"My mistake. To be honest, I was just guessing." Patrick didn't sound as if he believed his own words but at least he left the subject behind.

Edmund nodded, unwilling to speak in case he couldn't sound as calm as he wished. Patrick seemed to peel back his head and examine the insides with no effort—as easily as he'd peeled off Edmund's clothes.

Leave now. Go to bed, he ordered himself.

No. He would steady himself in Patrick Kelly's company because he was a man, and not a cringing ninny...under a table. He'd always disliked that wee, sleekit, cow'in' tim'rous beastie poem by Burns.

He forced a pleasant expression onto his face. "Tell me about other cases you've worked on?"

"All right. For now."

As Patrick Kelly talked, Edmund found he could actually listen, which was a great relief. And actually more interesting than he'd expected.

Patrick's assertion that he didn't push the rules for every case seemed true, at least according to his accounts.

"So you don't burst into people's lives for your own amusement," Edmund said.

Patrick had relaxed but now his gaze sharpened again; his stare made Edmund want to slink away, that blasted mouse again. "I haven't in the past. I believe you're the first. And believe me, that wasn't my original intention, no sir."

"Why me?"

"You're a puzzle. I enjoy figuring out why you say and do the things you do."

"I'm not sure I want to be a source of your entertainment."

"Oh? Not sure? Let me know if you decide you want to be." Before Edmund could respond, Patrick held up a hand. "I know, no flirtation. How about I tell you about a robbery that wasn't really a robbery?" He went on to describe the scene staged by the homeowner and how they'd first come to suspect the man. "The glass shards were on the ground outside, which means the man broke the window from inside."

"I'll take notes so I'll know what to do if I decide to break into my own house," Edmund said.

He felt charitable about his houseguest until Patrick said, "I can show you any manner of things, though I wish I could teach you what you need to know." The words might have seemed part of his playful vocabulary, but his voice was grave.

"What do you mean?"

"I'd teach you how to understand that crime is all the fault of the perpetrators and nothing you did, Ned. Nothing ever to do with you or I should say that little boy under the table."

Edmund had to say or do something. "Such a silly thing to say." He tried to laugh but it sounded like a gasp. "I don't expect you say things like that to the other people you interview."

Patrick didn't smile or look away. "No, you're right about that."

"I'm going to bed." Edmund rose, said a fast good night and left the room before Patrick could say something even more uncomfortable.

Lying in bed, Edmund conducted imaginary conversations with Patrick. He invented so many answers to so many questions, he had trouble sleeping. But at least he felt as if he could remain calm about any topic Patrick might bring up.

His calm state lasted until he discovered his guest had fled again first thing in the morning without leaving word. And when the doorbell rang at about noon with a telegram for Mr. Kelly, Edmund was near the front entrance. He waved off Becker and accepted the envelope from the boy who was still panting from his bike ride. He longed to rip open the telegram but he'd wait. After a while, he wondered if he'd need to hire a detective of his own to track Patrick down.

Chapter Seven

Patrick had slipped out of the house before nine. He found the distraction of his host kept him from concentrating on his work, although perhaps that was an excuse. Perhaps he had nothing else he could accomplish here. A long journey for his personal amusement wouldn't go over well. The thought of returning to New York filled him with gloom. A sense of defeat, he told himself. Nothing to do with leaving behind an intriguing new friend.

Funny to think of the rich young gentleman as a friend, but surely that description fit. Even if they never touched again, and chances were they never would, he had rarely felt so amused or amusing in the company of another person.

Patrick went to the hotel to drop off the key he'd forgotten to leave behind.

The man behind desk scowled and held up a box. "I have an item delivered to you here, sir. I was going to send it to your forwarding address when the delivery lad returned. The sooner the better, I'd say."

The moment Patrick took the small package wrapped in brown paper and tied with twine, he knew why the desk clerk had made a face of disgust. This was no prize.

"Patrick Kelly of New York City" had been scrawled on the paper in grease pencil. The thick packaging consisted of butcher's paper, and it looked like any package a meat seller would put together. It smelled of blood and slightly rancid flesh.

Patrick held it rather than stash it in his pocket.

He asked, "Do you know where this came from?"

"No notion." The clerk folded his arms.

"Did you see who delivered it?"

"A small boy, and no, I don't know him and he didn't leave his calling card or name. He scurried in here and ran out again."

Patrick thanked the man and gave him a tip.

He took it out to the street and laid it on low wall before cutting the strings with his pen knife.

Cloudy blueish eyes with huge pupils stared up at him—real eyes. Patrick cursed. His instinct was to throw the things as far away from himself as possible. Instead, he forced himself to study them.

Not human eyes, he told himself. But cow eyes would be larger, and goat or sheep eyes would have slit pupils.

Please, God, not human. With shaking fingers, he rewrapped the package. He reentered the hotel and asked for the address of the nearest butcher.

By the time he'd walked the half mile to the address, he'd calmed down, though just thinking of the package in his pocket made him queasy. It had to do with Ned Lawton, of course it did. Was Patrick wrong and the man who'd murdered the family still in England? Why would he send these to Patrick? At least he or she had sent it to Patrick rather than Ned.

And with every hurried step he took, the phrase echoed through him: *Please, don't let these be human eyes.* Weren't the pupils too large? But what did he know of dead eyes?

Please, let them be animal and not human. He ignored the row of carcasses hanging in the windows of the shop and managed to ask an expert without sounding too panicked.

"Pig," the butcher declared, and Patrick almost sobbed with relief. The burly man with the red face and red-and-white mustache and red-and-white apron continued, "Not ours, I can guarantee that. We use a better quality of paper and white string. Is someone playing a nasty joke on you, sir?"

"A joke," Patrick agreed. Better that than a threat. He wondered if he could throw away the package—best to save the wrappings and dump the contents. He did not wish to carry rotting eyes around the city. The butcher agreed to take the eyes and add them to his offal or catsmeat pile.

Patrick thanked him and handed over a few pence. He pocketed the twine and the now-empty wrapper with his name. The scent of dead animal filled the shop, so he didn't know if it also filled his pocket. It took a half-crown and couple of sixpence to get the butcher to scrawl a list of his competitors in the area. The man ripped a piece of paper from the roll next to some hanging chickens, and took up a pencil from the brim of his bowler cap

"You'd best start with that meat market." The ruddy man poked the paper with a blunt fingertip, leaving a blood smear on the paper.

"Only two streets away, and his products aren't nearly so fresh as mine."

It took three visits to three butchers. At last he found a man who recognized the package. This butcher did his business standing at an outside counter. He was thin and cheery. "Yes, I delivered fresh eyeballs. Not so strange as you'd think. They make a fine addition to a stew. I have a recipe if you wish for it."

"Can you describe the person who'd bought the eyes?"

"Office boy, no more'n fourteen, fifteen years old, nothing unusual, I'd say. Probably a dark-haired chap, yes, I think that. Flat plaid cap."

Patrick handed over some money, but even as he gratefully pocketed the coins, Mr. Belson declared he couldn't elaborate on the description. The boy had paid for the eyes, hadn't put it on an account. He'd told Belson where to deliver the package, turned, and was gone. "My son handles our deliveries. The office lad scampered off right away."

Patrick walked off wondering who would want to send him a message and what exactly the message could be. *Come find me* seemed right.

The killer had never sent any sort of message before, not after the Lawton murder nor the ones in the United States. And why send something to Patrick of all people? Perhaps whoever had sent those awful eyes wanted Patrick to think the murderer was here. Perhaps it was some other kind of threat. Perhaps the murderer truly did walk the same streets Ned did.

That might be the connection. He wouldn't put it past the lawyer who'd seemed mighty determined to keep everyone away from Ned.

When Patrick went to visit Sloan the lawyer, he was turned from the door, told the gentleman wasn't home to visitors. He briefly considered using some strong-arm tactics, but those wouldn't work here.

He returned to Ned Sloan's house and found he had no need to do anything of the sort anymore.

The butler met him at the door with a silver salver holding a telegram. Patrick thanked him and took the flimsy Anglo-American Telegraph Company envelope. As he tore it open and read the typed capital letters on the yellow paper, Ned strolled down the corridor.

"Hullo, you got your message, I see," Ned said. "Anything interesting?"

Patrick flipped the paper back and forth. The sender's location on the left side was scrawled in pen: New York. "Damnation," he muttered.

"What's wrong?" Ned asked.

"No, no, it's good news," he reminded himself. If it was the truth. He handed Ned the yellow paper with its simple message.

SUSPECT CAUGHT STOP RETURN NY SOONEST SHIP STOP

What the hell were the eyeballs, then? A joke after all? Perhaps he'd annoyed someone and they had a strange way of trying to unsettle him.

"Are you well, Mr. Kelly?" Ned asked. "You look quite distressed. May I offer you a drink?"

Patrick followed him into the library. He longed for a whisky, truth be told, but needed to keep his head clear. He told Ned, "No, thanks, but no, nothing's wrong. I'm relieved the guy has been caught. I guess my boss is kicking himself about allowing me to come here." He tried out a laugh. "He'll kick me for good measure when I get back to New York."

He'd been about to tell Ned about the eyes but decided not to. If there'd been any mention of Ned or some indication that it was directed at him, he might have. But the eyeballs were for Patrick. Maybe that damned investigator he'd annoyed on his first day in the country thought it was a funny joke. He'd check and not bother Ned—the poor guy was already on edge about the past being dredged up.

"I should get ready to leave," Patrick said. "The sooner I get out of your hair, the faster you can return to regular life. You'll be glad to leave he past behind, I imagine."

He'd have to take a train to Southampton, and he could make that take up most of the next day. If he was unlucky, he'd find a transatlantic ship almost at once. The thought of returning home with his tail between his legs annoyed him.

His hunches and ideas usually were on target, but this mess of an investigation would undo the credit he got for others he'd done for Greene. The price of the journey would come up in every conversation his boss would have with him from the moment he landed in New York forever and ever—or until he slugged Greene.

"Anyway, if you'll excuse me, I guess I'll go pack."

Ned didn't answer. He sat on a plain wooden chair and stared off into the middle distance, a small frown corrugating his forehead. A scowl on that pleasant face made Patrick want to beg his pardon.

Patrick tucked the telegram paper inside his jacket. "I guess I owe you for everything, and I think I should offer to do some*thing*... I supposed there's no point in my offering to pay for my stay."

Ned shook his head, and something like a growl escaped him.

Patrick adopted his most beleaguered look and gave an exaggerated sigh. "Fine, if it will help, I'll apologize, and by golly, I'll mean it this time." He couldn't resist adding, "I hope you believe I shoved my way into your life for what I thought was the best of reasons."

Ned still glowered at him.

"What's wrong?" Patrick asked.

"You don't truly have to rush back to New York, do you? You said you wished you could take some time and explore London and perhaps other parts of England. Stay for a few days, and I could show you some of the city."

Patrick's jaw dropped. He closed his mouth. Opened it again. "Really?" he asked. "You'd do that?"

Ned examined his starched cuff, not meeting Patrick's eye. "If you are uninterested, don't feel you must say yes or—"

"Please. Yes, yes, that would be wonderful." He thought about days and days with Ned, nights too, and reluctantly gave up that idea. "I won't be able to stay more than a day or two. I'm already in trouble enough with Greene. At the moment, I don't much care, but I like the work and will want to keep the job once I get home."

Patrick wanted to celebrate with a kiss or at least ask Ned what he expected from the rest of his visit, but he didn't want to push his luck. His mood had suddenly lifted. Really, why not enjoy himself?

And maybe find the idiot who'd sent the eyes and batter answers from him.

As he went up to the room to change his collar and cuffs, and to scribble a note to a source, he went over the reasons he should be singing instead of grumbling. A killer had been stopped, and that had to be good news, no matter how the bad guy had been captured.

A man Patrick admired and liked wanted to spend time with him, despite exposure to his rudest manners, part of his relentless hunter's approach. Now he could concentrate on a day or two of a different sort of hunt. He wondered if he could manage this change of attitude without making Ned think he was lying or putting on some kind of flimflam.

He took the butcher's paper from his pocket and stared it. A joke, a terrible tasteless joke, and if it proved something else, he'd be able to keep an eye on Ned. Ugh, not that. Keep watch on Ned, Patrick amended.

He decided to leave the fact of the eyeballs out of the note to his friend the reporter, who wouldn't be able to resist a dramatic touch like that. But as long as he remained in London, he'd do some looking—no, no, *searching*—about the truth of those eyes.

He trotted down the stair, and Liam, waiting at the bottom, directed him to the library. "Can you deliver this?" he asked Liam and handed over the note.

The footman looked at the address and scowled. "It's fine," Patrick said. "It's a friend who works at a paper. Nothing sordid, I promise. I just asked for information."

Liam nodded, and Patrick walked into the library.

Ned stood by the smaller and neater of two desks, frowning again, this time directing his serious expression at a slender man in a heather tweed suit that was a bit too broad in the shoulders. The man had a carefully trimmed mustache, and hair parted exactly down the middle and slicked to his scalp. He clutched a sheaf of papers that he held toward Ned. "Sir, I hope you'll look over the corrections you wished for the dinner speech."

The man glanced at Patrick and gave an abbreviated bow. Some sort of servant, then, Patrick decided.

Ned ignored the papers. "The corrections can wait, Peters. I'm going out now." He strode toward the door where Patrick stood waiting. There wasn't an introduction. Did that have something to with a secretary's status, or Patrick's?

As they left the house, Patrick said, "That guy was your secretary, right?"

"Yes, and a pest. The most efficient secretary in the world seems to produce more work for me to do than the lazy gentleman who held the place before him. Does that make any sense?"

Patrick schooled his annoyance—stupid to feel hurt—before asking, "Why is it you didn't introduce us?"

"Oh. I thought you'd met. I needed to get out of there before he realized that I hadn't actually looked over the notes from the meeting he attended for me two days ago."

All right, if Ned could be so breezy about this, so could Patrick. He didn't care about the niceties of society, he reminded himself.

Ned clapped a sleek bowler to his head, buttoned his frock-coat, and trotted down the stairs.

Patrick followed and found himself asking, "So the reason you didn't say anything before wasn't because you are…unwilling."

Ned paused, one gloved hand resting on the marble balustrade on the fence surrounding his front garden. "Unwilling to do what?"

"Introduce me to the people you know."

"Do you care?"

As they walked, Patrick thumped his own battered hat onto his head and fished his gloves from his pocket. "Whatever you think is suitable. I'm still learning how to get along over here."

"What the devil? Are you suddenly turning into a gentleman?" Ned glanced over at him, wearing a peculiar half smile. He slowed then stopped. "Please, don't, I beg you. I feel positively free when you behave…when you act like a…"

Patrick, unaccountably relieved by the explanation, narrowed his eyes. "I bet you're too polite to finish that sentence."

Ned squinted right back at him, twisting his face in a silly imitation, so very different from the emotionless gentleman he'd first seemed. "I am far too polite, Mr. Kelly."

"Remember, I'm Patrick."

Ned smoothed his jacket and began to walk again. "Indeed, Patrick. Now let us put a plan in place. Would you rather see art? Books? Relics from another age? Or should we simply have a meal and discuss your case?"

"Not mine any longer." Patrick even managed to sound cheerful about his failure. "I'm not going to work today or tomorrow, and I'll take whichever tour you prefer to give."

"Hmm." The sun came out of from behind a bank of clouds. "We'll stroll wherever our legs take us and enjoy the weather." Ned stopped, pulled off his straw boater, and tilted his head back. He seemed to soak up the sun. The small smile on his face might have been knowing. Maybe he knew that Patrick was gaping at him, unable to look away from the gilding of sunlight on his fresh-shaven face.

Patrick moved out of the way of a nanny pushing a perambulator. He and Ned continued to stroll down the pavement.

Patrick said, "You're lighthearted today. It's because the book is closed on the past?"

Ned's frown… Patrick had a strong and ridiculous urge to lick that divot between those eyebrows. "Yes," Ned said slowly, and he wasn't frowning any longer. "But I have other reasons to feel this way, I think."

"The nice weather," Patrick offered.

"Indeed. But I have other, more personal reasons."

"Mr. Sloan, that tone of yours. It was positively…"

Ned eyed him. "Flirty?"

Patrick's bark of laughter was so loud, two ladies strolling nearby stopped and gazed at him. He covered his mouth with his hand. Ned's eyes were bright with merriment, and he made small fizzing sounds, holding back his version of hysterical laughter.

"This conversation is not at all amusing," Ned managed to gasp out. "Why do I feel as if I might succumb to a fit of hilarity?"

"We're a couple of idiots?" Patrick wheezed.

That only made them both laugh even more.

Edmund pulled out a handkerchief and wiped his face. It wouldn't do to cross Trafalgar Square looking like a lunatic.

He'd made the offer to be a guide without thinking, but now he was positively pleased to be walking next to the brash American.

Odd. He should have been glad to say good-bye to the one person who knew his sinful nature and more alarming, the details of his past. Leaving the bad dreams behind had been a goal he'd desired above all others. He stared up at the clouds and wondered at the calm that filled him now. Usually the mere thought of those nightmares created an echo of terror, but his heart did not race and his hands remained steady.

As they walked up the steps toward the National Gallery, he gingerly tried to conjure the familiar horror, the images that seemed to lurk and spring on him at the oddest moments. He poked the monster that slept inside him. Nothing happened.

They strolled through the front doors and made their way down a long, arched corridor, stopping to view the paintings. Perhaps it was his imagination but under Patrick's jovial air, he still seemed tense, as if looking for some sort of danger.

"What is wrong?" Edmund asked.

Patrick shook his head. "Thinking," was all he said.

"Go on, tell me. I know it has to do with the Lawton case."

"Oh? How do you know so much, Mr. Sloan?"

"You get a sort of tight expression on your face. Wary, I think. Your mouth tucks in and you avoid looking at me."

Patrick gave a loud enough laugh other people looked around. "And here I thought I was the only one making close, personal observations." He lowered his voice. "All right, Detective Sloan, I wonder who the hell they have caught in New York. I can't help wondering what the connection is to you. There must be one because I didn't make it up, did I?"

"What can you do? Is there someone you can talk to?"

"I'm waiting a bit first."

"Waiting for what?"

Rather than answer, Patrick walked ahead of them to point at a Giambono. "Say, this painting is from the 1400s but looks more modern, huh."

Ned half listened.

He returned to the other exercise: trying again to summon the worst of the images he'd seen night after night. In the past, he'd always shied away from that exercise. The pictures of blood and mutilation his mind conjured had seemed too dreadful to contemplate, but now they might have been among the paintings on the wall in front of him, with no power to horrify.

"Judging from the expression you got on, you really loathe that Madonna and that piglet she's holding." Patrick touched his shoulder. "Do you want to leave? I like this place, but wherever we go is fine with me."

They stood in front of a medieval portrait of Mary with an infant Jesus, who did indeed look slightly porcine.

"No, the painting is lovely. I'm distracted. I shall pay better attention now."

"No need," Patrick said. "As long as you're not looking so bleak because you want to attack me, I'm fine."

"My appearance is that forbidding, is it?"

"Grim as a grave," Patrick confirmed. "What are you thinking about?"

Edmund described the portraits of murder in his mind, wondering at their curious new lack of power. His words came out in a rush. He needed to speak before he had second thoughts about sharing such things.

Patrick listened without interrupting.

Edmund finished with, "I feel as if I've exorcised demons, or at least dulled their claws."

"You probably have," Patrick said.

Edmund moved to the next painting, another Madonna. He said, "If I have, then it's because I've talked to you. Thank you."

"You're welcome." Patrick shoved his hands into his trouser pockets and edged closer to Edmund. "It feels wrong to get a pat on the back when I wasn't even trying to help you. It feels worse to know that."

They walked through the galleries and looked at the paintings and sculptures. Edmund was pleasantly surprised to learn Patrick recognized many of the artists whose work they saw.

Patrick paused in front a Dutch master's still life. "You have one of his works in your collection in that front parlor."

"So I do. I'd forgotten that painting."

Patrick snickered. "Some collector you are."

"I'm not, really. Mr. and Mrs. Lawton loved and collected art." And they hadn't lived long enough to pass along their appreciation to their son. Perhaps he'd make a better study of what they'd treasured.

After a couple of hours of art, they returned to Edmund's house for a meal. He wasn't ready to eat in public yet, but he found he could manage with Patrick. His new friend seemed distracted somehow, lost in less than pleasant thoughts, but denied any such thing when Edmund ventured to ask.

The afternoon was devoted to going to bookstores and then visiting Bond Street. Patrick refused to allow Edmund to purchase him any sort of clothing. They visited Edmund's club.

"Another thing I can cross off my list," Patrick whispered to him. "A real gentleman's club in England. I've been to societies and clubs in the States, but this is even better."

Edmund enjoyed his company and felt freer with him than even with Wensler. Had he anything to hide from Patrick?

Nothing.

He wondered if Patrick had something hidden from him. When they returned home, a note had been delivered to Patrick. He opened it, read it, and tossed it in the fire.

"Bad news?"

"Probably not," Patrick said. "Shall we play cards?"

A clear avoidance, and Edmund decided to respect the message. Odd that he'd even consider pushing the subject of the telegram. He'd been better trained than to be so obtrusive. But when it came to Patrick Kelly, good manners were less important than honesty.

Another reason to relax with the man as he never had with anyone else.

After dinner, he and Patrick retired to the library. Should he suggest cards or chess?

He looked over at Patrick, who'd picked a book off a shelf and flipped through it. Good, he wouldn't have to entertain his guest. And the sense of disappointment was nothing more than fatigue.

Edmund stared into the fire of the library and thought about the plant room again and the chair and massage that had been so much more than he had known. He leaned forward and rested his arms on his knees until he recalled he was sitting in Patrick's customary informal slouch and straightened.

Patrick had brought something new and rather threatening into his life, and it wasn't simply the way the American had dug up the skeletons from Edmund's past and delivered them to him, dropping them on his lap like a happy dog. His touch was dangerous. Edmund's hurried episodes with other men had always seemed wonderful, bright moments of sensation, a dark need fulfilled in dark, anonymous surroundings. The risk of discovery made them even more charged.

But that such a thing happened in Edmund's own home, and accompanied with all that conversation... Dear God. Conducting that activity under light so he might make out the features of the man touching him and whom he stroked and kissed and... All those things seemed too powerful. Rats preferred the dark. And too much light would make them grow agitated and mad. Shine too much light on what he did, and he too might go crazy. More insane, since he supposed his taste for men was a disorder. He'd read that men like him were prone to fits of morbid sorrow, and he believed it.

Except, no. He couldn't imagine Patrick as insane or morbid. The American seemed to be a hectic, lawless spirit, but he was sane and certainly not unhappy. The thought of a quiet or morose Patrick was odd enough to make Edmund snort at the fire.

*

Patrick put down the book, a novel about a dead Russian, and looked at his watch. He wished the note from Drury had said more than "looking into it." What was there to look into? Drury would contact the New York bureau and get a story. Simple enough. She had plenty of contacts back in New York.

Ned was glaring and then grinning at the fire.

"What are you thinking about?"

"You."

"I'm glad to see you looking so happy when you think about me. The scowl, no."

"You've been watching me for a time, then?"

"Oh, yep, I have."

He considered the chair next to Ned, but instead he crossed over to the door and locked it.

Ned rose to his feet at once. Of course he'd have to protest. And of course Patrick would listen.

"I'm not going to repeat what happened between us before."

"All right," Patrick said. He pulled off his jacket and placed it on the chair behind the desk.

Ned bit his lip. "What are you doing?"

"This room is too warm," he said.

"It is not."

"It is for me." That was true enough. All his blood sang with heat as he carried out his absurd impulse.

He undid his cufflinks and put them in the pocket of his jacket. Then he unhooked his watch's chain and fob and dropped them into his watch pocket.

When he'd unbuttoned and removed his vest, Ned made a soft noise. A kind of whimper.

Patrick grinned at him and slipped his braces off his shoulders, untucked his shirt, and started in on unbuttoning it.

"Oh," said Ned. "What?"

Patrick sat and pulled off his socks and shoes. Since he didn't wear sock garters, this was easy. He wiggled his bare feet in the thick carpet and considered putting on a display there. No, better to go to the sofa near the window. Thank goodness the drapes were drawn, or he'd give passersby a fine show. He set the shoes and socks on the floor next to the chair where he'd draped the jacket. The rest he'd take off over by the sofa. If Ned should grow upset, he'd at least cover up some of himself.

"What are you doing?" Ned asked.

"What does it look like I'm doing?"

"Taking off all your clothes in my library."

Patrick snapped his fingers and pointed at him. "Huzzah! You win the prize."

Ned gave a nervous laugh. "I hate to ask what that prize might be."

Good. If he was able to joke, his host wasn't offended, yet.

Patrick walked to the sofa, unbuttoning his trousers. He peeled them off and placed them on the arm of the sofa. Dressed only in an undershirt and drawers, he sat and waited several seconds for the next protest.

None came, but when his eyes met Ned's, Ned turned red.

"I don't know why you're blushing. I'm the one embarrassing myself," he said. With that, he unbuttoned and removed his undershirt and untied his drawers. He didn't bother to fold those cotton garments and only tossed them on the arm over the shirt.

He tried to recall some of the draped nudes they'd seen that day in paintings, all women, of course, and arranged himself on his side on the sofa, propping up his head. He suspected he looked ridiculous, but he didn't care.

"Go on, keep staring into the fire," he said. "I'll find something to do."

He looked down his chest and belly and mimed surprise to see the half-erection he sported. His surprise was somewhat real; an erection of any sort was a minor miracle considering the peculiar situation he'd set up.

Ned seemed unable to look away. He licked his lips, and that encouraged Patrick's ever-hopeful prick.

"What…what will you do?" Ned whispered. His eyes looked fathomless, huge and pleading.

Apparently, Patrick's prick liked the way Ned looked at him. Patrick reached down and gave it a stroke.

Ned's attention remained steady. He took a few steps closer, slowly, as if in a trance or he didn't want to startle a wild animal.

Perfect. His gaze briefly moved to meet Patrick's eyes and then lingered where Patrick stroked himself hard, and slowed because he grew too ready. He slid a finger over the dampness at the end of his cock, hissing, and pushed up into his hand. Another stroke under that hungry gaze, and Patrick grew close to exploding. He didn't want to let go until he had Ned's skin under his palm. Or any part of his hand, mouth, prick, rear—he didn't care which bit Ned touched which piece of him. Patrick craved contact, and more skin would be better than none.

Halleluiah, his absurd actions were having even better results than he'd hoped.

Ned knelt by the sofa and grazed his fingers over Patrick's busy hands and arms. He grasped Patrick's wrists and tugged. "Let me. Please." His voice cracked.

Patrick let him draw his hands away. Ned leaned close and his breath brushed over Patrick's naked skin. When he laid a tentative kiss on the underside of his engorged and interested cock, Patrick shivered, repressing the urge to shove up and clamor for more.

Kisses and soft licks were almost too much and not enough. He groaned and stroked Ned's hair.

"Is this all right?"

"Christ. If you knew what you're doing to me. The answer..." He broke off when Ned kissed and licked again then drew away. "Oh, Ned. The answer has to be no, you tease. I'm going to go mad."

Ned took him in his mouth then, with no hesitation, and drew Patrick deep. He gagged but when Patrick tried to pull back, Ned went after him and continued to suck and lick like a starving man.

So intense and magnificent—no, the feel of that hot mouth would bring this experience to an end far too soon. Patrick fought his instinct to thrust. He threaded his hands through Ned's hair and gave a tug.

"You too," he demanded. Ned raised his face, and the sight of his reddened cheeks, his eyes heavy with passion, his lips wet and parted, made Patrick's heart throb. Other bits as well, but his cock was used to feeling too full near Ned.

He reached down and stroked Ned's cheek, gasping when Ned turned and nipped then sucked his finger into his mouth.

"Take off your clothes," Patrick said.

Ned rose to his feet and undressed quickly, only stumbling a little in his haste.

They lay on their sides facing each other. Ned's cock was hot and dry against Patrick's damp one.

"Both of us," Patrick said.

Ned, all rumpled and hot, stared back, wearing a confused frown. So Patrick untangled their limbs and kissed his way down to Ned's erection. He twisted his body so his groin lay near Ned's face, and Ned understood immediately.

He returned to his hungry exploration.

Patrick buried his face in Ned's soft pubic hair, licking the crease where his leg met his body. He kissed Ned's tender inside thigh. He stroked with his mouth and hands all around that area, pausing now and again to enjoy the busy work Ned continued on his own body, drawing Patrick closer to the edge.

Not yet.

He loved the soft sounds Ned made, the sweet musky scent of man. He wanted to savor it. He moved his hand to the base of Ned's cock and pumped, determined to bring him off

But then Ned did something with his tongue and Patrick knew he would spend any second.

The release swept through him and he squeezed his eyes shut and threw his head back. Even through the moment, his fist moved jerkily.

In his grip, Ned's cock grew harder and larger. Warm liquid hit Patrick's chin and cheek.

When he could breathe again, he groaned, a ridiculous sound to express his amazement and pleasure.

"Oh, my Ned," he whispered.

The other man lay still for several long heartbeats. "Well, that was …" He shook his head.

Patrick attempted to hold back his desperation and sound only amused. "Good? Bad?"

Ned pursed his lips. "Good."

They cleaned, then dressed almost at once and in silence, but Ned smiled at him and moved easily. The ramrod-straight back and stiff motions were gone.

Before he could suggest a rematch however, Ned bid him good night and slipped from the room. Patrick hoped that a host retiring before his guest was another sign that Ned had relaxed even more and not that he had to escape shame.

Chapter Eight

The next morning, Patrick was in the breakfast room when Edmund came down the stairs. Edmund had spent quite a while before drifting off to sleep wondering what it would be like to wake up next to a man. Would they kiss? Climb out of bed as soon as they could scramble away from each other?

Occasionally, when he'd had nightmares in the school dormitory, Edmund had awakened and climbed into Wensler's bed. They'd slept side by side on Wensler's narrow cot, and that warm, breathing body had been a comfort. He hadn't felt the need to touch Wensler, though, except when the nights were cold. That form of well-being had ended when Edmund realized that his fantasies about other boys weren't going to go away. Even if Wensler wasn't the object of his dreams, he felt as if he could somehow harm his friend in his sleep.

A strong man like Patrick would be able to keep Edmund from any unwelcome touches. A naked Patrick holding Edmund's arms and pushing him down on the bed, directing him, forcing him, kissing him and falling into—oh good Lord, he was arousing himself.

Edmund knew his face was burning as he sat at the breakfast table, but his visitor was leafing through a newspaper and didn't look up for several minutes. Patrick was a quiet man in the morning? Edmund wouldn't have guessed that.

Edmund dismissed Liam. He never liked eating with servants in the room.

Patrick folded the paper and laid it aside. "What shall we do today?"

"We shall go explore more of London."

Patrick grinned at him. "You sound sad about the idea. I wonder if we ought to stay here and explore each other instead?"

Not so quiet after all. "No."

"Later on, then? This evening?" Patrick lifted his cup of tea and kept his attention on Edmund as he drank.

Edmund gave a single nod, and even that felt outrageous, an acknowledgment and acceptance of what they could do together. His mouth watered, his skin prickled—he couldn't wait.

"Good." Patrick rose and rubbed his hands together. "We'll go soak up art, beauty, learning and all those fine civilized parts of your city. The place is chockablock full of culture. You eat, and I'll be back momentarily."

They walked through Hyde Park and visited an art gallery where Edmund had sold a couple of Lawton family pieces he disliked. The proprietor greeted them with enthusiasm and offered them refreshments. Edmund was just as glad when Patrick said he wasn't hungry. Yet the thought of food hadn't created nausea in Edmund. Perhaps Patrick's presence kept him from his usual responses. He might conduct an experiment or two.

Perhaps he should face his ghosts in physical form. He thanked the gallery owner and, as they walked out the door, asked Patrick, "Shall we visit the wax museum now?"

"From high culture to low," Patrick said. "Hey, didn't you make a sneering comment about that place."

"I merely said I hadn't seen it. I am not a snob," Edmund said indignantly.

The new location on Marlybone Road was more than two miles away. Edmund hailed a hansom. They took a round-about route, and during the ride Edmund began to regret his suggestion. Despite what he'd said to Patrick, perhaps he *was* a snob. Nearly everyone he knew derided the museum as coarse—appealing to the worst of common tastes. He drummed his fingers on his leg and cursed himself.

Of course, that wasn't the reason for his discomfort. The Chamber of Horrors awaited, with a depiction of his own personal nightmare.

"I'm having a great time," Patrick said. They sat side by side in the small space of the speeding carriage. "What about you?"

Edmund made what he hoped was a sound of agreement, but Patrick leaned forward and studied his face.

"You're still grim. Heck, you look like you'd have more fun attending your best friend's execution. Shall we go visit a dentist and have a few teeth extracted instead?"

Edmund tipped his hat forward over his face. "Oddly enough, I am usually quite good at hiding what I feeling from other people."

A sharp elbow dug into his side. "Go on. You can tell Mr. Kelly all about it. What's the problem?"

Edmund spoke with the hat still hiding his eyes, because he didn't want to see either pity or disgust. In the last few days, he'd grown extremely tired of his "delicacy" and guessed that anyone else would see him as a quivering mess. "There is a special rogue's gallery there."

He paused, trying to think of how to put the rest, but Patrick understood. "Oh," Patrick said softly. "And Weller is in there."

Edmund pushed the hat back. "I am a full-grown man and am not afraid of a wax dummy." He defiantly met Patrick's steady gaze and read only warmth and humor.

"We'll skip that part if you want, or, hey, I'll walk with you so we go through it together. Put your hat over your face again, or I can tie my handkerchief over your eyes if you think that'll help you ignore that part of the exhibition."

The brisk amused tone he took suited Edmund more than ignoring the topic or growing gravely sympathetic, the only two responses he'd imagined possible. How could Patrick have known exactly what to say?

"If anyone else is visiting the exhibition, a patron touring the exhibit blindfolded would provide an amusing side show," Edmund said and, incredibly, felt like laughing.

Patrick pulled out his handkerchief and shook it in his face threateningly.

Edmund snickered. "If a blindfold doesn't work, you ought to shove it into my mouth if I start screaming like a ninny."

"If I shove anything into your mouth," Patrick whispered, "it won't be some piece of cloth."

A frisson of desire ran through Edmund. "Good Lord," he muttered back. "And wouldn't that be a show for the paying customers."

They were still laughing as the hansom drew to a halt in front of Madame Tussaud's.

After years of decorous behavior, Edmund had come loose from some sort of mooring. He was behaving like an idiot schoolboy, and his prick seemed to have reverted to those days when it grew hard when another boy grinned at him. Patrick had a very attractive smile indeed.

Edmund paid their admissions, and they entered the wide hall and climbed the stairs. Once they pushed through the brass turnstile and admired the huge mirror, he couldn't avoid the exhibits. A fascinated little boy asked his father if the pope laid out on a bed was truly dead. "And that's his body," the man said solemnly. "Covered in wax to keep the flies off."

The mother started to argue with him about terrifying the boy, and Edmund and Patrick slipped past.

"These things give me the shivery horrors," Patrick said as they shuffled past some wax figures of British royalty. "Not quite human, then again, not quite *not* human. Take a gander at Henry and his wives gazing at nothing. Soulless, empty things."

Edmund shrugged. He didn't enjoy the crowds of real people, but the wax beings didn't bother him. He wondered how much effort it took to create one and if the people who sculpted them enjoyed their work.

The sound of a small orchestra drifted down the hall, and they made their way past effigies of popular authors, skirting the crowd at Dickens. A lady in a bright purple dress spoke to the statue.

"She's reciting passages from *Little Dorrit*," Patrick informed him. "The one about debtor's prison."

"I haven't read much Dickens," Edmund confessed.

"I bet your foster father said he appealed to the masses." Patrick said.

"Perhaps, although I wish you would cease portraying me as an overrefined aristocrat," Edmund said. "I imagine you've read everything Dickens wrote?"

"Every last word. And some of them twice."

At last they arrived at the Chamber of Horrors. Edmund's head ached a bit, but not from fear. It was likely due to the crowds, a small boy's shrill temper tantrum, a stout lady's floral perfume, as well as the off-key blaring and scraping of the orchestra. Yet he wished he could grab Patrick's hand. He'd drag Patrick back to his house, where they'd strip off all their clothes and indulge in more massaging. Naked. On a bed, or the floor, or a sofa. He didn't care where, as long as they were alone.

Within minutes, he stood in front of the exhibit of past notorious murderers. He'd imagined this moment, but never before had he pictured himself with a cock half-erect. The thought made him want to crow because he was alive. The man who'd done it all was long gone, and he, Edmund Lawton Sloan, had survived.

He didn't recognize any of the faces on the wall. The only exhibit of full figures was near the guillotine.

"Weller is up there?" he whispered to Patrick.

Patrick pointed. Edmund inched closer. "I don't know that face," he said at last. "I don't remember it at all."

He scanned the rest of the masks and knew none of the rest of them either. An etching and a photograph were near the portrait of Weller. He'd seen the etching before. It was a recreation of the scene in the Lawton house from a newspaper. Wensler had shown him a copy years earlier. The photograph, though. Looking at it, he felt something punch him hard in the chest.

Before.

A woman sat in a chair with a sleeping baby on her lap. A man stood behind her, and on either side of her were two small girls. His vanished family and him. He realized that he had not seen a single picture of the Lawtons, his family, since he was a small boy. Had he asked Papa Sloan to see them? He didn't recall asking or being refused. But he knew he hadn't seen those people alive or even in a photograph for many, many years.

He studied their faces as if he could memorize them. They looked as glassy-eyed and blank as the wax statues, the way people do when they posed for photographs, though the man wore a faint smile. *My father*, he thought, and moved even closer.

A hand rested on his shoulder, warm, strong, and offering comfort. He resisted the urge to close his eyes and rest his cheek on Patrick's fingers, and he inched closer to the photo.

He stared at the figures in the photographs one by one. A fragile blonde woman with a sweet face holding a blob of a baby. Edmund tried to memorize them all, his mother, those fragile blonde girls with distinctively large eyes, and a dark-haired man with Edmund's nose and the same large eyes. "My mother clearly didn't cheat on my father. We all look just like him," he whispered to Patrick.

He must have taken too long examining the photograph, because someone in the crowd behind him made a throat-clearing sound, and someone else complained in a loud mutter about needing to get on with it. Edmund had gotten off the path through the exhibit, but when he'd moved closer, he blocked anyone else seeing the Lawton family portraits, before and after death.

He glanced at the artist's rendering. *After.* Body parts and teacups of blood. So much blood, hand-colored and the badly proportioned bodies at the table, a standing man sawing off a seated man's head. Not exactly fine art. And under the table, a small boy lay curled, his face turned toward the viewer as he screamed. Of course, little Ned Lawton hadn't made a noise, or he would have been caught. Maybe his mouth was open in a silent cry. Maybe the artist wanted to get as much pathos and fear into the print as possible.

"That's not a very good piece of art," he told Patrick, who still stood comfortingly close. He took one long last look at the photograph, then, at last, he backed away from the pictures—and the mask of a man he'd never seen.

The rest of the museum was a blur to him. Only the photo remained clear in his mind. It seemed to reveal other memories beyond vision. Could he recall the way his mother cleared her throat? And his father's deep laugh might have been something he'd heard very recently, an echo in a room he walked through regularly.

A family. He'd been a part of them and loved them. And that photo, again—the way his mother held him in her arms drew up something ancient, a love he'd forgotten or had locked away.

Her face had resembled the one he saw in the mirror. She'd been real. They'd all been more than hazy dreams. He'd walked, squabbled, and played with them—the children and the adults too—every day. Family.

He and Patrick walked out of the dark museum into the cool, fragrant day. Edmund briefly thought of the stupid etching, but then he considered how pretty his family had been. The girls would have been married and settled with children long since. He'd have been an uncle several times over. His parents' hair would be streaked with gray, perhaps.

He realized he'd never before attempted to consider what might have been if his family had been spared. A jolt of anger hit him, at himself. It didn't seem fair that the only remaining member of the Lawtons hadn't even given that much thought to those lost futures. He should have at least thought of them on occasion.

"We shouldn't have done that," Patrick said. "You look sad, and that's even worse than angry."

"No, it was time. I hadn't seen them, and I couldn't remember them. I don't mean that horrid scene set up by Weller. I mean before he paid his visit." Edmund knew he was blithering and walked quickly toward a waiting carriage at the stand. "We'll go home, have some food, and make plans for later in the day."

"You'll be all right?"

I haven't been fine for a very long time, he felt like saying, but then decided that was the wrong answer. "Yes, I will. Thank you."

Patrick stopped near a small boy who held up a copy of a newspaper and shouted incomprehensible phrases. "That's the afternoon edition?" Patrick asked.

The boy nodded. Patrick dug into his pocket and pulled out a tuppence. He traded the coin for the paper. He stood and looked through it, frowning. Then he tucked the paper away. "Hold on," he told Edmund. "I have to check something out."

He strode down Marylebone a short distance to where a different boy waved another publisher's paper, and bought that one as well. Flip, flip, scan, scan. He folded it up and handed that one to Edmund. By the third paper, the fingers of his gloves were smeared gray with ink.

"What are you looking for?"

"News of the arrest in New York."

"Perhaps that story wouldn't make it into London papers yet. Or ever."

Patrick shoved the last paper into his pocket. "I'll come clean. I've been in touch with a couple of reporters since I've been here in England."

The automatic revulsion hit Edmund. He closed his eyes for a long moment, then began to walk toward the row of hacks waiting for passengers. "You didn't tell me about that."

"No, I wouldn't. Not when you hate newspapers so much."

"What did you promise them? A story about me?"

"Of course not."

Edmund growled. "Don't lie to me. One receives information from reporters only by promising to give stories in return." He kept his voice steady, though he wanted to turn and swing at Patrick, hit him hard enough to cause pain.

"Naw, I didn't promise a thing about you, Ned. The only information I gave them was about the similarities I already noticed between the murders, the scene setting, and so on. I didn't say anything about you or talking to you. They were annoyed their own guys hadn't picked up on the story."

Edmund wondered if Patrick was a fluent liar. And then he wondered what was the worst thing Patrick Kelly might say about him. The worst, of course, would show Patrick himself in a bad light. *He and I were naked, and I sucked his genitals* would hardly make it into a story in any newspaper.

He pulled off his hat and wiped back his hair. "Tell me what you said."

"Edmund. Ned. Please, there's no need for that hopeless tone. The information I wanted from them wasn't about you."

Edmund put his hat back on. "What did you want, then?"

"I wanted access to their old records and went to introduce myself. I did that my first day here. I figured I'd need their help, so, to get their interest, I pointed out just a couple of the similarities between the crimes in the United States and the Lawton family." He grimaced. "All right, I admit I did some finagling you might not appreciate. I said it was only a potential story, and that unless they held off printing anything until I'd made some progress on the case, I wouldn't talk to them again. I wanted to get as much information from them as I could, but if they ran a story, it would make it more difficult to talk to you Sloans."

"So very clever," Edmund said, though he felt less angry.

"Yesterday morning, I tipped them off about the arrest in New York and told them they should go with the story about the murderer being caught—but first they ought to check with their New York-based reporters."

Edmund asked, "And did they check?"

"Yes, I got a note from Drury. She'd sent a telegram asking about the arrests yesterday and that's the last I've heard. Last night and today, I've looked in the papers and haven't found anything about the arrests. That's made me suspicious."

"I don't understand."

"If there had been an arrest, it would take hours, not days, for the New York reporters to dig up and wire back the news. I think it's time I found out the truth."

"About the arrest?"

"Perhaps. Now I wonder about the telegram I got." He sighed. "It would have been easier just to send one to my boss, Mr. Greene, asking for details, but I didn't want to annoy him any more than I already have—not to mention spend too much money on useless telegrams. The problem is, there's another thing I didn't tell you about." He looked grim. "I should have told you, but it was directed at me, not you. I was sure of it. And I thought it wasn't relevant because I knew the murderer was in the United States."

He stopped speaking and looked so unhappy, Edmund demanded, "What?"

"Pigs' eyes. Delivered to me."

The phrase "in a pig's eye" flitted across Edmund's mind. Eyes though. That stopped all amusement. "Delivered to you?"

"At my hotel and, no I didn't find out who sent the grisly package." Patrick related a bizarre tale of receiving pig eyes in a delivery.

"Good Lord. Why didn't you say anything?"

"I might have, but then the telegram arrived. And I was convinced that it was someone trying to give me the shivers because I was poking my nose where it didn't belong."

"So you don't know? Aren't you at least curious about who was doing that?"

He shook his head. "I have some ideas. But I only wanted to make sure it had nothing to do with a threat to you and the murders in New York."

"What? How can you avoid looking into it, tenacious Mr. Kelly? And why didn't say anything to me? Or do anything about finding the perpetrator?"

"Because I figured it was just a distraction," he said shortly. "I wasn't surprised someone is trying to jar me. It's a nasty bit of business, but once I got the telegram, I supposed it was just someone with a godawful sense of humor and the desire to get to me. I only wanted to be certain it was directed at me and not you."

"Is that why you walked around with me?"

"More the opposite—that's why I wanted to take off the moment that telegram arrived. Keep you out of it, but I was selfish and wanted to spend time with you."

"But now."

"Now that I see the telegram is false, there could be danger after all. The pig eyes and the telegram—I don't think they were sent by the same person. Both seem interested in what I'm up to. One seems to want to send me away, and the other wants me to think there is a connection to the murder here in London. Or maybe it's just one person who acts without thinking. A madman?"

Edmund had relaxed too soon. His heart began to thump hard again. "What do you want to do?"

"Go to the office where this telegram came from and find out the details of its origin."

A wave of impatience, or perhaps actual fear, twisted through Edmund. If the telegram was intended to send Patrick back to the US, he could think of only one person in England who might try to get Patrick to leave and who had the interest and time to mislead him. "What do you think? What?"

"If I'm right and the telegram didn't come from my boss, someone wants me out of England. Probably because I'm snooping too much. I haven't made any reports back to Greene or anyone else in the States."

Edmund snorted. "That seems like a silly way to get you to leave, sending a false telegram. You'd figure out the truth with a simple word back to New York."

"I know. It might be the move of someone desperate. Or maybe the telegram is real and my boss will be annoyed that I'm not on my way to Southampton already."

"I hope to God it's real and the killer has been caught," Edmund said.

Patrick directed a long serious gaze at him. "Yes, that makes sense you'd wish for that. I do too."

He walked briskly down the pavement toward the waiting hacks.

"I suppose we ought to go visit the post office," Edmund said, grimly.

For a moment Patrick seemed to consider the idea, but then he shook his head. "The telegram didn't come to me at the hotel." Patrick waited until they were in a closed carriage, not a hansom, before he pointed out the other far too obvious fact. "Ned, I sent a report to my boss and told him that I wasn't at the hotel, but he wouldn't have gotten that report already. I didn't go fancy and use a telegram."

"What is your point?" Edmund stared straight ahead. Why would his uncle do this? He'd been acting oddly off and on during his illness, but this telegram business was so very strange. Oh God. Could he have sent the eyes?

Patrick pulled out the envelope from his pocket. Edmund gave it a quick glance and then looked into Patrick's serious face. The worry and kindness was directed at Edmund, who didn't interrupt when Patrick spelled it out. "This wasn't delivered to my hotel. The message was delivered straight to your house. That means it was sent by one of the few people who know where I actually stayed, and all those people are in England. I don't think we need to bother to visit the post office, do you?"

Chapter Nine

Ned pushed into the corner of the carriage and closed his eyes. He didn't answer.

Patrick leaned forward and slid the window open. "New destination," he told the driver and gave Mr. Sloan's Mayfair address.

At first, the butler refused to grant them entrance, but Ned did a fine job of imitating a young sultan.

"Kindly allow us to wait in the sitting room. We shan't require any refreshments," he said and brooked no possible answer other than "Yes, sir."

"Please inform my father a guest awaits. No more than that."

Patrick had expected that imperious manner when he'd first approached Ned, and he was glad to see he hadn't been entirely wrong. He considered telling Ned that he was quite the rajah, but the grim look on Ned's face stopped his mockery.

They sat near to the fire, for it was a chilly day despite the approach of summer. Patrick felt chilly from this whole thing. He didn't want the dark crime in America to be connected to Ned's family. He wanted the murderer to have no association with the Sloans, and he could tell by Ned's drawn face and blank eyes that he was haunted as well. Mr. Sloan could not be the perpetrator, but he must have a connection.

The bump and shuffle of his approach sounded from the hall. Mr. Sloan entered the room. He seemed even more hollow-eyed than before, if such a thing was possible. Patrick wished he could move closer to Ned, squeeze his hand for comfort.

"Well then? What do you want?" Mr. Sloan sounded querulous yet unsurprised to see Patrick still in the area. "Oh, it's you, Edmund. I thought only this one was here. How are you, my boy?" He waved the servants off and dropped heavily into a chair.

"Good morning, Papa Sloan. I'm here to discover why you sent a telegram to Mr. Kelly here."

His eyes, set too deep in his head, were hard to read, but he remained calm. "A *telegram*? Why would I do that? I have no interest in communicating with him."

The emphasis on the word "telegram" settled the answer for Patrick.

Edmund said, "Perhaps it wasn't a telegram but only the semblance of one."

"What are you talking about?" His lack of surprise at seeing Patrick and his befuddlement now seemed genuine.

And then when Mrs. Sloan entered the room and said, "Gracious, me. You!" Patrick began to have his suspicions.

He and Ned rose to their feet.

"No, dear, please," she said. Mr. Sloan seemed to think that meant he shouldn't try to stand.

Her quavering voice was enough to convince Patrick to pull the crumpled yellow paper from his pocket. "How do you do, ma'am. I believe you sent this?"

She shook her head, but obediently took the paper and read it. Her hands trembled.

Ned walked to her side and briefly laid a hand on her shoulder, hardly the great hug Patrick would give his own mother, but it seemed to help her. Her spine straightened.

In a gentle voice, Ned asked, "Why?"

She examined the paper in her hand as if it was the most fascinating thing in the world. "He would have told you the truth, and I couldn't bear it."

Ned frowned. "What do you mean?"

"He is my brother," Mr. Sloan began.

"What?" Mrs. Sloan said. "Why are you speaking of poor Gregory?"

Clearly, the two of them were as confused as Patrick felt.

Patrick felt like interrupting too, telling them all to shut up and then forcing them to explain one by one.

Ned sounded nearly as impatient as he felt when he said, "Mother Sloan. You sent the telegram. But why would you send Patrick, Mr. Kelly, away? Surely it has no connection to the murders in the United States."

She looked shocked. "Gracious, no. I knew he was here for that investigation, so I knew how to leave you and your poor foster papa alone. I worry about your father's ill health, and I didn't wish this…this person to overtax him."

The old man raised his heavy head. "Judith. It is not your role to protect me. I should have kept you safe, and, God help me, I didn't."

She gave a sniff and a furtive glance at Edmund. "I don't know what you're referring to."

Ah-ha, she did know the truth and didn't want Edmund or London society to find out about her husband's affliction. She must have thought Patrick would announce to the world that Mr. Sloan had a venereal disease.

"You know that misleading me about a murder investigation is a far more serious deed than the illness you were trying to cover up? Particularly since I think the murderer is still at work." He looked at Mr. Sloan. "And that's what you're talking about, yes?"

But Mr. Sloan wasn't paying any attention to him. He'd shuffled to the edge of the chair and seemed to be trying to stand. She rushed over to him and laid a hand on his shoulder. Really, these Sloans seemed to have only one way to express affection.

Mr. Sloan stopped trying to rise to his feet and settled back with a soft grunt. "I'm ashamed that you know the truth and it didn't come from my lips. How did you discover it?"

"My sister is married to a doctor."

Mr. Sloan began to laugh, a wheezing horrid sound. "Oh my, my. The things I've done. How long have you known?"

"Years. Since you, ah…" She crumpled the paper and turned pink. "A very long time."

"What are you talking about?" Ned said. "I say, isn't Gregory dead?"

Patrick was tired of standing. He went to a chair, picked it up, and let it drop again next to Mr. Sloan. "Sit, if you please, Mrs. Sloan."

She handed him the now twisted and slightly ripped telegram and sat. "I shan't beg your pardon for the deception," she said, though she sounded apologetic rather than indignant.

"No, it was kind of clever of you. Trouble is, I don't expect you knew the half of it. Mr. Sloan will tell us that part. Then let's get back to the blessed murder. Which I think is more important, don't you?"

"If that's true, yes, it is, then you don't need to say the rest... Please don't say anything more." She lowered her voice. "Edmund doesn't need to know."

"Are you still trying to protect me?" Ned snapped. "That's ridiculous. I'm a grown man and don't require coddling."

"You've always been a sensitive sort of a child. Quiet and..." She began to snuffle. "So well behaved and darling."

Ned sat across from his foster parents. His mouth was tight and thin. "I was frightened. I'm not any longer."

His glance at Patrick just about finished the thought: *I'm not frightened because of you*, or perhaps that was Patrick's own desire.

Patrick sat next to him. Two couples facing each other, he thought. There was one secret he wouldn't share today or ever. He spoke to Ned's foster parents. "Do you want me to talk about what's going on with Mr. Sloan, or will you?"

"No one needs to say anything." Mrs. Sloan's voice wobbled. "We have been so happy, and there's no reason to change that."

"Mother Sloan, we will still be happy," Ned said. "Since you mentioned your sister's husband, Dr. Peck, I assume this has to do with Papa Sloan's illness. And since you wished to keep it a secret, I must believe it is something...unsavory."

She shook her head so hard, her dangling earrings gave a faint tinkle. "Edmund, it is a private matter and hardly your concern—"

"Syphilis," Mr. Sloan said, still wheezing, a handkerchief blotting his cracked lips. His laughter sounded nearly hysterical, so he was difficult to understand. Sloan could well be insane on top of everything else. It was a symptom of the disease. "I have done so much to keep the truth from you, my dear. And you have known for years." He began to laugh again.

"You refused to—" She stopped and bit her lips. "My dear, you must calm yourself."

Patrick guessed she'd begun to say something about sharing a bed, but decided it wasn't relevant. He moved on to the more important topic. "And there is a connection. Gregory Sloan knew about your health, I guess?"

Mr. Sloan sobered almost at once. He nodded. "He threatened to tell my wife," he said quietly.

Her eyes widened. "No. He was always such a quiet, gentlemanly sort of person."

Ned gave one of his short, dry laughs. "You once remarked that I reminded you of him."

"I should hope not," Patrick couldn't help remarking, since at last they'd come to a man who might be the murderer.

"The poor thing went to Canada and died very soon after you came to live with us," Mrs. Sloan said.

"No. He's alive and I *thought* in Canada," Mr. Sloan said. "He'd deteriorated in the last few years, and after I got sick, I lost track of him. But..." He shrugged. It was an easy journey over the Canadian border into the US.

"Oh my God." Ned sat up straighter. "Your brother. You sent him away to recover from a nervous disorder. Why would you say he died if..." He rose to his feet and began to pace. And Ned, who seemed able to connect dots faster than his foster mother, understood what Mr. Sloan had meant when he'd said it was Gregory.

"He worked at your law firm for a while before the Lawtons' death, didn't he?" Patrick asked. "He was at your home while you were at school. And he and Weller would have met at your home. Did they meet again later on, when he delivered messages? Did they become friends?"

"I don't know." Mr. Sloan touched his mouth with his handkerchief. "Perhaps. Probably."

Ned rose to his feet and began to pace. "What have you done, Papa Sloan? You might have unleashed a terrible thing on the world."

He shook his head. "One had no notion that one's own brother could do such a thing."

Mr. Sloan's forehead wrinkled, and he looked at Ned, pacing. "He changed as he grew into a man, became very odd, but I didn't think he was particularly clever or violent. Until he made those threats about telling the world about...about..." He made a sweeping gesture up and down his body.

"It wasn't your fault." Mrs. Sloan ran her fingertips over his knuckles, then rested her hand on his. "You tried as hard as you could to help the poor boy."

At least that was one story husband and wife had shared. But truly, what a bunch of closemouthed ninnies. Patrick said, "I've never met such a group for hiding secrets to protect each other."

"Oh no, you are wrong in my case. I've come to understand I hid my secrets to protect myself and no one else." Mr. Sloan was slumped against the back of the chair, his eyes closed. His skin was chalky, and yet he wore a small smile.

"How can you be amused?" The Sloans started and stared. Patrick assumed Ned never shouted, and yet his voice rose to a thunder. "It's possible that your brother is responsible for those deaths in London and in the United States. He is the one."

Patrick said, "I expect he's relieved rather than amused?"

Mr. Sloan gave the smallest twitch of his head, chin going down, and Patrick decided it was a nod of agreement.

Patrick raised his voice. "But you didn't really want me to stumble onto the truth, did you? Not when you sent those eyes. You wanted to mislead me into believing the murderer was still in Britain."

"Perhaps. Perhaps. I was wrong to do that. It wasn't sporting."

Ned yelped, "You? You sent the pig eyes to Patrick?"

"He deserved them, forcing everyone to see things. Forcing the issue." He sounded like a fussy old man again. "And I didn't want him overturning any more rocks."

Mrs. Sloan's face creased into a mask of worry. "He hasn't been himself of late," she whispered as if he was asleep.

Patrick didn't point out that syphilis brought on madness. It seemed fairly obvious and, like the damned pig eyes, wasn't pertinent to the case.

*

Edmund couldn't hold still. Everyone else sat, watching him pace back and forth. "We can't simply lounge around, Papa Sloan. If the killer is your brother, you must do something."

Papa Sloan opened his eyes and glared. It was almost a relief to see that familiar haughty expression.

"I regretted those blasted eyes. Those were a mistake." That was as close to an apology as he would come, Edmund supposed. The real regret filled his voice as he added, "Once I understood I must do so, I had a telegram sent to that Mr. Greene and then wrote a letter with details."

Patrick spoke up. "Did you send a photograph of Mr. Gregory Sloan?"

Mr. Sloan pursed his lips, another familiar expression. "I hadn't thought to do such a thing. Do we have any photos of my brother?" he asked Mother Sloan as if asking if there was any tea left in the pot.

"I don't believe so," she said faintly. "He didn't care to have his likeness taken. I was sad we had no photos or memento mori of him. But now... He's alive, truly?"

No one answered. Perhaps by now he was dead, Edmund thought. That would be a relief for them all.

"Why did he dislike pictures?" Patrick used the past tense, so perhaps he didn't think of Gregory Sloan as among the living.

"He thought himself ugly in them."

"Do you suppose he resented people he believed to be more attractive?" Patrick asked the question casually. *The perpetrator went after pretty people.*

"I have no notion. I'm seven years the elder, so Gregory and I were hardly playmates as children." Papa Sloan waved a bony hand. "Come to that, I don't understand why I felt responsible, but one does have a sense of obligation."

Responsible for what? Taking care of his brother? Discovering if he was a murderer? Edmund wanted to know. *Is that guilt over your obligation why you sent him to Canada? Did you know?* Before he could ask that loaded question, Patrick asked one with less condemnation attached.

"If you didn't know him well, how'd you notice he'd changed when you came home on holiday?"

"He'd grown very quiet," Papa Sloan said after a moment's reflection. "He didn't tag after me, which was a relief at the time. He stayed in his room much of the day. He didn't smile or talk." Papa Sloan chuckled and, for a brief moment, seemed more like himself than he had in weeks.

"What is funny?" Edmund asked when he realized Papa Sloan was gazing at him.

"The description of Gregory is precisely how I'd have described you when you came to us."

"But dear Edmund soon improved beyond measure," Mother Sloan protested.

"Yes, much to our vast relief."

Last week, Edmund would have dismissed the question that rose inside as ill-spirited, but today, after Patrick, after everything else that had happened, he didn't mind asking rude questions. "Why were you relieved? Was it simply because you didn't have to care for a thoroughly damaged child, or was some of your guilt relieved, Papa Sloan?"

"What can you mean?" Mother Sloan put a hand to her mouth, and her eyes widened.

Patrick rested his hand on Edmund's shoulder, a comforting weight. "He couldn't have known what would happen to your family, Ned," he murmured. "That means something."

Edmund swallowed the hurt and betrayal that threatened to rise up like acid in his heart. After the fact, yes, that couldn't be as horrendous. But still... "I think Papa Sloan knew or suspected that his brother was involved in my family's demise. There were two people there that day. There had to be--to be more than one killer." He stuttered to a stop.

Patrick gave his shoulder a squeeze and stepped away from Edmund. He must have read Edmund's thoughts, and he spoke them to

Papa Sloan. "You suspected or even knew your brother was involved. You saw something when you were summoned to the scene, perhaps?"

Papa Sloan stared ahead as if he didn't hear. Patrick raised his voice a little. "But instead of telling anyone of his connection to the murder, you sent Gregory overseas and then did your level best to forget the Lawtons had ever existed. You've got a lifetime of dirt swept under an ocean of carpets."

"A terrible analogy," Papa Sloan said dryly. "One does what seems best at every moment of one's life." He shifted in his chair so he faced Edmund, who'd begun pacing again.

"Best for whom?" Edmund's voice trembled. "For yourself, I'd say. At every moment, you have picked the options that made your life easier."

"Please, both of you must stop. He was quite naughty for sending those horrible pig eyes, but he has done nothing more," Mother Sloan pleaded. "There is no reason for dramatics. I do wish you'd left well enough alone, Mr. Kelly. And the situation is dreadful. There is no need to hurt your poor foster father, Edmund."

"He's hardly injured. He's as cool as always." Edmund actually pointed at his foster father, something he'd never have been rude enough to do before today. "He's smiling."

"Ah. That's a sign of my illness." Papa Sloan's smile widened. "I seem unable to respond in an appropriate manner. The eyes were stupid. Stupid." He raised a shaking hand and covered his mouth.

"This is painful, and I beg your pardon for barging in, Mrs. Sloan. I couldn't leave a killer to carry on." Patrick seemed remarkably composed and polite. Perhaps the overly calm Sloan way had rubbed off on him as well.

She sighed. "No, I suppose you can't. The damage has been done now, so you'd best be on your way."

"What damage?" Edmund startled even himself with the shout.

"This. You are so angry, Edmund. This is precisely what I worried about."

He felt a rush of impatience at her fear of strong emotion. "I shall be fine, and Papa Sloan is certainly not upset enough, sitting in that chair while men, women, and children in another country were slaughtered. Good Lord, I still find it horrible to believe he sent those eyes because he wanted Patrick, an investigator, to think that the murderer was still in this country."

She touched her mouth with two fingers, an old, so familiar gesture and a reminder of his affection for her. He gave her a short bow. "We're going. Don't expect to see me soon." His throat was tight.

Papa Sloan pursed his lips and managed a shade of his old imperiousness. "You'll come back. You must, for your mother's sake." *Your mother.* Not *your foster mother.*

Edmund felt dizzy and he heaved a shuddering sigh. Already the powerful surge of his pure anger had turned into something more ambiguous.

"I'll return. I couldn't walk away forever. Don't you understand that? You're all I have of family."

He walked toward the door and was stopped by Papa Sloan's call, his voice reedy and high. "Surely you must see? That statement you made—that's how I felt about Gregory. I couldn't know for certain that he'd been a part of what happened in that house."

"You saw him there?" Patrick said.

Papa Sloan didn't bother to answer. "He was my brother, all that was left of my family."

Edmund had opened the door, and now he gently closed it. No need to bellow the news to the servants. "You'll never convince me you took the right action to cover what you knew and perhaps allow a murderer escape."

Papa Sloan sucked in a breath and coughed. "He was there. Yes. He needed money and was there to take it. He told me later." He coughed some more. "But he grew frightened and ran."

"Did you believe him?" Patrick asked.

Papa Sloan ignored the question.

Edmund ignored his foster father's hacking cough. He moved closer to Papa Sloan. "I didn't see Weller. I saw another man and you told me I shouldn't think of it. You told me to forget. And now I know why."

Papa Sloan stuttered, "That is, I don't say... I-I thought it was best for you to never think of the horror of that day. And I swear, I didn't believe he did—"

Edmund was suddenly too weary for this conversation he'd imagined for so long, when he could finally talk with Papa Sloan about the day his family died and perhaps get answers to fill in some of the blanks in his memory. He couldn't bear to hear more of that useless lack of contrition. "Stop!" he interrupted, and once again, an out-of-character shout was enough to startle his foster father into silence. "Enough." And at that moment, he knew it was beyond enough. He walked to the door, ready to leave again. Edmund looked into Papa Sloan's lumpy gray face and burning eyes. He seemed far more ill than ever before. "We are quits, Papa. We owe each other nothing, and no more need be said."

He'd spent most of his life treading so carefully in the Sloans' world, worried he didn't deserve a family. And now he must reassure that family he wouldn't slough them off? How odd. "I care too much for you to bring in the authorities about your silence."

"Good." His foster father's whisper was hoarse. "Thank you for that." His eyes suddenly grew old and rheumy. No, oh God above, those were tears.

I don't owe you fealty, you don't owe me love, and yet we are bound together. For half a second, Edmund considered embracing Papa Sloan, but that seemed too false for them. "Good-bye," he said. "I hope you..." He sighed. There was no good way to finish the statement. "I hope you feel better," was the best he could manage.

"I'm going to die soon," his father whispered. Edmund started at the certainty of the words. That nearly swept away the rest of his anger of course. He could not act against a man who was dying, especially not Papa Sloan.

Patrick put his hat on his head, then took it off again. "It's been nice to meet you." Ridiculous Patrick sounded entirely unironic.

Edmund stifled a laugh. What an astounding person Patrick Kelly proved to be.

Patrick aimed a frown at him before turning his attention back to the Sloans. "No, I mean it. You did a fine job raising Ned, Mr. Sloan, Mrs. Sloan. And I don't blame you for trying to get rid of me, coming in here and beating all the filthy carpets. Ha. That telegram was clever as can be, missus. Getting me to go away."

She made a faint, polite sound.

"Go away, sir," Papa Sloan said. "Go, you bloody bastard."

Mother Sloan gasped in astonishment. Papa Sloan would never normally be so rude or use foul language. It must be another symptom of his illness.

Edmund murmured an apology, but Patrick only shrugged.

"I'm going. Here's the thing." He cleared his throat. Patrick would say something and reveal far too much. But Edmund was too curious and too free of his own usual restraints to stop him.

"Your son and I have become friends over the last couple of days. I shall do what I can to convince him to come back with me to New York."

"I say," Edmund exclaimed.

"But I doubt he'll come with me because of his loyalty to you. So I imagine I'll have to hang around here. And that probably means I'll see you again."

He sounded mild as toast, but the grin on his face was fiercely triumphant. He must have thought his announcement would dismay the Sloans. Perhaps that was his revenge for their treatment of him. Or perhaps the smile was because he was certain that he had Edmund. That was an odd idea, to think of himself as a rag tugged between a dog and a child. Edmund was obviously the toy, but which was the dog and which the child, Papa Sloan or Patrick?

Papa Sloan looked at Patrick with open loathing and said nothing.

Mother Sloan only murmured faintly that she would be glad to see him and she did hope he begged her pardon for that silly trick.

Patrick and Edmund left the house together without exchanging a single word. Edmund tried to think of a way to apologize for his foster father, while Patrick was apparently lost in gloomy thoughts.

"I have to send word, you know. And look for pictures of Gregory Sloan."

Edmund nodded. "Of course."

Chapter Ten

"I'm sorry. That he called you a bastard," Edmund said.

"Mr. Sloan must have done his research. But I'm not worried. You already know I'm a bastard." He shook his head smiling. "The things families do to keep their children safe and happy."

"He was sick, and that's why he said that."

"It didn't bother me. And, at any rate, I didn't mean him, not entirely anyway. I was more thinking about Mam." His good humor vanished, and those blue eyes were entirely somber. "She used to tell me all about my father, lots of stories that made him seem like a kind, gentle soul who died before I was born."

"So even if they weren't married, she was left with good memories." Weak solace, he supposed, but he had to say something to shift the bleak expression from Patrick's face.

"No. It was all lies. She had never so much as seen his face. She was ravished, ruined, and nearly destroyed by a stranger."

Edmund gasped.

Patrick bent his head and kept walking. "She tried to protect me from that truth for most of my life. I only found out a few years ago."

"I'm so sorry. For you. For her. I don't have the words to express how…how…"

"Don't worry. It's quite a thing to learn about a person, I know. I had trouble knowing what to say to my poor mam for a time afterwards." He rubbed his arms and looked at Edmund without a trace of his usual warmth. "Hardly a big surprise—it's not an easy thing for me to discuss."

"I don't think less of you because of that truth. And I am honored that you chose to share it with me," he said and immediately felt stupid. But the darkness cleared from Patrick's face, and he slowed his pace, so it must have been the right thing to say.

"Thank you for that. I guess I told you because I figured, in a way, it fits you. No, that does sound pretty bad." Patrick grimaced. "You're not the son of a rapist. I mean that Mr. Sloan tried to hide the truth from you in order to protect you. He didn't do all that just for himself. People do the damnedest things for family. Also, I'm trying to distract you."

"Oh?"

"Because I'm so sorry, Ned. For what it's worth once Weller was caught, I don't think your foster father believed his brother was the man who killed your family." Patrick frowned and shook his head. He came to a stop again. "So much for distracting you—I brought up the damned subject again. Very suave, huh?"

Edmund's chest tickled oddly, and he realized strong emotion was bubbling below the surface. Standing in the middle of the pavement under the shade of an old battered oak, he gave in.

"God, I'm sorry." Patrick stepped close and peered at him. "Oh. You're laughing, not crying? I really don't know what I should do about that. Is it hysterical laughter? Should I slap you on the back?"

"Thank you, no, I'm fine." Perhaps an edge of hysteria had flowed through him, but it was gone now, and he had regained his balance. "You've no need to worry about me any longer."

"What sent you off into that strange fit?"

"You. Because, lately it seems you would keep me safe in the oddest ways. You. Of all people, trying to help me feel better."

"It worked if you're laughing."

Edmund wiped his eyes. "Why, I suppose it did. Thank you."

"I'm going to go the telegraph office now," Patrick said. "I'll make sure Mr. Greene knows what's going on. And I better write to my mam and tell her I'll be here a bit longer."

"I don't recall offering you an invitation to stay," Edmund protested.

"I'll wait until you do, of course." He pulled out his watch and looked at it. "Any minute now."

"You're very confident."

"Aw, you're right." He settled his hat back on his head. "I guess I shouldn't work so hard at anything. I'm done. My job is over."

"No! Wait, no. Patrick, you said you'd remain in London." He winced at the pleading in his voice. The long-lost five-year-old still hung about, rising to the surface now that he had the confidence to allow such a thing. He mustn't let the little beast out often.

"Ah-ha! Is that my invitation I hear?"

"Yes." Edmund drew in a long breath. "Please, Mr. Kelly, do stay with me."

"Thank you, I hope a week won't be too long?"

"I say, that's not nearly long enough." Edmund wondered at his own alarm. "Didn't you tell my parents you planned an extended stay in London?"

"That was probably the devil speaking. They don't approve of me as your playmate."

The word *playmate* gave Edmund such ideas—which sadly vanished when Patrick continued. "No, I must return to New York to earn my bread and stop my mam from sending me pages and pages of worried letters."

They walked in silence to the post office. Edmund stood next to a wooden desk, watching Patrick compose his message and take it to the telegraphy window. What would Edmund think if he passed this man on the street? He'd notice the dark hair, the fine shoulders—and Edmund quickly looked away, for he realized he was outright gawking.

Did Patrick look in the mirror for traces of the father who'd ruined an innocent girl?

The words Patrick handed to the clerk would cross half the world in far less time than it took to sail to the United States. A sea voyage… Edmund had never attempted such a thing, and what had stopped him?

But then Patrick finished and came to his side. "You're frowning. I'm sorry about your father's…um…unsettled mind."

Edmund shook his head, unwilling to voice his thoughts of New York. He said, "Who would have guessed that Mother Sloan would be so crafty?"

"She seems the sort of person who remains timid and mild until she sees a threat to her family, and then she strikes. I was a threat. I'm lucky she didn't have me arrested."

"From what I know of Papa Sloan, that seems more his style, at least until he stopped making sense and started sending eyeballs." He sighed. "I wonder if the people who died in New York could have been spared..."

"I get the impression Mr. Sloan wonders the very same thing. He looks considerably more ill than he did when I met him just a day or so ago. He seemed relieved that the matter is out in the light. Could be guilt is eating at him."

That wasn't the only thing that had consumed him, Edmund thought with some bitterness. "To learn he has such an awful disease..." He stopped speaking, raised his hat at an acquaintance, and waited until the gentleman had long passed before quietly adding, "I have been purposefully blind."

"He's a powerful man and clever at keeping his secrets."

Edmund glanced at his companion, who gazed with bright interest at a lady wearing what appeared to be a coat of fox fur with several heads still attached. "Patrick, will you argue every point I mention? I say I was blind, and you say he blinded me."

"Yes. It's my contrary nature." Patrick turned his attention back to Edmund and smiled at him. "I'm in a bad mood because I just spent a fortune sending a message abroad. I gave Greene your address, by the by. Hope you and your butler won't mind getting irate messages from him there."

"You look quite cheerful for a contrarian in a foul mood."

"And now who's the one contradicting everything? No, I agree with you. You're right, of course. I'm in a terrific mood."

"Why is that?"

"For whatever reason, you don't hate me, which stumps me, what with that scene with Mr. and Mrs. Sloan. You still liking me is reason enough to tip back the hat and whistle at the blue sky with pleasure."

"You weren't the one holding secrets."

"Messengers have been shot before for less unpleasant messages."

Edmund strolled along, wondering how he'd recovered so quickly from the jolts inflicted during this shocking morning. "I think that even before today, I must have discerned at least a portion of the truth. Why would Papa Sloan hide his diagnosis if it weren't something dire? Why would he always insist I forget my past? I didn't want to face reality, and he didn't want me to know it, so we worked together. And now…" He fingered his lower lip and recalled the tingle of kisses. "Thanks to you, another truth about myself I've tried to ignore is often on my mind. One that has nothing to do with my family."

"Oh? And what is that?"

Edmund licked his lips. "We shall return to my house, and I will demonstrate rather than speak of the matter."

*

Patrick couldn't believe his luck. Not only did Edmund actually speak of their mutual attraction, he could be humorous about it. He'd stopped looking and acting like a guilt-stricken martyr.

Naw, unfair, Patrick scolded himself. A guilt-stricken gentleman—that seemed a more fitting description. Ned hadn't adopted the prayerful silence of the sanctimoniously injured.

Patrick moved closer, and as they walked, his sleeve brushed Ned's, the knuckles of their gloved hands touched. He tried to imagine other ways he might get more contact with Ned right out on the street. A conversation that allowed him to put a hand on the back of his neck? No, far too much.

A slap on the shoulder that lingered? Hard to engineer.

Another stranger interrupted his thoughts. A stout gent wearing a top hat and spats hailed Ned and bid him a hearty good day. He inquired after everything, from Ned's opinion on the weather to the stock exchange. Patrick stood a little apart, waiting. He considered yelling and grabbing Ned's arm and pulling him away, maybe pretending they needed to run to an emergency. But that silly thought, and even the simmering lust, vanished when Ned motioned to him to come closer. Ned grabbed *his* arm, pulled him to his side, and introduced the man to Patrick.

"This is my good friend, Mr. Patrick Kelly from America," Ned finished the introduction. "He's here in London for as long as I can convince him to stay."

Patrick shook hands with the pleasant, round-faced gentleman, who then bowed over his hand like Patrick was some sort of visiting royalty. "Ah! Any friend of Mr. Sloan's is a friend of mine," the man declared as if he'd only just now thought up the phrase.

"Glad to meet you." Patrick managed to extricate his hand and wished he'd thought to listen to the man's name. He'd been too caught in astonishment that Ned, of all people, would come right out and admit they were friends.

A few more predictable phrases were exchanged, and they escaped. Patrick sped up. If Ned was truly ready to admit they were friendly in public, he couldn't wait to discover what he'd reveal in private.

They returned to the house and ordered luncheon. Patrick had no appetite because he was wound too tight. For once, Ned ate, though he took his sweet time. Patrick sat across from him, watching the tidy way Ned carved and chewed the tiny pieces from the roast grouse and the croquets of rice. They ate in silence except for the clink and scrape of silver against china. The squeak of Patrick's chair as he shifted about.

Ned looked up at him occasionally and smiled. After Ned nibbled a piece of meat, swallowed it, then licked his lips, Patrick had had enough.

"You rat! You know what you're doing to me," Patrick protested.

Ned's eyelids lowered. "I have a fair notion, yes. I expect it's no more than you've done to me."

"Turnabout is fair play." Patrick picked up an ornate silver luncheon knife and licked it up and down from the haft to rounded tip.

A long, audible breath escaped Ned. He tossed his napkin on the table and rose to his feet.

That ended the meal.

"The servants," Ned whispered. "They will suspect. We must remain so quiet no one will ever know, not even the mice in the wainscoting."

"I have a cat in New York that's a champion mouser."

"Eh, what? Oh yes, the mice in the walls." He smiled at Patrick. "Poor Becker would faint at the suggestion that we actually did have mice. But do you suppose... Would your puss like Britain?"

Did that count as an actual invitation? What a thought. Never mind the cat, Patrick wondered if his mother would consent to life in England. He doubted it, but Ned's pull was more than he could fight. That battle would be faced eventually. No need to look out for it yet.

"Let's give the rodents a show." Patrick rose to his feet. "Let's dance."

"I beg your pardon?"

"Dance. The waltz, perhaps? A polka?"

Ned laughed. "You're a lunatic."

"Dancing is hardly crazy." He held his arms wide.

"But a man with another man?"

"Come on, Ned. Step up. I'm a fair dancer."

Ned shook his head, and Patrick went to him, bowed, and held out a hand. "Monsieur?"

With a long, and no doubt impolite, answer in French, Ned let Patrick pull him up.

But it was Ned who pressed close and grabbed up Patrick's hand and wrapped his arm around his middle...and pressed close. He hummed a tune in a pleasant baritone.

"Do I hear a milonga?" Patrick said, laughing. "I don't know much about dance, but I know that your sort of people would call it a vulgar dance. Where would you hear such a thing?"

"My sort of people, naturally. At a rather fast dance held by a friend of mine. It's the tango andaluza."

They didn't get very far—both were too accustomed to taking the lead. A few steps into it, the pulling and laughter began. Ned's humming died away, and soon his touch turned into something as passionate but even more interesting than an intimate dance with a desirable partner. Patrick was giddy with laughter and wrestling. He pushed forward to land a smooch on the corner of Ned's mouth. Ned turned his head, and then they truly kissed, soft and slow. Almost at once, Ned's kisses turned from tentative to wild. They were deep and tasted of desperate need that lit an answering hunger in Patrick.

They sank to the ground with some difficulty, because two grown men going to the carpet is awkward and because Patrick didn't want to release his hold on Ned. They lay on their sides, facing each other.

"Please," Patrick begged as he ran his hands up and down the cool fabric covering Ned's chest and belly, fumbling for buttons. Of course his gentleman would wear studs on his silk waistcoat. It took a goddamn valet to cope with these clothes, but Patrick was determined and wrestled the waistcoat and shirt and undershirt aside, tangling Ned in a mess of fabric caught by his braces. Ned groaned as Patrick dove down and began kissing all the exposed flesh he could reach, licking at the warm flesh and delicate hair on Ned's belly. Patrick happily cupped Ned's solid erection through his wool trousers. He leaned down and breathed against Ned's bollocks. The way Ned whimpered and bucked was profoundly satisfying.

"Hush," Patrick murmured.

When he undid the buttons of Ned's fly, a hand suddenly appeared to block his access. Patrick licked the fingers and bit them. "What's wrong?" he whispered.

Ned sighed. "You've done that already."

Patrick lifted his head and grinned. "I would do it again. And again. And again." After each "again," he stroked Ned's cock and nibbled those long fingers. Mm, he would dearly love to see those on his body and a second later Ned cupped his cheek and thrust his thumb into Patrick's mouth, in and out.

Once again, Ned went from shy to enthusiastic in a single breath. Patrick sucked on his fingers, on the skin between his thumb and forefinger, but when Ned arched up again, Patrick managed to get the last scrap of fine gentleman's undergarment out of the way and found his prize, hard, hot, and thick.

Ned groaned when Patrick licked him from base to apex. "Hush," Patrick said. "The mice."

He lapped the tip of Ned's erection and licked along the underside to suck on his balls, but they were already tight and high, ready to release.

Ned squirmed under his touch and mouth and, to Patrick's dismay, pushed away.

He came back a moment later, an attack on Patrick. Ned was far more deft at undoing buttons and peeling back clothing than Patrick had been. Ned escaped long enough to shuck his own shoes and clothing.

He stood over Patrick as soft light filtered through the mostly closed curtains and gleamed on Ned's flesh, which looked as rock-hard and impressive, and nearly as pale as a Grecian statue—with the added pleasure of that impressive erection.

Patrick tried to stand but was too tangled in his clothes. He sat back, and Ned grinned down at him.

"Lie on your back," Ned commanded.

Patrick obeyed.

Ned knelt by his feet. As he slid Patrick's socks from his feet, he spoke in a low voice. "Once, in a library, I found a book of ancient art." Ned cleared his throat. "It excited me beyond all reason. I believe it must have been pornography hidden in that library. It showed two men who lay together like dogs, and also like a man and a woman. I've thought about that book every time I look at you."

"Ah. Hey. You mean buggering me?" Patrick had indulged in the act several times, but always as the penetrator. He wasn't sure if he was interested… Those dark eyes watching him gleamed with purpose and such desire. Patrick swallowed. Sure. He'd do whatever Ned wanted when he wore that look.

"All right. It would be nice for something to ease the way in, if you know what I mean." Patrick lay back and stroked his own mostly hard cock. That strangled sound from Ned made him forget any worries of discomfort.

Ned muttered something under his breath. He went to the luncheon table, and dishes rattled.

He returned and knelt again on one knee by Patrick, like some sort of supplicant, Patrick thought. "What should I do?" Ned whispered.

"What feels good?"

"Oh, that's a strange question. Everything. Feels good…far better than good, I mean." Ned opened his hand and showed the pat of butter. He gnawed his lower lip and seemed to wait for Patrick's instructions.

Patrick wasn't going to take over. He put his hands behind his head and looked at Ned with a smirk.

"Ah." Ned blinked and held up the hand with the butter on his palm. "And now?"

Patrick gave in. He rolled onto his stomach and issued instructions. "You do the work, then. Rub that on you. And on me." He waggled his rear. "And we'll take it from there."

Ned's eyes wore that greedy look again. He gazed at Patrick up and down, then touched the butter with one finger. "I could simply decide to lick this from your body."

"Mm, if you'd like." *That, yes. Please.*

Ned brushed his fingers across his palm, and they came away slick and shiny. He stroked his cock with his buttery hand. Soon, his eyes closed and his head went back.

"Not too much of that," Patrick said. Although, why not? He'd love to watch Ned spend.

"You're too loud." Ned shook a glistening finger at him.

He leaned over Patrick now, and that finger went down between Patrick's cheeks, down, down, and then slid around and in.

Patrick closed his eyes against too much sensation. This would be good, and he needed it to last.

Those fingers explored. Something hot and wet brushed Patrick's cock. His eyes shot open to see Ned bobbing on him. Ned's tongue and mouth and the slight scrape of teeth, then tongue. Ned, who'd been so unwilling to even speak of masturbation, had shed his stodginess—and for Patrick. Brave lad and oh God…that felt amazing.

He needed the rest now. "Come here," he whispered.

Just as he'd hoped, Ned crawled up and kissed him so their bodies and cocks met, Ned naked against him. He ran his hands up and down Ned's back. That slippery hot cock pushed against his, just more, only more, please…but he didn't protest when Ned moved away to sit up again.

Patrick had moved his hands from behind his head to grasp Ned and palm his rear as they'd kissed and writhed, but he returned them to the back of his head now. He presented himself by spreading his elbows and knees wide. If he hadn't been so excited, he might have felt silly, but he didn't have time for anything but pleasure and exploration.

Ned's fingers at his arse pushed in. Something scraped, and Patrick hissed. A fingernail. But even that slight pain made him harder.

"Sorry." Ned fumbled and tilted forward. Not sharp any longer, blunt but immense, and before Patrick could say *wait, not so fast,* a sensation that wasn't quite pain seemed to overwhelm him. He writhed and clamped down, and they both gasped.

"Oh," Ned said. "Sorry. Sorry."

"No, not sorry." Because now Patrick could move, and it was no longer so harsh or even uncomfortable. "It's..." He rocked against the huge cock filling his arse. "It's amazing. Oh holy... Yes."

"Yes?" Ned came forward, his face hot against Patrick's neck, and his breaths fanned Patrick's jaw.

Patrick moved ever so slightly. Another ripple of sensation and excitement rolled through him. "More than yes. *Fuck* yes."

Ned took that as instructions and began to rock inside Patrick, who grabbed at him and urged on each thrust with his hands. The muscles under his palms tightened and writhed as Ned pushed into him.

He slid a hand between them and touched himself. Ned's taut belly slid over his fingers and cock. He'd drawn so close to Ned, so close to orgasm, on top of skin and life and...Patrick, who'd always known to be quiet when with another man, realized he'd shouted. And then he couldn't give a damn, for he erupted under the weight and invasion of *Ned. Ned. Ned.* Hell. He was saying the word but couldn't give a damn. He nearly cried with the relief of the orgasm.

Ned murmured, "Not so loud," and put his lips over Patrick's mouth for another hungry kiss. Patrick slid his hand from between them and slapped Ned's arse, urging him on, because fast and hard still felt fine.

Several powerful thrusts later, Ned groaned and pumped so deep into Patrick, he might have been going to the other side. He froze and shivered in Patrick's arms, the best armful it had ever been Patrick's pleasure to hold.

Patrick smiled, closed his eyes again, and wiggled until he could wrap his legs around Ned. The angle was uncomfortable for his body, his balls, and his now-trapped penis, but he wasn't about to allow any air to come between them.

Ned made a protesting sound and rolled to the side. They lay sprawled on the scratchy wool carpet, staring at each other.

Patrick rested his hand on Ned's side claiming all that warm breathing flesh as his own. He wanted to make sure he knew every inch and scent, every limb and taste. He planned to memorize his Ned.

They dozed for a time. And when they woke again, they spoke of nothing in particular and of games they played in school and people they'd admired as children.

"My foster father was my hero, of course. He seemed almost too strong to be human, even when ill. I had never known him to make a mistake. Until very recently, that is to say." Shadows and smiles passed over Ned's face as if he'd never held back a secret sorrow or a moment of joy in his life.

Patrick reached over and pinched Ned's upper lip.

"Ow. What on earth?" Ned batted him away.

"Lost all that British starch in your upper lip, my friend."

"For the moment, perhaps." Ned's full mouth curved into a brilliant smile, all softened pleasure and white teeth. "With you."

Well, that was a fine thing to hear. Patrick wanted to slap himself on the back for a job well done.

By the time they cleaned themselves using their handkerchiefs, a glass of wine, and a glass of water, it was late afternoon.

They checked each other up and down after they dressed. Something was different in Ned, and Patrick made him go in a slow circle to see if he could figure out the change.

"It's your posture," he decided at last. "It's not just your upper lip that's lost stiffness. You seem looser."

"Hmm. And you're a bit more stiff. As if you've..." Ned broke off. He turned pink, looked away, then smoothed his jacket cuff.

"As if I've had a branch jammed up my rear?" Patrick guessed. "Well, boyo, I guess I have."

"Perhaps." Ned flashed him a cheeky grin. He glanced at his watch, adjusted his fob one more time, and went to the door to unlock it. "Now we shall pretend to be normal."

This could be normal for us, Patrick wanted to argue. *This could be how we lead our lives.* But he was arguing with himself as well, because who'd want to uproot his life for a dangerous and probably temporary alliance?

Edmund had never had a holiday like this one. He felt as if he had walked out into sunshine for the first time after a long imprisonment. An odd response when the day was miserably damp and chilly.

He and Patrick went to places he'd often visited before, but now they seemed to be imbued with something important, and he saw them more clearly than he had before. The spreading elm tree in a square seemed far more impressive and lovely than it had when he'd walked past it a fortnight earlier.

He supposed he understood what it all meant. A response to the release he'd been given in his room and the less crass and more subtle release he'd felt since Patrick muscled into his life. His life had changed for the better, even though one of his dearest connections, a man he admired as a father, had lied by omission. But no, he wouldn't think about Papa Sloan as he and Patrick walked under the still-dripping trees of Hyde Park.

The day passed gloriously even though it consisted of nothing more than walking and conversation.

Edmund even managed to eat a pastry in a shop. They attended a play near Covent Garden and walked and talked before and after the performance. Edmund's legs ached from all the walking and other activity he did that day. By the time they reached home, he was quite tired. They sat and read in companionable silence. A last Patrick said he needed rest. Edmund bid a reluctant good night to his new friend. But it wouldn't do, of course, to go to bed in the same room. No doubt they'd already stirred the below-stairs gossip pot with the door locked for so long that afternoon. And some of those shouts... He blushed to recall them. He undressed and climbed into bed. The slight scratch on the door startled Edmund awake. Patrick, still fully dressed, entered his room. He began removing each piece of clothing, and Edmund sat up to watch.

Afterwards, they kissed and touched. Each kiss and each touch grew more urgent and Edmund's head spun with anticipation as they lay side-by-side. When Patrick took them both in his large hand, Edmund knew he couldn't last long. He wanted more. He needed more. But then the soft guttural moan that came from Patrick proved too much. He spent in the firm grip that massaged him until he shivered.

He waited for Patrick to leave but after a sigh and a shift, Patrick seemed to doze off.

Edmund felt ridiculously pleased as he listened to his breathing, slow and measured, occasionally interrupted by a snore and a mumbled word and an impatient shift of his body. Patrick was not an easy sleeper.

Edmund ran his hand down Patrick's side, and his own heart thumped hard the instant Patrick jolted awake and spoke into the dark. "What? Hey?"

"Hush," Edmund reminded him. It had become a game. "Quiet," he commanded as he slid down the sleep-warmed body, brushing his mouth against the hair and skin. "And again," he murmured.

Patrick slipped back to his own room before dawn and slept late. When he went downstairs at last, he found that the idle had come to an end already. The outside world invaded in the form of a telegram from Greene.

Chapter Eleven

"Mr. Sloan is meeting with a gentleman in the library. The cook has been instructed to prepare you a late breakfast," Becker told Patrick.

"No need. I don't want much to eat."

"Shall a light repast be sufficient, sir?"

Becker apparently didn't want to take no for an answer, so Patrick agreed to a cup of tea and some toast in a drawing room. The tray held the usual lovely bouquet of flowers, plain white toast, and some spicy and rich pastry, and a large pat of butter that had been shaped like a leaf. The sight of butter made him smile.

"I could get used to this sort of life," he told the butler, who gravely inclined his head as if agreeing with some piece of wisdom. Patrick wondered if the servants had been lectured again about the importance of the American upstart.

A few moments later, Becker reappeared with the telegram on a silver tray. He lingered as if he hoped Patrick would share the contents, so Patrick obliged with, "I guess I won't get used to life in Mayfair after all. I have to return to the States."

"Oh, too bad, sir."

Patrick almost believed the butler's sympathetic tone. He went to his room to pack, wishing it was yet another false telegram, but the abbreviations were distinctively Greene. He'd never simply trust a telegram again. He smiled at the thought of that seemingly harmless old lady, Mrs. Sloan, trying to send him on his way.

He came back down and found Ned waiting at the door with a young man, probably his secretary, shaking hands with another older man, who had an impressive gray beard.

Ned looked up and gave Patrick a distracted nod. Not precisely lover-like behavior. For the best, he supposed. But he wished he could think of a way to drag Ned back to New York. It would do the man good.

*

Edmund had trouble meeting Patrick's eye. During his call, Mr. Grady, his foster father's friend and colleague, had made it clear that Edmund must pick either his family or his new friend.

"I have been informed that you know all," Mr. Grady had said as they sat down together.

Know all of what? he'd wondered, but remained silent waiting for Mr. Grady who said, "And I must say it is a relief to know Mr. Sloan has decided to tell you about his brother."

As he spoke, it became apparent that the lawyer had kept Papa Sloan's secrets well. Mr. Grady had long known about the murderous brother, and about the real cause of Mr. Sloan's illness. Edmund supposed he should be grateful the lawyer—his own lawyer—kept his clients' secrets.

And then Mr. Grady cleared his throat and divulged another secret. "Last night, your father, Mr. Sloan, revised his will. He doesn't wish to leave you anything because your pursuit of the truth has driven his wife to take desperate measures. Also, he has made it clear that certain of your propensities are not acceptable to his... What you have done is not acceptable."

"You mean my friendship with Mr. Kelly? Did he say as much?"

Mr. Grady tilted his chin and seemed to examine the leafy flower medallion around the ceiling gaslight fixture as he spoke. "I am making this call because he wished me to, and because I am not sure he is sound of mind and certainly not of sound body. I am worried for your family, Mr. Sloan."

"Don't worry for my sake. I don't require his inheritance. I don't need money." Edmund realized he didn't even require his foster father's good opinion—although he did desire it.

"I plan to see him in a few days." He'd go after Patrick left and Edmund had time to recover from that loss. He'd received his mother's note, but for once he wouldn't drop everything and run to the Sloans' house.

"You should go sooner, I think." Mr. Grady pressed his lips together and touched his necktie with one gnarled finger as if he wished he hadn't spoken. No, that wasn't his problem. Mr. Grady fought back tears.

Edmund swallowed. "You believe he is going to die very soon."

The lawyer flinched, but Edmund wouldn't apologize for plain speaking—Patrick's influence, whether for good or bad, he didn't know.

Mr. Grady said, "I believe he is not long for this world. I've been told perhaps a matter of days or even hours."

And who'd told him that? But Edmund didn't object as he rose from his chair. "Very well, I shall go make my peace with him. And don't worry. I shan't mention this conversation with you."

Mr. Grady stayed in his chair. "I think I must tell you more. His brother, that is to say Gregory Sloan, was a strange boy." He blurted out the words as if it hurt to speak.

"Ah." Edmund hadn't even known the man had existed until recently, but admitting ignorance wasn't the way to coax more information from Grady. He said, "I understand as a child, he had a sudden shift in behavior."

"Yes, I'm glad you know about that. After Gregory was unconscious for hours, he woke a changed boy. Because the injury happened as Gregory tried to follow his brother, and Mr. Sloan didn't immediately go to his aid, Mr. Sloan has felt responsible for him ever since."

Edmund sat again. "My father said he didn't know what had happened to his brother."

"Oh, too bad, too bad." Mr. Grady turned red. "That will teach me to never gossip. I beg your pardon for speaking out of school—"

"Please do not balk at telling me the truth."

"I have said too much. I wished you to understand exactly why Mr. Sloan has some great worries for you. He wondered if the trauma that took place when you were a child, that is to say what you witnessed, could have somehow turned you... Could have given you a nervous disorder as well."

"I have no desire to murder or mutilate anyone," Edmund said. "I find it difficult even to be rude."

Mr. Grady coughed into his hand.

He was so gifted with subtle communication that Edmund immediately guessed the truth about what qualified as strange behavior. "Does Papa Sloan think my lack of interest in the ladies comes from witnessing my family's demise?"

Since he'd wondered the same thing once or twice in his life, it felt odd to grow so indignant at the idea. But once again, he had Patrick to thank for that. A man like Patrick was alive and vibrant and the very opposite of mentally defective... Edmund's heart clutched tight. Oh no. This would not do. He had fallen in love with Patrick Kelly. This would not do at *all*.

Mr. Grady was gabbling again. During this visit, he'd gone from an articulate, quiet professional to a babbler. "I should hesitate to ascribe any thoughts about the subject, I mean my own opinion on the matter is not what one could call a certainty about any sort of cause or—"

"I understand," Edmund gently interrupted. "You are speaking of my father's view, are you not? And this is what he believes? That a trauma can produce a change in a man's personality or his desires?"

Mr. Grady nodded so hard that his beard rasped against his stiff collar. "He also spoke of a bad influence ensconced in your house, and in that, I think I must agree. I have had some contact with Mr. Kelly, the private inquiry agent of New York, and he is not a gentleman."

"No, I believe you're right. He isn't." Edmund thought of all the amazing ungentlemanly things he and Patrick had done together. No time to indulge in those memories. He rose again, and this time, Mr. Grady did as well. Edmund said, "I'd best go see my father."

"Oh dear. You appear so distressed, I'm not at all sure I should have come here."

The poor man looked so distraught, Edmund said, "Mr. Grady, please don't think that I will storm into my father's house and demand explanations. I understand he is very ill."

For the first time, Mr. Grady smiled. "You have always been the pattern of fine comportment, m'boy. I'm glad my old friend is wrong and you aren't changed in your nature."

"I am the same as always." Edmund steered him to the door and offered his hand. *I am utterly changed forever.* "I thank you for coming to me despite your misgivings."

When Patrick met them in the hall, Edmund knew at once that Mr. Kelly the investigator had returned, abandoning Patrick, the heavy-eyed smiling lover.

"What is it?" Ned asked.

Patrick announced, "I have to go back to the States."

Ned closed his eyes for a long moment. He'd known this was coming. "I shall miss you," he said quietly.

Patrick ducked his head and folded his arms. "My boss asked me if you could identify the other man who, uh, did that to the Lawtons. We would buy you passage."

"I doubt I could identify Gregory Sloan or any other murderer since I didn't even recall his existence." Ned scowled. "And why do you call him the man who did that to the Lawtons? Why are you suddenly restrained? Patrick? You'd do better to call him the monster who slaughtered my family."

Patrick wrapped a hand around Ned's upper arm, a reassuring touch. "Are you all right?"

"No, and I must apologize for being beastly." He twisted under Patrick's grip. He couldn't afford to draw comfort from that warm hand any longer.

Patrick let him go. "You have a long way to go before you qualify as that. Any notion why you're so jumpy?"

Ned rubbed at his face, which felt hot. "I have again tried to ignore the facts."

"Which facts in particular are bothering you?"

"You must return to America. My father is quite ill. Mr. Grady advises I visit, and a note arrived this morning from Mother Sloan summoning me. I'll go immediately."

"I've heard that name. Grady. Who is he? The man with the biblically big gray beard?"

"Yes. My solicitor and my father's partner. No doubt you communicated with him whilst trying to track me down."

"That seemed like another lifetime ago." Patrick moved closer. "Want company to visit Mr. Sloan?"

Edmund longed to plead, *Come with me. Hold my hand.* "I think I should go alone."

Patrick stepped closer. "Are you worried about last night?"

Edmund shook his head but didn't speak.

"I don't regret a single moment," Patrick said.

"We shall talk when I return from my father's house." Edmund avoided his gaze. He hoped to see hunger and love in Patrick's face almost as much as he dreaded seeing them.

Edmund took his hat from Becker and walked out to his carriage. He wanted to walk, but the day spat rain, and if he got wet, he'd have to listen to Mother Sloan fuss at him about catching chills.

He touched the end of the wrought-iron railing the way he always did for luck, though today, his luck had apparently run out.

From the carriage, he gazed at the damp streets and the dripping trees and again thought about going to New York. Obviously, he could not while his father was so very ill. And the abrupt way Patrick had announced he must leave added to his bleak spirits. Edmund had had the best time of his life with Patrick, but perhaps that was the sort of experience Patrick had encountered over and over.

Would Patrick move on and never think of what he left behind? Edmund imagined him being sent to Chicago or some other American city on his next job. He'd smile and be blunt while charming some man—or perhaps a woman—into taking him into their bed.

Edmund closed his eyes and wished he could not so easily conjure the image.

The butler met him at the door and led him to his father's room, a place he'd rarely seen.

Mother Sloan sat dozing in a wingback chair pulled to the side of the big mahogany bed. They had separate rooms, and now he understood why. Syphilis.

When Edmund entered the room, Papa Sloan stared as if he didn't recognize him.

"Good morning, sir," Edmund murmured when he came to the bedside.

Papa Sloan's lips moved. Edmund bent forward to hear. The bed was old-fashioned and quite tall, so he didn't have far to bend.

"You came. You can be saved."

"Yes, of course." Edmund patted his cold, lumpy hand and noticed the nailbeds had gone blue.

"Promise you'll leave that man alone."

"Certainly," Edmund said. Would he obey? Easy enough to do now that Patrick was going. But even as he stared into his father's pain-filled face, he understood that, given a choice, no, he wouldn't keep such a promise. The dutiful and wary boy was gone, never to return.

But he wouldn't announce the fact to his father.

Papa Sloan gave a tiny nod. "You didn't bring him."

"No. He's returning to America." How surprising—to say the words aloud hurt.

"Good." The old man closed his eyes. "That's what I require." He fell into a doze almost at once. Edmund fetched another chair to wait.

By three o'clock, the doctor arrived. Edmund had always liked the youngish man who had taken over the practice for the Sloans' crotchety old doctor. Dr. Davidson had a pointed beard and spectacles. His brisk, forthright manner allowed him to deal well with the autocratic and stubborn Papa Sloan, and his gentle friendliness endeared him to Mother Sloan.

After greeting Mother Sloan, he examined Papa Sloan, who did not wake up for the doctor's inspection.

The doctor tucked away his instruments but didn't put his hat on. Instead, he crossed the room to Edmund who rose at once.

"His time is coming," the doctor said in a low voice. "I shall remain because I promised his wife."

"Surely it isn't normal for a doctor to remain at a patient's bedside for what could be days?"

The doctor looked sheepish. "She requested it of me, and, to be honest, they have been most generous with a clinic I am associated with."

Edmund knew this already—the money had actually come from him. He liked the doctor for admitting it. His mother, the doctor, and Edmund stayed by Mr. Sloan's bed, reading or talking quietly. Edmund requested paper and writing materials and jotted a note to Peters telling him to cancel any appointments and a note to his valet, Giddings, about fresh linens. An hour or so later, he wrote another to Patrick. He wished he had a seal so he could say what he wanted in the note and avoid curious servants' eyes. Although even a tamperproof seal should make no difference: a sensible man would never put down on paper such feelings and thoughts that filled Edmund.

He wrote *Mr. Kelly. I beg your pardon for abandoning you, but my father is indeed quite ill, and I feel I can't leave his bedside at this time. I am disappointed I am not able to visit with you and continue our interesting conversations and tours of London. If you have need of any service, I and my staff are at your disposal. Yours etc.* He wanted to sign the note as Edmund or even Ned. He longed to say more about his feelings and how much he'd miss Patrick but knew too much affection expressed would do him or Patrick no good.

The patient moaned now and again, causing everyone to jump up and lean over him, but he did not wake. The doctor had Mother Sloan leave the room as the servants turned Papa Sloan. "Although I don't expect he'll remain with us long enough to develop sores," the doctor informed Edmund.

"Oh." He'd known, but it still seemed shocking to hear.

The doctor gave the standard comforting responses, and Edmund made the proper sounds as well. He sat again to wait.

The room smelled of old man and illness and the faintest whiff of the familiar expensive soap Mr. Sloan had always used. Edmund closed his eyes and tried to recall his earliest memories of his foster father. He dozed off and dreamed the old man scolded him for his affection for Patrick.

"It's not so very bad. He's not a murderer."

"Who's not a what?" That wasn't his father's voice, and Edmund was confused. Could Patrick be visiting? How badly he wanted to see Patrick, and what a mistake it would be to allow him into this room.

But it was Dr. Davidson who stood near Edmund's chair and gazed at him. Even in the dark room, Edmund could see the puzzlement on the man's face. "Are you well?" the doctor asked.

"I had a dream," he explained.

"Ah."

His mother slept, and so did his father, his slow breaths coming loud and far apart.

"How are you, Mr. Sloan?" the doctor whispered. "I suppose that's a strange question, considering the circumstances of this meeting." That seemed such a Patrick-like remark, Edmund smiled for the first time in hours.

"You look quite robust," the doctor whispered. "Is something changed in your life? A better diet? Regular exercise?"

"No, nothing has changed." Edmund rubbed his eyes and rose to his feet. "Although. I do wonder…"

"Go on," the doctor encouraged.

Edmund glanced at the bed. They spoke in quiet whispers, but not far enough away from his father and sleeping mother for him to feel comfortable with the conversation.

The doctor tilted his head at the door at the far end of the bedroom, and they quietly walked into Edmund's father's dressing room. It felt odd to be closeted with the smells he'd known for years.

Dr. Davidson crossed his arms. "What are you worried about?"

"I wonder what you think of some forms of depravation."

Davidson blinked but otherwise didn't appear disturbed by the question. "Do you mean something in the nature of sexual fulfillment?"

Just through the other door of the small room, his father's valet lay asleep—his snores didn't quite rattle the door, but they were loud enough.

"I am thinking of something that is sexual in nature and is not perhaps..." He tried to think of a word. "Wholesome."

"I assure you, I have heard of plenty of issues between men and women." Davidson examined Edmund for a long minute. "With men and their solitary pursuits of pleasure. And also between men and men. Perhaps you are asking for a friend?"

Because Davidson didn't smirk or raise his dark, bushy eyebrows at the last word, it would have been easy to agree that yes, Edmund sought advice for a friend.

But the words poured out of Edmund. "No, I speak of myself. I-I find men attractive. I like ladies, that is to say, I enjoy their company, so I don't disdain them." In for a penny, in for a pound, and for once he could be honest with a safe confidant. A doctor must not spread rumors after all. Edmund said, "I think of men no matter how I try to counteract that desire. I know people have managed to grow out of such impulses. But when I have tried to pick more appropriate subjects for my, ah... It hasn't helped. I can't seem to change what I crave."

There. He'd said it aloud. He hadn't been struck dead with shame, and the doctor hadn't expressed shock or even stepped away from him.

Davidson remained silent for a full minute. "I have met others like yourself."

Another long moment passed, and Edmund wished he'd kept his mouth shut.

Davidson continued, "I think the fact that you are willing to speak of it with a calm and open manner is a good sign. Although, of course, it is only good when you talk with a doctor. I do hope you don't speak as openly with most people?"

Edmund had to laugh. "Good heavens, no. I have told no one." Or almost no one. *Patrick, laughing and naked...*

The doctor gave a solemn nod. "Good, good. You do not have the air of the unmasculine brethren one so often sees, so you should be safe from sneers and distrust. Otherwise, I cannot say it's the healthiest of passions, but I have seen worse, far worse. I wouldn't despair if I were you. Obviously, you mustn't allow yourself to form an alliance with a man who will blackmail you, for you are wealthy. And I beg of you to remain discreet. It would spell ruin to be caught by the wrong people." He gave a weak smile.

"That is the sum total of your advice?"

"Yes. I think so. Perhaps I'm not a reliable font of information on this topic." The doctor hesitated. Was he going to admit his own interest in men? Edmund wondered what he could say in response if the doctor admitted as much, but Dr. Davidson said, "I have a bias. Two of my near relations prefer the company of his or her own gender."

"They are open? You've spoken with them about it?"

"Ah, well. We haven't broached the subject. Because I am closely related, I can't be their doctor, and one wouldn't trespass on such a private matter otherwise. I should say they are respectable, yet one who knows them well can easily see the truth." Edmund expected him to say something about their unhappy lives, but the doctor finished with, "I can only see them as good and caring people."

Edmund felt a welling of gratitude for the doctor's generous outlook.

"I must leave for my surgery hours but I will return as soon as I can. And I'll send Nurse Tomkins in my place."

Edmund bid him good-bye and returned to his seat. Time passed slowly after Davidson left and Edmund composed letters to Patrick and to his secretary. He reassured his foster mother and looked through some papers Papa Sloan had left behind. Sure enough, Grady was correct. Every penny went to Mother Sloan who was upset that Edmund had been written out of the will so very recently.

"I assure you this is just how it should be," he told her. "I don't mind at all."

It took two days before the last breath left Papa Sloan's body, and the dying man didn't wake again in the meantime. He slipped away soon after Edmund had returned from bathing and donning fresh clothes, which meant Edmund was ready an hour later to receive the condolence callers and order the crape over the door.

Edmund summoned Peters, Giddings, and Grady and helped Mother Sloan organize a funeral. He didn't think he should ask Patrick into the Sloans' house, not yet.

By the time he felt he could leave his trembling foster mother in the hands of her maid and good friends, it felt as if a month had passed. Odd to discover it had only been four days altogether.

When Edmund returned home, he discovered the several notes he'd sent to Patrick still lay on the silver salver. He probably shouldn't have written so many notes—Peters and Becker would have noticed the constant correspondence, but Edmund had nothing else to do in that dark bedroom, waiting for his father's end. And none of his notes spoke of his attraction and affection for Patrick.

Peters entered the library as Edmund tossed the notes he'd written on the fire. After expressing more sorrow at Edmund's loss, Peters said, "Mr. Kelly left soon after your second missive arrived. I gather he was going to do some more business in London and then depart for Southampton."

Edmund shouldn't appear too upset. Still he had to ask, "Did he even read the notes?"

"Yes, and he said there was no answer because he didn't wish to disturb you when you were busy with your father and mother," Peters said, sounding slightly aggrieved. "One suspects he was wrong and you wished to receive word."

"He is an idiot," Edmund said.

Peters handed over a slip of paper. "He left this in reply."

Edmund read it several times. Formal and stiff, the paragraphs were nothing like the breezy Patrick he'd come to know. It seemed a standard-template thank-you note for a guest at a country house. Perhaps Patrick was not good at expressing himself on paper?

The only personal words came at the end. *"Thank you for your generosity in allowing me to remain in your house so long. Should you ever find yourself in New York, I hope you will visit me. As they say in Mexico,* mi casa es su casa, *although in this case, my cold-water flat is your cold-water flat."*

"My father's funeral is tomorrow." Edmund stared at Patrick's angular, slashing handwriting. Mr. Kelly possessed a decisive sort of hand, no surprise there.

"At nine o'clock," Peters confirmed. He'd made most of the arrangements, after all.

"Yes, I am a little hazy about time at the moment." Edmund rubbed his forehead.

"No need to worry, sir. Giddings and I have arranged it all."

Giddings the valet would likely have put a huge crape bow on Edmund's hat. "Good. Then I shall need to make travel arrangements for as soon as possible afterwards."

Mother Sloan. He'd be abandoning her…but only temporarily, and he had to do this. He must or risk losing Patrick. He'd contact her bosom friend and see if she'd stay with Mrs. Sloan during his absence.

"Travel?" Peters asked.

"I shall take a ship to the US."

"Sir?" Peters leaned forward. "You never travel."

That was true enough. The thought of going on a train or a ship made him mildly queasy. The thought of never seeing Patrick again was far worse.

"Are you ill? Is anything wrong? I mean other than…" Peters blushed.

Edmund took pity on him. "No, nothing other than Mr. Sloan's death. But I require passage on a ship. As fast a ship as possible, if you please."

As he ate his lunch, he read the *Times* and saw a headline about a man charged with murder. The etching made the man look like a rat-faced individual. That pointed nose could remind anyone of Mr. Gregory Sloan.

The article identified him as DePayne and made the connection to the horrible scene of the murder years ago.

There was a quote from an American investigator who'd come to England and was part of the agency that helped identify the terrible killer who'd struck in two countries.

We had seen an echo of the crimes in New York and London and decided we'd best investigate. We received help from several people here in Great Britain, which helped the American authorities capture the dreadful murderer. That hardly sounded like the Patrick he knew.

Another paper had more lurid renderings of the murder scenes, and he swallowed his coffee, suddenly nauseated.

Patrick hadn't made the connection for the papers and had missed a chance to look even more clever.

Edmund supposed that if the story grew any larger, the DePayne investigation would lead back to his foster father and himself and the murderer would be given his real name of Sloan. Ah well, Edmund had avoided notoriety for years. He could survive anything now. As long as he found his American gadfly.

*

Patrick had been too damned pushy. When he first heard about Mr. Sloan's illness, he supposed it was more conniving on the old man's part.

But after Ned left the house and didn't return for hours, Patrick commenced snooping. As a young policeman, he'd learned to cultivate the servants on his beat, and those helpful old habits remained. He'd managed to make a few contacts on the staff here, though this group was far stiffer and less friendly than the people he knew in New York—not just because he was a houseguest. They kept up the role of servant even on their off-hours.

He tracked down Liam and tipped him a full crown, explaining he just wanted to be friendly, of course. No obligation to speak... No speaking out of school... But what had Liam heard was truly wrong with old Mr. Sloan?

Liam had some information. The housemaid at the other household had told a footman delivering a message that the old man was, in truth, dying. "Our Mr. Sloan won't come home until the old man has passed," Liam predicted. "Giddings packed a few of our Mr. Sloan's items and is hauling them to the other house even now."

Soon after, a note came to Patrick. Ned's missive was stiff and formal. *Dear Mr. Kelly?* That was the first hint that their time was over. Easy enough to see what he meant when he mentioned their parting and how he had enjoyed Patrick's company. Ned was obviously consigning their time together to the past.

Patrick read the note a couple of times, looking for information between the lines. As he read, his anger grew. He wasn't used to being sloughed off like this. In fact, he'd never been dropped. He'd never held on either, and that was the part that made him want to go find Ned and demand he take back whatever it was that had made Patrick into some kind of a sap, a drip of a person full of emotion and anxiety.

His instinct to go after Ned and tell him exactly what he wanted was ridiculous. The poor man had to sit by a deathbed—ha, and Patrick showing up to make a scene would put an end to the old bastard of a lawyer for sure.

Patrick should have kept his mouth shut when he visited the Sloans. Going to their house in search of Ned would be in the poorest of tastes.

He sank onto his bed with the letter in his hand and tried to banish his own prickly anger. Patrick wasn't the one facing the death of a loved one. *Ned.* What did Ned need? What would be the best answer for the poor gent who was so averse to conflict? Patrick smiled at the thought of his genteel lover, so quiet and well behaved, except when they were alone together. Oh yes, that mouth on his, those wild and deep kisses...

His anger fled. Now he was stuck with unwelcome arousal and the understanding that he must think of what Ned required, at least for now. Sure and how awkward to remain in Ned's house when the man himself wouldn't even return home to bathe.

Patrick really should heed the message. "Be gone," Patrick muttered to himself and got up to pack his bags.

He returned to the library and ignored the curious glances of the secretary as he labored over the note to Ned. He'd pressured the poor man enough, a gentleman who'd been only generous to him, yet Patrick had to make his own interest clear. They'd been apart for only two days, and Patrick had a hankering to hear that laugh, embrace that excellent muscular form, and watch Ned take the better part of a decade to devour a small sandwich. Thinking about Ned made him smile and his insides twist with longing.

Mr. Becker interrupted his thoughts. "Another note has come for you, sir."

Patrick unfolded it. Another impersonal sort of letter from the man himself. Although what did Ned mean when he wrote that he'd spoken to a doctor about his own circumstances? Was Ned sick? He'd been pale, but that had been a lack of sleep, hadn't it?

Patrick tapped the paper and read again. Ned wished that his father might wake up so he could tell him he was right to subtract Ned from his will. What the hell? Patrick hadn't heard that. So that was what his own obnoxious behavior had done, created a rift between an old man and his usually obedient son.

Patrick couldn't stay here any longer. He stood in the library, his unpolished boots on the gleaming floor, surrounded by the luxury and the hundreds or perhaps thousands of books, all leather-bound and—even more shocking—entirely dust free. Yet the library no longer felt intimidating, which in Patrick's eye meant a challenge. He'd gotten used to extravagance, and even more than that, he'd grown accustomed to the presence of Ned. Not much time had passed since Patrick had arrived in England, but he knew that he'd been changed, perhaps permanently, by this new friend of his.

He'd turned damp with emotion and lost all the starch in his spine.

He went back up to his room, and grabbed his bags. After he bid the butler good-bye and left his forwarding address, he strolled out of the house.

The hotel where he'd originally stayed upon his arrival seemed small and dingy. When would the world readjust to normal?

After he signed the large register, the clerk pulled an envelope from a pigeonhole. "Mr. Kelly? We have a letter for you."

He grabbed the letter, ready to read something wonderful from Ned. *"Come back to my house. Tell me where you are, and I'll find you. I love you, I love you..."* Not likely, but a man could be silly in his thoughts all he wanted.

No, alas, the letter was from Greene. It hadn't been forwarded to Patrick at Ned's house and had apparently had been sent the same day he'd left the United States. Perhaps it had even traveled on his ship with him.

In a few terse paragraphs, Greene told Patrick he was to check two loose ends while he was all the way across the ocean. If Patrick did the job, Mr. Greene wouldn't have to hire an outsider inquiry agent in London. *No need to go to the continent for these requests,* Mr. Greene had written. *In fact, don't even leave London if it interferes with the case you're there to investigate.*

That was generous, Patrick supposed. There was nothing about extra pay, but he'd do the work.

The first case was about a man who was supposed to have died back in New York but was very much alive and had apparently had taken another identity in London. Kelly was to go at once and gain proof that the man calling himself Mr. Plummer was either the long-lost and presumed dead gentleman of Long Island or some other gent with a hook nose. The description was fairly thorough. That would help.

The other job was also simple. A lady with a cousin living in the East End of London wished to ascertain the condition of this cousin. She wanted a description of the cousin's workplace and home.

Cases unrelated to the Lawtons or murder—it felt odd to work on anything else, but he would obey his orders.

Patrick read the cousin's address in the poorer part of the East End. Did the client want to gloat over her cousin's misfortune or rescue him? Never mind. Patrick would do the work and then catch a boat back to New York as soon as he could.

He'd left his address with Ned's butler. And if he never saw Edmund Sloan again... He swallowed that depressing thought. He got out his map of London and his notebook and sat on a dusty sofa to plan his two jobs for Greene.

As he sat in the hotel's lobby with the potted palms and the faded oriental carpet, he heard someone give an exclamation of disgust. A moment later, a young lady dropped onto the armchair across from him. In her elegant bottle-green gown, she looked like a fashion plate, though under her green cap, her dark hair was unfashionably short and curly. She fished a pencil and a pad from an old leather satchel slung over her shoulder. Flipping open the pad, she glared at him. "You're a difficult fellow to locate."

"Good morning, Miss Drury. You're looking well. London suits you."

"Yep, you too. What do you know about Adam DePayne? Other than that name has gotta be an alias." Her New York accent sounded strong. He wouldn't have noticed it if they'd been back home.

He stalled by carefully folding up Greene's note, sliding it into the envelope, and putting it in an inside pocket—all the while considering how he might deflect her questions. His prevarication and evasion about the Sloan connection to the man calling himself DePayne would be his gift to Ned and Mr. Sloan.

"The man in the United States calling himself DePayne used methods identical to the murderer who killed Edmund Lawton's family," he said. "Um. Put that any way you want."

234

"What do you mean?"

"Have me use words like *dreadful, horrendous,* and *despicable,* whatever you like."

"Any more directions, boss?"

"As usual, I'd rather you didn't identify me in your articles, but talk up Mr. Greene to the skies."

She narrowed her eyes. "So what do you think? Did they hang an innocent man in the Lawton murder?"

"No, they hanged a murderer. Maybe they should have been looking for two killers, and if they had, then DePayne wouldn't have been free to kill again. There, that sounds nearly dramatic enough to be something you'd write."

She ignored his dig. "Why didn't the Lawton child say there were two killers?"

"Probably because he was a sensible boy and hid? He didn't see much, now, did he? Ask him."

"Ha, as if he'd talk to the press. That's precisely why I'm asking you. So there's a connection between the kid and the murderer—did he remember something?"

"Not that I know of."

"Ahem." They looked up to see the clerk hovering near them. "Madam, we don't allow unescorted young ladies in our lobby."

She rolled her eyes, dug into her bag, and pulled out a few coins. "Will that get you to go away?"

The clerk slipped the coins into the pocket of his sponge bag trousers and pointed at the clock on the wall. "Fifteen minutes," he said and returned to his station behind the counter.

She turned her attention back to Patrick. "The truth now. Did you alert the New York police with a telegram?"

"I don't know what you mean."

"Was it something Mr. Sloan told you?"

"No, and I don't understand your point."

She tried other ways to get him to admit he'd made the connection or had been the one to send the tip to the United States authorities, and he refused to say anything more.

At last, she sighed and slipped her notebook into her battered satchel. "I could have sworn your visit here in London would be more directly tied to DePayne's capture. I guess you're not lying, because there's no way your Mr. Greene would let a triumph like tracking down DePayne go unheralded. He loves publicity." She rose to her feet. "You're a useless interview after all that help I gave you, but I'll find something in this. Say howdy to New York for me, would you? I miss the place and will visit eventually, but not as soon as you."

He stood as well. "Have fun tracking down your story. I appreciate all you've done for me during my visit."

"And you have a funny way of showing appreciation, Mr. Kelly."

"If I think of any interesting details, I'll write."

"I'm sure you will."

She waved her kid-gloved fingers at the clerk and strode out of the hotel lobby.

A few days later, Patrick was done with the side jobs for Greene. He sat in the lobby and wrote a short note to send ahead.

1. Unless the Long Islander managed to chop off a chunk of himself, Plummer the Londoner in question is not him. Mr. Plummer is about 5'6" not 6'.

2. Tell your curious cousin that her East Ender relation is doing well. His house on Cannon Street Road is actually fairly nice. I've tracked down a photograph of it, which I will bring back with me. You might inform her that the cousin owns three tobacconists shops and he lives above one of them.

I bought him a pint (not in my expenses, so you don't have to grumble), and he told me he's planning to open a fourth shop next year. He was particularly chatty, and when he learned I was an American from New York, he said his least favorite relation lives in New York. I was discreet and didn't mention that she's our client. I told him I was in London as a tourist.

I'll be back on a ship leaving in two days from Southampton.

He wanted to give himself extra time to visit Ned. Just to say good-bye and perhaps beg him to visit.

Becker's mouth almost twitched into a smile after he opened the door. "Good morning, sir. I'm afraid Mr. Sloan is not here." The trace of human emotion vanished as if it had never shown. "He is at his mother's house."

"His mother's house and not... Oh. Do you mean to say that the elder Mr. Sloan is no longer among the living?"

Becker tucked his chin as much as he could in the tall stiff white collar, a version of a nod. "The funeral is this morning."

And Ned hadn't contacted Patrick. Becker appeared to be waiting, so Patrick gave a solemn nod in return, as if not hearing from Ned didn't hurt. *Nothing to do with you, idiot. Think of the man whose father just died.*

The butler asked, "Shall I inform Mr. Sloan you called?"

"Please. No. Um." He rubbed his face, at a loss for words for once. "No, I left word earlier. He has enough on his plate. Thank you. Good day, Becker. Nice to meet you," he added before he turned and walked away.

Would a sympathy note be welcomed or simply created awkwardness for Ned? The gentleman was scrupulously polite and would no doubt feel he must answer the note no matter that he was relieved to see the back of Patrick.

Funny, he'd seemed a sentimental sort. Not like Patrick, who didn't need an emotional connection to enjoy another man. That was what he told himself as he plodded away from the quiet little oasis of Ned's street back to the jangling streetcars and cursing cabbies and wagon drivers of the real city.

Patrick walked back to the hotel, unwilling to spend the extra money on a cab. He moved slowly, caught in his thoughts, and didn't recall much about the walk other than nearly getting bowled over by a hansom and being called "sweet boy" by a lady selling some kind of seafood from a wagon.

By the time he'd reached his hotel room, which smelled of cigar smoke and dust, he still hadn't managed to budge the subject of Ned from his mind and wasn't sure how to leave their time together behind without feeling bereft. At least he could reassure himself he hadn't been a terrible friend, well, not entirely.

He'd helped Ned in many ways, mostly untangling him from his past.

As he folded his clothes and shoved them into his bags, he almost convinced himself to go back to Ned's house one last time just to tell him no hard feelings.

But the problem that had arisen with Ned's foster father—all those secrets revealed had made a rift. Well, that was Patrick's fault. Or at least he hadn't done much to keep the father and son on good terms, and now the old man was dead.

No, he was right not to bother Ned at the moment. But as soon as he was in his cabin on the ship, he'd write another note.

He composed the letter in his head as he hailed a hansom to the train station and as he took the ride to Southampton.

The next day, he boarded the boat. The ship was hardly the fastest or newest in the Red Line, but he was glad to get a berth aboard her. He was pleased to find he had a porthole and a writing desk, practically the height of luxury in his second-class cabin.

He left his cabin to watch England vanish, and the man in the cabin next door stepped out at the same time. The man tipped his straw boater, tugged at his mustache, and winked. His spotless white flannels made him look as if he should be on a cricket field, but they fit him beautifully.

An obvious sort of a gentleman, Patrick thought, amused. The man sniffed the green carnation in his button hole, then walked to the deck rail.

"Lovely day for it, eh?" He waved a hand at the disappearing pier. He turned and leaned his back against the rail. Patrick was so lost in thought, he almost missed the man's up-and-down examination.

"I'm Beaton," the man said.

"I'm Kelly and uninterested," Patrick said.

Beaton tugged at his mustache again. A nervous tic rather than something flirtatious, Patrick decided. And at the sight of that tiny unguarded habit, Patrick *was* tempted. But all that work of talking and negotiating just to fumble around with a stranger…

He sighed and must have looked thunderous.

"I say, no need to worry about me. I didn't mean to say more than good day," Beaton began. He inched along the rail away from Patrick. Probably a smart move since Beaton was a scrawny sort, at least sixty pounds lighter and several inches shorter than Patrick.

"Peace." Patrick raised his hands. "I'm not going to go after you. And since you're brave enough to show your stripes, I'll tell you that you weren't entirely wrong. I could have been a jolly molly, I think you English call them? I have been anyway," he said, feeling a jolt of nostalgia.

"No one I know of calls anyone that." Beaton gave Patrick a wide smile. The man had bright white teeth and dimples and seemed far younger than Patrick had first guessed. "But I don't mind! If you want to call me that, I won't protest. Call me whatever you wish, hmm?"

Patrick raised his eyebrows. "I think Beaton will do."

"It's a long journey. We have a shared wall. If you grow bored, do give a hard slam or two, and I'll bring along a deck of cards or whatever else you could want." Beaton stuck his forefinger in his mouth and gave it a suck.

Patrick laughed. "You are an obvious lad, aren't you?"

Beaton looked offended.

"Seductive too," Patrick hastened to soothe the man—the youth's—injured pride. "If I weren't..." He shrugged.

"Weren't what?" Beaton asked. He left the rail and strolled toward Patrick.

In love, Patrick thought, annoyed at himself. It seemed late in life to learn he had a troublesome streak of monogamy. "I'm busy," Patrick said. "I have to write some letters. A letter. I'll see you later."

And, like a coward, he went into his cabin and locked the door.

Chapter Twelve

Edmund arrived in Liverpool on a day that threatened rain but never seemed to deliver the promise. The Cunard line ship seemed gaudy compared to the hardworking vessels around it.

But he'd requested the most modern ship available—and the SS *Oregon* could make the journey in a week or even six days, or so the ticket agent informed the footman who'd fetched the tickets.

Edmund was shown to his saloon cabin by a dignified steward who reminded him of Becker, but with a far more impressive and unwelcome flow of conversation as he demonstrated the luxuries of the cabin to Edmund and a fascinated Giddings.

The man spoke of the Spanish mahogany-and-mosaic floor of the smoking room on the upper deck as if he'd helped design and build it. Edmund suppressed a sigh as the steward talked about the glories of the soaring lines of the first-class saloon's dining area, the satin wood and walnut, the light and airy feel of the cupola.

Giddings gave all the appropriate responses of admiration and awe, while Edmund stared absently at all the white-and-gold carved decor on the wall in his cabin, which might have been inspired by the elaborate cake served at his old friend Wensler's wedding. The mirror, nearly hidden by gilded plaster versions of flourishes and fruit baskets, seemed a bit much.

A porter brought in the trunks, and Giddings fussed at him to be especially careful. Edmund shot the valet a quelling glance. He really shouldn't have told him he'd packed the sculpture. Edmund didn't know much about sea travel, but he knew it was best to keep quiet about one's valuables or use a safe. He preferred the first.

After the steward demonstrated turning on and off the incandescent electric lamps around the room, he finally excused himself. Edmund wandered off to the deck to watch Liverpool vanish into a dense and dripping fog that covered the piers.

The fog seemed to enter his brain and not leave for the entire week of the journey. Giddings had a fine time and mentioned various entertainments on board, but Edmund paced around the deck and smoking room and his cabin as if he were walking to New York.

He made and unmade plans. If he found that Patrick was uninterested in seeing him, he'd still explore the new city.

Patrick had expanded his world, broken him free of constraints Edmund hadn't even known had bound him. He'd at least force Patrick to hear his thanks and then…Edmund might take rooms somewhere in the city and learn what this new life meant. That plan cheered him a great deal but didn't release him from the grip of restless agitation.

He read the short bits of news that showed up in an onboard newsletter. His stomach congealed as he read about DePayne's upcoming trial—the authorities still hadn't released the man's true name of Gregory Sloan, which was interesting. And there was no mention of his connection to England.

When he woke from a nightmare of Papa Sloan turning into a murderer, he glared up into the darkness, wishing he could still run away from his pain. No. That wouldn't work. Somehow he'd have to arrange to see Mr. DePayne.

Would Patrick come with him? He turned his face into the pillow and groaned. He'd had more than enough thoughts of Patrick Kelly, thank you. As he shifted and the nightmare faded from his mind, another pressing urge came over him.

He rarely indulged in the habit of touching himself, but he needed a way to relax and that… That.

"Patrick," he said into the darkness. He felt foolish, but a strand of excitement grew stronger. Thicker. So did another part of his body.

He reached down and untied his pyjamas and ran a hand over his penis. Did Patrick like the way it tasted? He'd been eager enough for it.

Edmund pushed off his covers and bared himself to the chilly ocean air, which prickled on his skin. His arousal felt hot and hard under his fingers. He tried to think of another, more anonymous, body. A woman. A man. Two men. Figures in the dark, grappling, filled with an eagerness he'd finally experienced. The excitement built and his breath came faster. Patrick threw back his head as he pumped into orgasm. The desire curled and tightened at the picture of Patrick. Edmund tightened his grip, his balls drew up, and his climax came faster and harder than he was used to. He thrust again and again, wanting to keep the moment with him. A false Patrick was better than none.

He fell asleep still damp and uncovered and more relaxed than he'd been in days.

When he arrived in New York, the customs sheds were well organized, and he had nothing to do but wait for Giddings at the other side of the line while the valet handled the baggage. They piled into a cab—after arranging for the trunks to be sent in a different conveyance. Giddings should have been named Giddy, for the man had remained in a constant state of near-swooning pleasure since they'd spotted the shoreline of Manhattan and the jagged shapes of the tall buildings.

Funny how Edmund had barely noticed Giddings a month ago, but since he'd met Patrick, the whole world and the people in it had become more interesting.

The hotel would do for the day. He didn't propose to move everything in, just himself and a few objects.

He didn't know which ship Patrick sailed on. Perhaps he'd already arrived. So Edmund armed himself with only a good suit, his favorite homburg, and a hopeful smile when he gave directions to the address where Patrick lived.

The apartments were jammed tightly together, tall and forbidding, at least seven stories of red brick and likely no lift. The city seemed dirtier here than it had on the docks or near Fifth Avenue.

The address had a men's apparel store and a bookshop dividing the space on the bottom floor. The trouble seemed to be that while he could get into the hallway and climb the stairs, the door to Patrick's apartment was locked and no one answered his knock.

He made his way back down to the first floor and went into the badly lit bookstore. The shop was dark and smelled like damp paper, not a good sign for the books. The clerk, a large young lady in a blue serge gown, leaned against a ladder, a pile of books at her feet and one in her hand.

When he asked her who was in charge of whole building, she answered in a surprisingly loud, deep voice, telling him about the lazy stupor. As she complained about the stupor, wishing they had the old one back, Edmund understood she'd been using the word *super*.

"He's next door," she said and jerked a thumb at the men's clothing shop. "You from England? One of the tenants upstairs, Kelly, is in England. Or maybe he said Ireland?"

"Ah," he said. "Thank you for your help."

He left, and she went back to leaning against a ladder, reading a travel guide to Rome.

The super, or stupor as Edmund knew he'd always think of the man, was fat, bald, and dressed in funereal black. Edmund was also in black for Papa Sloan, though his suit was less worn.

The shop owner/stupor greeted him with a happy cry and, before Edmund could ask about allowing him entrance to Patrick's apartment, began to ask questions about Edmund's suit. The round little man practically drooled on the fabric, and Edmund at last took off his jacket so he could inspect the seams and lining. Edmund looked away when the man buried his face in the cloth and took a long sniff.

"Excellent dye. And the wool, so fine. Such tiny stitches! Obviously made for you. We do bespoke work here, and I'd try to sell you one of ours, but that would be an insult to yous. I know that," the man said after he handed back the jacket.

Edmund, who left matters of this sort to his valet and couldn't really tell a well-made jacket from a superior one, said, "Not at all."

He'd expected he'd have to bribe the stupor for entrance into Patrick's apartment, but apparently the man took him at his word when he said that he was a friend of Kelly's. Perhaps the suit convinced him? He handed over the key. Edmund handed him the bribe anyway and called it a tip.

Patrick's rooms seemed much too small and bare for such an expansive person. Edmund walked through all three of them in no time at all and examined every surface and the gray-and-pink wallpaper. He stopped in front of the photograph of a woman holding the arm of a young man. She was older, but they might be brother and sister. And then he realized it must be Patrick and his mother.

In the faded portrait, Patrick grinned. His mother wore an elaborate hat and a pained expression. After that long gaze, Edmund went to the kitchen table and stared longingly at the stack of mail there. He wouldn't so much as look through it, though he was greedy for every detail of Patrick's life.

He went back to the hotel and sent Giddings out on a reprehensible errand: to get a copy of the apartment key made.

The valet, who never remarked on such odd tasks, came back speaking excitedly of a man selling hot chestnuts from a wagon.

Edmund handed over several days' wages. "If you wish, you may charge meals to my account here at the hotel," he told Giddings. "Enjoy yourself. You are free to explore New York as you please. I'm going out, perhaps for a day or perhaps three."

"But sir, who will dress and shave you?"

"I can manage."

He opened a valise and began to pack. Giddings almost pushed him aside. "At least allow me this, sir. Three days at most, you said?"

A few minutes later, Edmund grabbed the bag, some books, and the little sculpture, and returned to Patrick's apartment.

He went to the men's clothing shop, gave the key back to the stupor, and ran up the stairs again before the man could ask him why he carried baggage—or begged to see his trousers or waistcoat.

Then he settled the marble figure on top of a small coal stove, because there was no mantelpiece. It looked bizarre in its surroundings, far better than he'd hoped. He grabbed a book and settled in a comfortable but worn overstuffed chair to wait.

At one p.m., he grew hungry. The kitchen had nothing but some dried beans and a shriveled piece of fruit that might have once been an apple. He clumped down the stairs out into the bright sunlight and, just around the corner, he found a restaurant that offered good grub at good prices.

The food was plain and not awful, a sort of stew, a slab of bread, and a glass of bad wine. Apparently, hunger and anticipation made anything delicious. He bought a loaf of the bread and went back to the apartment, whistling. This was freedom, he thought. No one knew him, and he knew no one, except Patrick—and he was responsible for Edmund's liberation.

He climbed the stairs to the apartment and stopped at the top of the stairs. Sounds came from inside the apartment. Heart beating far too fast, he tried the door. Unlocked.

He went inside…and nearly ran into a short woman with dark hair and blue eyes. Patrick's mother gave a loud shriek.

He tried for a smile and held out a hand to steady her. "I'm sorry I startled you. It's fine! I'm a friend of Patrick's."

She covered her mouth and backed away, whimpering. Recalling the story Patrick had told him of her attack, Edmund raised his hands and backed up until he hit the door. "I beg your pardon. I should have knocked. I was, er, rather hoping to surprise Patrick, you see."

She lowered her hands, placed them on her hips, and glared. "You're English."

"Yes, I'm afraid so."

"You came back over with him? With Patrick? You say you're Mr. Sloan?"

"Did I?" He hadn't said any such thing. "I mean yes, I am."

She fell silent and looked him up and down. "I came to New York for a visit because I thought he'd be back by now. But apparently, you were too interesting."

"He said that?"

"I can read between lines. How is it you're here without him?"

"Ah. Well, he, ah. Um…" Had Patrick actually told this woman the truth about their relationship? "I took a faster ship, I believe."

"What are you doing here? And did you bring that?" She pointed to the sculpture on the stove.

He nodded.

She sniffed and produced a handkerchief. "'S lovely. Beautiful."

He cleared his throat. "I'm glad you like it. Your son said it reminded him of something he could get at Conley Island."

"*Coney* Island, and he was funning you. *That* there is real art. The mother and her child love each other. Aw, gee, I was all set to hate you, but with that…" She pointed at the mother who sat with arms open, ready to embrace the toddler rushing to her. "You came all this way to give that to Patrick? And just to see him?"

He nodded.

She wiped her eyes and blew her nose. "That is something. Ha. No one who owns and loves that mother and child can be all bad."

He didn't bother to tell her the truth: that he'd inherited the piece and he had rather agreed with Patrick about the vapid expressions on the faces. "I'm glad you think so, ma'am."

She picked up the sculpture, squinted at the details, and with extra care replaced it on the stove. It reminded Edmund of the first time he'd seen Patrick.

"I came to the city just for a couple of days to see Patrick and another friend of mine." She ambled over to him. "But if you're here, I think I should leave."

"Please stay. He'll want to see you."

She gave him a warm smile. "That is the right answer, young man."

"I know one oughtn't speak of a lady's age, but I'm sure you're not old enough to call me that."

She laughed and poked him in the chest. "You'll do, despite being English. I've been waiting for him to find a nice person."

"Um. Ah."

He hunted for words but didn't need to find any, for she blithely carried on. "I mean, of course I'd rather you were a girl, but after all this time, I want him to have some sort of companion. Don't you think? For a person to be all alone, oh, that would be terrible. He thinks he doesn't need such a close friend, and, well, you know he says he won't marry, and I must believe him. But I say that's nonsense about not requiring affection."

Good Lord, could her eyes be filling with tears again?

"I'm not sure if he'll be glad to find me here," Edmund confessed, hoping to distract her. "We didn't travel together, after all."

"How'd you get a key?"

He ignored the question. "Perhaps it would be better if I left and you stayed? I have a hotel room not far away."

"A hotel!" She sounded impressed. "Patrick stays in those all the time, but it seems to me to be a wicked extravagance when you know someone in the city."

"I don't have any friends here in the city."

"You have Patrick." She went into the kitchen, then poked her head around the doorway and gestured at him to follow, apparently fully cheerful again. "Come on. We'll make tea and play cards. Is that a loaf of bread? Perfect, we'll have toast too. Do you know how to play rummy?"

"Sai rummy?" he asked.

"'Tis another name for it, yes." She flashed him a narrow-eyed look of happy anticipation, and Edmund recognized that mischievous look. "We won't play for high stakes, Englishman."

"Must we play for any money at all?" He had no interest in taking her hard-earned coins, nor did he want to cheat to lose. Edmund had played many more hands of cards than most people. It allowed him to be in company without the necessity of consuming meals.

"Of course we have to. Otherwise the game is dull."

He returned her big smile with one of his own.

Chapter Thirteen

Patrick's ship docked almost a full day later than it was scheduled to arrive. The line of disembarked passengers at the customs sheds shuffled along at the pace of a constipated snail. Patrick allowed a harried young mother with three children to stand in front of him and almost regretted his generosity when the baby in the mother's arms began to cry and wouldn't stop. But then Patrick distracted the baby's two older sisters and himself with some thumb-wrestling and playing Miss Mary Mack, and the time passed more quickly.

He should have been glad to be home, but New York seemed dirtier and noisier than usual. Too full of people who didn't give a damn.

In the early evening gloom, he swung onto an omnibus, found a seat, and hoisted his case onto his lap. He could only hope his mother hadn't arrived yet. He needed time to clean his apartment and cheer himself up. If she'd arrived when Patrick wasn't at home, perhaps her mother would spend time with Mr. Balsan, an old friend who'd recently moved to New York from Boston. Patrick had high hopes that their ex-neighbor would become his stepfather someday. Balsan was calm and easygoing, the perfect foil to Patrick's mother's emotion.

Someone ought to find a permanent love.

He clumped up the stairs to his apartment, feeling as if nothing had changed in him or his world, a gloom made worse when he caught the scent of expensive soap and lemons. Edmund's scent.

When he opened the door, his heart sank at the sound of his mother's voice coming from the kitchen. He loved the woman, but didn't need her sharp eyes boring into his soul to find out why he was not in high spirits.

But why would she be talking to herself? Had she invited Mr. Balsan over? That didn't seem like the sort of thing she'd do. And then he saw a white object on his stove. He went over and stared at it. He'd seen such a thing before. Not at a museum. Recently, though.

There came the sound of clinking coins and his mother's laugh. At that second, he recalled where he'd seen the little marble sculpture.

A copy? But how had Mam known? His heart began to beat so hard, he felt the thumps in his throat.

"Mam, where'd this come from?"

In the kitchen, chairs scraped against the bare wood, and Mam came into the room. "Your friend brought it along."

"Ned?" The word came out as a croak.

Because there he stood in the kitchen doorway, already so familiar and dear, and far too beautiful for Patrick's shabby place. Ned grinned at him. "I don't know if I'll ever grow accustomed to that name again."

"It's a good pet name," Mam argued.

"Mm," Ned said. "How about this. Winner of the next two out of three hands gets to decide if Patrick calls me Ned or Edmund."

"Ned? What?" Patrick gaped. What the hell? His mother and Ned strode back into the kitchen and pulled up to the table. They sat on the chairs Patrick had collected from an out-of-business bar. Ned looked thoroughly out of place on the scratched and worn chair at the even more battered round table—but he didn't appear to notice his surroundings as he dexterously shuffled cards.

Patrick recovered enough to follow. His head swam, but he swallowed his strange joy and bewilderment. "Ned, don't ever gamble with my mother. She's a regular cardsharp." He even sounded like himself again.

"Too late," Ned said cheerfully. Judging from the plates and cups, they'd been at it for a while. And the piles of coins—at both places. Perhaps his mother had more. "Sit down for a minute. This shouldn't take too long."

"Yah, so you say, Mr. Sloan." She wrinkled her nose at him, then winked at Patrick.

This could have been a scene from a peculiar, fever-induced dream, the man he'd longed for but believed in England sitting in his kitchen playing cards with his mother.

"But…but why are you here?"

"You invited me," his mother said.

"No, I mean Mr. Sloan."

"Same answer." He looked up from dealing the cards, those long fingers dexterous. "*Mi casa es su casa*? Recall?"

"Yes. I do." He blinked at Ned, still caught by the miracle of the man's presence in his home.

"I hope you're glad to see him after he's made such an effort to see you," Patrick's mam scolded.

Patrick ignored her. "And that thing on my stove? That's from your house?"

"Yes, you'd admired it, so I brought it as a gift. Unfortunately, I underestimated your mother's ability, and I'm afraid she won it during the first few rounds of cards."

"Naw, don't worry, young fool. I won't keep anything we gamble for today."

"Oh-ho? You're so sure you'll win? Don't you think for a moment you'll get a chance to keep a single penny, old woman."

A small squeak escaped Patrick. "Did you two just insult each other?"

"Nonsense, just a bit of whatchamacallit, intimidation. Mr. Sloan says that when men play, they often try to throw each other off with words," his mother said. She lifted a cup of tea, tasted it, and made a face. "'Tis cold. Make another pot, would you, love?" She tapped her cup and pointed at his cracked white teapot. "Then sit down and join us."

"Oh no, no. I know better than to play cards with you."

"Then sit down and tell us about your journey... Wait, now, ya foul Englishman, I haven't cut the deck."

"Bother," Ned said, and gathered up the cards to shuffle again.

In the end, Patrick's mother won a nickel more than Ned, and the sculpture, and the right to give Ned a nickname. The end came only because Patrick demanded that they stop playing.

"From now on, you shall be Ned or Eddie," she declared as she threw down her winning cards.

Ned made a terrible face. "Ned it is, then. Never let it be known I'm a poor loser."

"Really? You made a face like you're sucking a lemon," Mam pointed out.

"I am expressing my gratitude at escaping the name 'Eddie.'" Ned rose and held out a hand to Patrick's mam to help her up. She used his hand to stand and didn't let go. She pulled him into a hug and dragged his head down so she could whisper in his ear. He laughed and turned red.

Patrick's mam pulled away. She left the kitchen and gathered up her sculpture from the stove.

"I shall call upon Mr. Balsan, then," she announced. *This time of the evening?* Patrick wanted to protest. But then he decided he wouldn't.

She must have seen his expression, for she rolled her eyes. "Miss Balsan, his sister, is also there, so no need to pucker up, lad. No scandal will be attached to me."

"Allow me to hail you a hansom," Ned said.

"A cab? Never. Such waste. It's an easy streetcar ride away."

"Now it is your turn to be gracious in the face of my demands, ma'am." He scooped the sculpture away from her and offered his arm.

They went to the street, and Ned hailed a taxi as if he'd been born a New York doorman.

Mam was unusually silent for the ride, looking up and down the leather interior and running her fingers over the brass handles. Patrick wondered if this was the first cab ride she'd taken. He'd only rarely indulged—and only when Mr. Greene paid.

Ned helped her out of the cab and insisted on walking her onto the porch of Mr. Balsan's narrow little house.

He got back into the hansom and ordered the cab to return to Patrick's house.

"What did she say to you right before we left the house?"

"She told me not to lead you on if I wasn't interested. She claimed that a bit of fun isn't worth breaking anyone's heart."

"Oh God." Patrick groaned. He'd been on the verge of excitement since he'd caught Ned's scent outside his apartment. The thought of his mother knowing they'd embrace and more was nearly enough to kill that edge of anticipation—nearly enough.

Then he thought of something else. Horror seized him, but he had to ask. "How much is that marble thing she's carting around worth?"

"A few thousand pounds, I think."

Patrick's belly turned over. "Christ. Turn this thing around," he shouted.

The driver stopped the horse. He opened the hatch and peered down at them.

Ned waved a hand. "No need. Carry on." Such was the authority of the man that the driver shrugged, closed the hatch, and they continued on their way despite Patrick's sputtering protests. "She can't keep that thing. She can't be liable for such a valuable object."

"Too late. It's hers."

"What if she breaks it?"

"I'll help her to get it fixed."

"But if she loses it?"

"She'd be far more upset about the loss than I. It's one less difficult pointy thing for my servants to have to dust. A mere object, Patrick. Not important. Not like she is, not like you are."

The fact of Ned's presence hit Patrick again. "You're here. My God, Ned."

He moved across the cab's leather seat to pull him into his arms for a fast embrace. The carriage was too open, which meant anything they did would be public. With some reluctance, he relaxed his needy grip and moved away. He kept one hand on Ned's knee. "You must have left England the day of your father's funeral."

"The day after."

"I'm so sorry about him."

Ned's mouth went tight. His gaze flickered to the ceiling of the cab as if it could give him a good answer. At last he said, "Yes, I am as well."

Patrick wondered if now was the moment to apologize about the way he'd barged into their lives and hurt the relationship between Ned and Mr. Sloan—but he'd already decided bringing it up wasn't the way to help Ned, only himself.

"It was all right, really. He forgave me at the end." Ned must have read his mind again. "I'm not sure I forgive him, but I hope I have more time to figure out how I must go about that task."

"How is your mother?"

"She is actually not as distraught as I'd thought she would be, perhaps because she knew the end would come soon. I don't think I believed he was dying."

"Your mother is probably a smarter person than she allows the world to believe."

"Ha, and when she heard that I would see you, she asked me to beg your pardon again for the trick she pulled with the telegram. I told her you thought it was rather clever."

"What? You told her where you were going?"

"I didn't say I was crossing the ocean to strip you naked and have my way with you."

Patrick gave a gasp and then a weak laugh. "We're almost back to my place. I don't want to stagger out of the carriage with an erection."

"Very well, what shall we talk of?"

He could think of one subject sure to kill desire. "Speaking of mothers, I'm glad you like mine."

"Who couldn't like her? She's funny, and she plays cards like a demon."

"Many people think she's too noisy and intrusive."

"But they'd be wrong, wouldn't they now. Ah, but I had no notion I could speak thusly." Ned had used a decent Irish accent. He grinned. "I've never attempted to imitate anyone. There is a great deal I've learned about myself lately. You've changed too. I'm more silly, and you seem more serious. Are you well, laddie?"

Patrick allowed himself to move close enough so their thighs touched. Beneath all those layers of cloth, Ned's heat practically burned him. Patrick longed to return to their simple teasing time with Ned Lawton/Edmund Sloan—whatever the man was called. He couldn't.

Patrick murmured, "It's hard to be careless when someone matters so much."

Ned only beamed at him, as happy as a man handed a gift, say a small sculpture, perhaps, worth thousands of pounds. His smile faded, and he said, "There is another reason I'm here, one that I hope you'll help me with."

That suddenly grim and determined expression was an echo of the one he'd worn when he spoke of the Lawtons, so it was easy enough to guess the direction of his thoughts. "You wish to talk to DePayne."

Ned's eyes widened. "Talk? No, I don't think so. Merely observe."

"I'll come with you," Patrick decided.

Ned's stiff shoulders relaxed. Patrick risked grasping his hand and giving it a squeeze. "We'll go to the Tombs tomorrow. Tonight I'll show you how glad I am you are here with me. I've spent several nights on the ship imagining what I'd like to do with you."

Ned cleared his throat. "Any particularly interesting ideas?"

Patrick nudged him with an elbow. "I never managed more than the very basic plans." He lowered his voice. "You excite me that much. Just the thought of a kiss with you…" He stared at Ned's lips, wished he could at least touch them with his finger, test how soft they'd feel on his skin. He moved away again and stared out the window because, oh dear, he'd gone hard again.

Ned gave an audible sigh.

They made their way silently up the already familiar narrow staircase. The smell of old books and starch mingled, and Edmund thought that he'd always associate it with this moment and this man. Now and forever, just the hint of that air would bring on the stirring of lust.

Patrick unlocked his apartment door and allowed Edmund to pass, but as soon as they'd entered, he slammed the door and was on Edward like a starving creature bringing down prey, but no, his kiss was suddenly gentle and searching, a way to communicate, not merely take. And then the kiss deepened, and Edmund stopped analyzing and allowed himself to enjoy and explore, his hands tracing the planes of Patrick's strong back under the rough fabric of his jacket.

They moved to a bed, which creaked like a tree in a high wind.

Gasping, Edmund pulled away. "This bed is far too noisy. Anyone will guess what we're doing."

"What we *will* be doing, you mean." The gleam in Patrick's eye made so many promises. "We won't let 'em join us, no matter how much they beg."

Edmund rolled to the edge of the bed and stood. "It's not something I'm comfortable with. Do recall that public knowledge of...of us might be dangerous." He waited for Patrick to grow offended or laugh him off.

"You're right as usual." Patrick rose to his feet and grabbed the mattress. With grunts and curses, he pulled the heavy flopping thing from the bed and its old-fashioned rope support.

It slithered onto the floor, and Patrick flopped down on it and bounced a few times. No squeaking.

"Come along. I've found an answer. Lie with me here on the floor, and the only sounds will be the ones from our throats."

He was wrong. They slid off the mattress in their heated embrace, and Edmund's head banged against the bed.

"Poor thing." Patrick rubbed his head and, with exaggerated gentleness, pulled a protesting Edmund on top of him.

"You are stronger than I. No need to show off," Edmund said and kissed him.

"I always need to show off, all the time," Patrick retorted and rolled them both again, so he lay on Edmund, who didn't protest this pleasant position.

They laughed and kissed and moaned. And took off every stitch of clothing.

They kissed and rubbed and discovered new secrets about each other. Edmund loved the smooth hot surfaces of Patrick, all of them. He wanted to wrap Patrick around his body. His cock begged for special attention, and he thrust it against Patrick's belly, sliding along the tickling hairs of his stomach and Patrick's erection. Edmund reached between them and held both hard poles together, marveling at the weight and heft of Patrick's.

When he rubbed his fingers over the tips of their cocks, back and forth, neither of them could remain still, and they thrust, groaning into each other's hands. So much more than when he took himself in his fist. So much... He gasped and gave a disappointed moan because Patrick had pulled away to roll onto his hands and knees.

"You do me. Now."

"I'm not sure—"

"I have ointment." Patrick reached under the bed. His back muscles flexed and stretched in the dim light as he grabbed a small blue jar. "I never imagined I'd use this with another man, especially a man like you. Christ, I want this."

He unstoppered the jar and slid his fingers through the glistening contents. Edmund watched, unable to move lest he spring forward and take matters into his own hands, too impatient to wait.

Patrick looked up, met his gaze, and that self-satisfied smile made Edmund growl. Patrick slowed his movements, rubbing the ointment on his own erection and playing with himself, watching Edmund.

With an impatient groan, Edmund leaned forward and grabbed the little jar from Patrick and dunked his own fingers in. The ointment smelled pleasantly like cucumbers, not that he cared about its scent.

He rubbed the stuff all over his own aching erection, then slid his slicked hands over Patrick's arms, his sides, trying to get him to move. So much slippery flesh to explore. At last Patrick returned to resting on his hands and knees. He lowered himself to his elbows and looked over his shoulder at Edmund.

"You do whatever you wish, Ned." In that voice, low with anticipated pleasure… Edmund decided that Ned was a glorious name, more than a ghost from the past that name was full of promise, especially when spoken with an American accent.

He would have planned, but now he could only think of coming pleasures. He needed completion so he could think and breathe properly again. He knelt behind Patrick, relishing the feel of the tight flesh of Patrick's bum against his erection and his belly.

Patrick rocked back against him. "Now." He spoke through gritted teeth.

"Mm." Edmund slid a tentative finger between Patrick's cheeks, and the tight heat surrounded his finger.

"Now." Patrick twisted, reached back, and grabbed his thigh, pulling him forward.

It took some fumbling and a muttered curse, and then he was sliding into the heat, and it was more incredible than he could have imagined, because the body under his was Patrick, moving and pushing.

He rested his cheek against the flexing muscles of Patrick's back and gently arched his pelvis, feeling every single inhalation and motion through his entire body. He had joined with Patrick. He didn't want to move too much, or the way they fit perfectly together would end quickly. Just the smallest wiggle sent pleasurable vibrations through him.

"Move," Patrick ordered.

And Edmund did. He pushed forward until Patrick grunted, and then he pulled nearly out until that ring of muscles grabbed him, and *yes...* He thrust hard and deep over and over, his skin gliding over Patrick's strong body.

He was close, could feel the tingle in his entire body.

"Not yet," Patrick panted, which was almost enough to send Edmund careening over the edge. He slowed. Edmund reached around Patrick's hips and found that Patrick held his own cock. Ah, that was even more arousing. He wrapped his hand around Patrick's and squeezed.

"God." The word shot from Patrick, and their smooth motion together stumbled, slipped, and crashed. Patrick's orgasm tightened all his muscles, especially the ones that clenched Edmund, who buried himself in Patrick over and over, going deeper with each thrust.

Edmund almost allowed the cry to escape, but at the last minute, he pressed his mouth against Patrick's spine.

He peeled himself from Patrick's back but didn't move away. They separated only when Patrick collapsed facedown onto the bit of carpet they'd ended up on. Edmund examined Patrick's glistening body smeared with ointment and sweat, his lovely buttocks, powerful shoulders and thighs. "This is far more precious than any work of art," he announced and slapped Patrick's rear, a gratifyingly loud sound and sting on his palm. "It's prettier too."

Patrick rolled over and yanked him down onto his chest. "Sweet-talking man." His mouth opened wide in a huge yawn.

"You're going to fall asleep, aren't you."

"Perhaps."

Edmund wanted to protest, to point out that they must decide what should be done, if they could stay together. But instead, he settled on urging a nearly asleep Patrick off the floor and onto the mattress. That was plan enough for now.

A few hours later, he woke to the pleasant sight of Patrick shuffling around naked, his hair standing on end and his beard nearly grown a quarter inch. Edmund lay on his back to watch. Pink dawn flushed Patrick's skin.

He dressed, and at the end of that interesting show, Edmund closed his eyes.

He woke much later to find Patrick leaning over him. When Edmund smiled, Patrick didn't smile back.

"What's wrong?" he asked.

"They're going to move DePayne to a federal facility because he's been accused in the Boston murders as well. I took a fast jog over to see Greene. He agrees it'll be simple for you to see DePayne just in case it does, uh…" He looked down at Edmund's shoulder.

"In case it stirs a memory for me," Edmund finished for him. He sat, and the blanket Patrick must have put over him at dawn slid down his body. Patrick watched its journey, and his interest shown in his avid attention. Good.

Patrick's hand lay on his thigh for balance. Edmund traced the lines of his knuckles. "This finishes your journey, doesn't it? You found me in England for this."

Patrick gave an impatient grunt. "You don't need to, you know. He's not talking much or making a lot of sense, but apparently he's said enough to put him away. They don't need you."

"I wasn't criticizing you. I just realized it would be the end of this for you."

"Me? Doesn't matter that it ends for *me*. You're the one I'm concerned about."

"I see, yes." Edmund had felt a spark of impatience too, but let it go out now. He'd managed to put aside all thoughts of the man who might have murdered his family—and who was Papa Sloan's brother. Now it was time to take them up again. "Thank you," he added. "I'll get dressed as quickly as I can."

The day was overcast and slightly muggy.

Patrick frowned as they stepped out of his apartment building. "You're far too well groomed to be visiting the Tombs."

"Hardly." Edmund wasn't used to dressing himself and knew his shirt looked wrinkled, his collar slightly wilted, and his tie knot less than perfect. "What is the proper dress for visiting a jail? A morning coat? Business attire?"

"The smell of the place might stick to your clothes, fair warning," Patrick said.

Edmund's steps slowed, and Patrick eyed him. "It'll be fine," he said, and apparently decided he must keep Edmund's spirits up, because as they walked to the corner to catch a cab, Patrick chattered. "Mr. Greene wanted to meet you, but I told him you'd rather not. He's sending along one of the office's clerks to take notes, a secretary named Chris Larson. You'll like Chris. He's a straightforward sort of guy."

Edmund stepped back while Patrick waved down a hackney, a large old thing that reeked of cheap hair oil. They climbed in, and for a moment, the sheen of the oil on the black leather seat reminded Edmund of the night before, the way Patrick's body had gleamed. The twist of yearning took him by surprise, but he was grateful for anything that distracted him from this errand.

The Tombs, with its enormous squat façade complete with peculiar columns, seemed to loom over all who came near the place. Once they went inside, the shouts and clangs added to a dismal atmosphere.

Patrick pulled him into a small office near the main entrance. "We can wait here."

"I don't want to wait. I want to get this done with." His skin felt as if ants crawled over him. He twitched, ready to be gone. This reminded him of the dreary times he'd had to sit through meals, except he'd thought those time had ended.

Patrick was speaking, and Edmund had to ask him to repeat the words.

"We'll wait for Chris, all right?"

Edmund nodded. He scratched the side of his neck and wondered why Americans used each other's first names so often.

Just as he began to wonder if Patrick would object if he ran from the dreadful building, gibbering, a knock came on the door, and a slight old man with a red nose and drooping ears entered.

Edmund must have behaved politely and given correct responses, because Patrick didn't stare or make remarks. But whatever Edmund said, or was said to him, vanished from his thoughts immediately.

They were admitted into the huge main hall with cells lining each side. The noise and stench didn't bother him as much as his own thoughts.

The large, bald orderly with an odd gray cap perched on his head led them up the metal stairs and along the passageway lit from above. Because they were walking, Edmund no longer felt the need to be sick. He even examined the men staring back from their dimly lit cells.

Their little party stopped on the second floor, where the sound was not so echoing and pervasive. Mr. Greene's clerk pulled out a pencil and small notebook. Patrick shuffled a little closer to Edmund, who was warmed by a sudden surge of gratitude for his presence. He didn't think he needed Patrick's strength and affection to survive, but certainly the world was a sweeter place because of them.

"There." The orderly indicated a corner enclosure. "He's a popular man with the newspapermen, but he won't say much of anything to the reporters or anyone else. The boss has ordered most people to stay away now. You all must be special."

Patrick inched so close that Edmund felt the heat radiating from him. He always seemed so much warmer than other people. All that life coursing through him, Edmund supposed. So very different from the prisoner he finally forced himself to look at.

A middle-aged man leaned against the bars, staring at nothing. He was entirely gray—gray hair, gray clothes, gray skin, gray hair, and dull, gray eyes. He might have had Papa Sloan's thin nose, but otherwise, nothing about him seemed familiar. His chin barely existed, his eyes were too close together—the man vaguely resembled a mole that had been coated in bone dust.

"He's so small," Edmund murmured to Patrick.

"Does he look familiar?" the clerk asked.

Mr. Larson must have been slightly deaf, for his voice rang out. It seemed to wake the prisoner from a kind of trance. He blinked and turned his head to study them.

"No," Edmund said with relief.

The man's gaze seemed to sharpen as he studied Edmund. "Do I know you?" he inquired with the polite tones of a gentleman.

"No, you don't." Edmund took a step closer. Patrick moved with him, lending him courage.

"I believe you're mistaken." The man's face brightened, but only enough so he looked less like a corpse. "Your eyes," he said. "Those eyes." He cupped his fingers. His smile showed only a few teeth and dark places where the others had been. "I have touched eyes like that. Put them in a bowl."

He'd gouged out the Lawton family's eyes. He studied DePayne's hands. Odd to think those skinny fingers held any strength, but then again, he'd done all that after the mother, father, and children lay dead. He couldn't have done anything of the sort to Edmund now.

Patrick stirred and cleared his throat. "Oh, yes?" he said. "That family in London?"

The man sighed. "Dear me, I miss London."

"I'm asking about the family you killed. The Lawtons in London."

"My brother asked me about that over and over. Ken did too. And here too—the talking wouldn't cease."

Edmund imagined slamming that little figure to the ground. He'd likely apologize for hurting such a pathetic creature.

Patrick's hand settled on Edmund's shoulder. Comforting him? Trying to pull him away?

Edmund leaned against him for a moment.

Larson must have thought he was about to faint, because he said, "Mr. Kelly? We must go. Mr. Sloan is not well."

Edmund straightened at once. "I am fine. That…" Not man, no, he was too far gone for that. "He's the one who is unwell." He pointed at DePayne, the nightmare come to life.

DePayne's head bobbed. "I think you're correct in that." He swallowed, and his Adam's apple moved.

"Are you sorry you killed my family?" Edmund asked. He realized his hands were trembling and wished they didn't. And what a stupid question to ask. Why had he bothered? Why didn't he just turn and leave?

Even over the noise of the jail, he heard the scratch of Larson's pencil on paper, as if this interview would do anything at all.

"Your family? Is that how I know you? Your family?" DePayne blinked.

"He's mad. So I suppose he won't be put to death," Edmund whispered to Patrick, who scowled at DePayne.

"Those eyes," DePayne said again. "I wish they'd stop staring."

Was that close to a yes, he was sorry? Edmund leaned forward. "Your brother is dead."

"Charlie? No, I would have heard."

"You're hearing now. I'm bringing you the news of Charles Sloan's death. I am his son, Edmund Sloan, and I'm telling you he's dead."

"Now I know who you are. Yes. I remember." He leered, and for the first time, he seemed entirely awake and alert. Dreadful joy filled his face, pure mad evil. But Edmund didn't feel anything like fear—his anxiety had all been used up.

"Sweet little boy," DePayne whispered. "That's what Ken said too. You're not just him, are you?"

"I have had another name. I'm Ned Lawton," Each time Edmund said this, his long-dead family seemed more real.

"Poor little Ned Lawton," DePayne said. "You have the eyes. That must be true then."

Edmund didn't bother to answer. His strength and contempt built with every moment he held that mad stare. At last, the man blinked. The light went out of his face. "Charlie. No, I must believe you. Oh no, oh no. My brother." DePayne finally did something that touched Edmund with horror. He began to cry. "Oh Charlie, Charlie. He hated me." He sobbed. Hitting himself on the head, he stumbled away to the platform that served as his bed. The gray man curled onto his side, his back to them, and cried like a child.

Edmund felt oddly like a bully as if he'd hurt an already injured animal. Seeing the monster cringing and in tears should have given him a sense of satisfaction, but DePayne looked pathetic and small as he writhed and wept. Under the rough gray shirt, he was so thin, his spine was visible.

"And who is this damned Ken?" Patrick began savagely, but stopped when it became clear that DePayne was lost to the world.

Edmund grabbed Patrick's arm and clutched it like a life preserver. He would not feel pity for DePayne. He refused. But he understood that the murderer's mind suffered…and how disappointing to learn it didn't help to know that.

This visit had been thoroughly unsatisfying, but could one ever gain satisfaction for what had happened to him and his family? Not likely.

He had gained Patrick through all this, he reminded himself, and pretended to feel faint so that Patrick had to gather him close, put an arm around him, and help him away from the sight of pitiful gray little Mr. DePayne/Sloan.

Outside, away from the sewage and swampy smell of the jail, all of them seemed to straighten and breathe deeply again.

Mr. Larson looked pleased as he read over his transcript. "He basically admitted Charles Sloan is his brother, so that will help with the identification. And the thing he said about the eyes…other victims." He abruptly stopped and looked up at that, perhaps aware that might reawaken bad memories for Edmund, who nodded. Larson finished with, "Well. That conversation should be helpful. And Mr. Greene will be pleased to have such a notorious case solved by us. I'll wager he'll come across with a bonus for you, Patrick."

"I hope so. I'll settle for less complaining about my travel bills." Patrick didn't seem happy. He frowned as he shook hands with the lawyer and parted ways.

Edmund and Patrick climbed into a large carriage. On this cloudy day, in a conveyance with dirty windows, it almost felt as if they sat in a dark little room, a pantry or closet.

Edmund didn't mind. He'd once disliked small spaces. Now he couldn't care less where he was, especially if Patrick was with him. Their sides were pressed together, so he felt the shudder run through Patrick's body.

"Are you all right?" Edmund asked.

"That was…" Patrick said. "He was…awful. But I'm fine. Jesus God, Ned, I should be asking you that. I'm sorry."

"I almost wish he'd been a giant creature, or that I even remembered him. Or he'd said something that would allow me to vanquish him." Edmund stared out the window.

Would that pathetic form show up in his nightmares now? And then it occurred to him that he couldn't recall the last time he'd had a nightmare. Perhaps the vanquishing had already occurred. He drew in a long breath, a relieved sigh, but then caught a whiff of the Tombs.

"I want to go back to my hotel," Edmund said.

"Oh Christ, I shouldn't have taken you there. I'm so sorry. I should never have forced you to face him."

"You didn't. Recall that this visit was my idea. And do relax, Patrick."

"I'm not sure I can."

"What's the matter?"

"He was so small and weak. The terrible acts he performed. They were tied, but still… How could he have done all that on his own? The acts in New York, I mean. And some of the things he said were…wrong."

"What?"

"It was a long time ago but the scene at your house—the Lawtons' house—was different enough from the ones here in the United States."

"What are you saying?"

"He said the eyes were in a bowl. That was a detailed described in the paper at one of the scenes here in the United States. But not at the Lawtons'."

Ned's head filled with heavy darkness as if he'd pass out. "No." Curious how his own croaking voice came from above their heads. "The Lawtons' were laid out by the killer, weren't they?"

"Yes." Patrick said. "That was a detail that been different. I think this man, Mr. Sloan, either has mixed up his own murders or …"

Edmund didn't want to say the rest, but he did. "Or he's not the man."

"Dammit, I should have kept digging. Once they found DePayne, I stopped worrying. But then this Ken he mentioned…" Patrick stopped and shook his head.

Edmund groaned. "Oh no. Please no. I did so want to stop thinking about this," Edmund knew he sounded like a cross child again and wished he'd kept his mouth shut.

"It has nothing to do with you, Ned." Patrick came out of his distracted fever for a moment to focus on Edmund. "You've been through the wringer and hung up to dry. That prison was bad enough, huh? Please don't worry. I just need to ask a few more questions, not that I'll get answers anyone will understand. Probably a waste of time. No need for you to waste yours too."

Patrick had provided comfort once more. Edmund borrowed some for strength.

"That's fine. I'm going to help." He pulled off a glove and allowed himself to touch Patrick's face. "If you're going to work on this, so will I. Consider me a member of your staff and tell me what we'll do next."

Patrick swore and pulled away. He began patting his pockets frantically.

Startled, Edmund said, "Clearly, you don't require my help. Did I do something wrong?"

"No, you said something right. Because we have to do something now. The staff. No one pays attention to the blasted servants. You've figured it out. I know that name. Ken." He pulled out a notebook and began to flip through it. "The nanny said her brother..." He ran a finger down the page. "He was working for your father—Mr. Sloan, I mean."

"Many people worked for him."

"Yes, but this devil has a connection to both of your families. The nanny with the Lawtons had a brother who also worked for Mr. Sloan. His name is Kenneth."

He stabbed the book. "Here it is. She called him Ken." He looked up from the book, his face turned to Edmund, though he seemed to be staring at something in concentration. "God, and she even said he was peculiar. Oh, and she knew how much it cost to send letters to America. A manservant sent with your foster father's brother, perhaps?"

Ned shuddered at the thought of more murderers walking free. "Good Lord, one wonders how all of these bad men managed to get away with it."

"The British authorities had already captured Weller, who was guilty as sin and kept his mouth shut about the other two murderers. Dammit, I don't have the London polices' excuse for not looking harder. I knew I was looking for someone else." Patrick sounded furious—with himself. "Ned, I'm so sorry. I can't go back to your hotel with you."

"I know. We have to return to the Tombs and talk to Gregory Sloan again."

"Not we." He thumped on the carriage ceiling to stop the driver. "You don't have to go back there."

Edmund managed something that sounded like a laugh. "Indeed, I'd hoped never to set foot in there again. I'm sure that's true of nearly everyone who enters that desolate place. But I must if we're to end this."

The driver opened the door on the roof. "Gentlemen?"

Patrick stared at Edmund. "You can face this again so soon? You're sure?"

Edmund silenced the last of his frightened child. "I am indeed."

Patrick ordered the driver to turn around.

Chapter Fourteen

It took all of Patrick's smooth talking and a nice bribe, but within an hour, they sat outside the cage that held the pathetic Gregory Sloan/Mr. DePayne.

"You again," the little man said with some interest. His eyes glittered. Too bad he seemed too interested in Ned.

Patrick would have to do something about that. "Hey, lookit me."

The pale eyes shifted briefly.

"Tell me about Ken."

The gaze went back to Ned.

"Ken," Ned said.

"He isn't around very often. We ran out of money."

Patrick took a step closer, blocking DePayne's view of Ned. "Is he American?"

"Now he is." DePayne scooted to the edge of his shelf. "Why should I talk to you?"

Patrick said, "I might keep the policemen from killing you."

DePayne's eyes widened. "They wouldn't dare. My brother is a well-known lawyer in London. A barrister."

The man's mind was slipping, and that might help them or end up giving them nonsense. Either way, Patrick wouldn't be the one to remind him that his brother was dead. "Of course your brother wants to help. In fact, it was Mr. Sloan who sent me. He wishes to know how the servant Ken..." He fought for the second name. Dalton? No that was the nanny's imaginary married name. "He wants to know if the servant, Miller, is satisfactory"

"Ken is not a servant. He is in charge. He told me so."

"So the manservant your brother hired for you treats you badly?"

"He lets me have fun now and then. The money stopped coming, and he grew angry. We had to go find some, and that's when we had some fun. He grows furious, though." He sighed and lay down on his side. "I'm tired. Leave me alone."

"I won't until you finish answering questions about Ken Miller. Has he abandoned you?"

"They found me on the street. They asked me about him, but I didn't say anything much. I don't want him in here with me. He'll kick me again."

"No! That is awful. Your servant behaved disgracefully."

Patrick had sympathized with villains before and had some good results, but the small man on the other side of the bars must have been too far removed from reality. DePayne only yawned.

Ned spoke up, sounding more like a bored policeman taking a statement than a man facing his own family's murderer. "What does Miller look like?"

"An enormous egg with wrinkles."

Patrick asked, "What color hair?"

"No, he's an egg. Though a bit of white hair." DePayne drew a circle around his head.

Ned cocked his head to the side, confused, but Patrick said, "Do you mean like a monk's tonsure?"

DePayne didn't answer. He drew himself into a tight ball.

Patrick tried some more, but Ned was the one who reached out to hit the bars. "Here, listen to me, Mr. DePayne, or I should say Mr. Sloan. Listen."

The little man untucked enough to look out at him. "Yes?"

"Did Miller make you do horrible things to people when you broke into their houses?"

DePayne's eyes filled with tears. "We have had fun." He buried his face in his hands.

Ned folded his arms and took a step backward, as if recoiling. "His sorrow is born of nostalgia, not regret. Do you suppose we'll get anything more?" He still sounded brisk and businesslike.

Patrick took a moment to squeeze Ned's arm before trying again with DePayne. "Your brother the lawyer asked me to find Miller. He must want me to remind Miller who is servant and who is master."

"He is master," DePayne said at once.

Patrick scrambled for another tack. "But you said Miller was upset when there was no more money. I have some for him from Mr. Sloan. That'll please him, I expect? And he'll be able to pay to get you out of here."

"You came from Charles?" DePayne looked up from his hands, his forehead wrinkled. "But...but didn't someone say he was dead? Charles is dead?"

"He'd want to help you," Ned coaxed. "Where did you live?"

DePayne said nothing, and Patrick wondered if they had enough to go with, when DePayne spoke at last. "Out our window we saw Colored people," DePayne said slowly. "They were ill. Colored people."

"Do you mean the hospital?"

"None of this is my fault," DePayne muttered. "Charles wouldn't care about that, would he. He stopped sending money, so we had to live where we could. Get money where we could. If you see Miller, tell him to come get me."

He didn't speak again, and soon the guard who'd accompanied Patrick and Ned said their time was up.

They managed to leave the prison with enough time to visit Greene's Agency offices near the Grand Central Depot. Patrick led Ned up the narrow staircase to the etched glass door.

Mr. Greene wasn't there, but Donwell, the clerk, stood at the tall, polished desk at the entrance.

"There you are, Kelly." He began to give Patrick bunkum about his long absence in England. With his pointed beard and pince-nez, Donwell seemed more like a schoolteacher than a clerk, and he did like to discipline the agents. He probably regretted not having a ruler to hit the back of Patrick's hand.

Patrick wasn't in the mood. He interrupted Donwell's diatribe about the weekly check-in procedures of an agent abroad. "No time, Donny. I'm in a rush. Gimme a City Guide or maybe King's Guide," Patrick said.

He grabbed the two-volume guide to New York and led Ned to his cubbyhole of an office at the back. "I hope this is all we'll need. The cops picked up DePayne in Manhattan, and he didn't have money to go anywhere else, so they figured he lived here."

They thumbed through the guides in silence. Patrick found what he was looking for in a couple of minutes. "Here are two addresses that might work. One is 65th and First Avenue—the Colored Home and Hospital. Or maybe this one, at 135 West 30th, the New York Colored Mission."

Patrick ripped out pages from his notebook. He scribbled the addresses, then began to write details of what DePayne had said for his boss. "The addresses are about three miles apart. We'll go to the mission first because it's closer." He wrote so quickly, his hand hurt, and he flexed it once or twice before going back to transcribing his notes. "I've got to get this to Greene as soon as I can."

"Why?"

"I need help checking both addresses."

"I'll go to one place and you the other," Ned said.

Patrick stopped writing and tried to think of a diplomatic answer. He couldn't very well say he didn't trust Ned to take care of himself. But the long silence must have said as much to Ned.

"I promise I won't try to accost Miller or fall into some sort of fit if I see him." Ned rose to his feet and began to pace. "I'm well, and

I'm finally doing something about the Lawtons—about my family's murder."

Patrick watched and tapped the end of his pencil on the desk while he formulated an answer that wouldn't insult Ned. "I trust you'd have nerve enough for the job, but I'd feel better if you came with me. Miller is a violent man, and you're not a brawler."

Ned growled something that might have been a curse, then added, "Fine, let's go."

They strode to the front, where Donwell listened to Patrick without interruption. He might be an ass, but Donwell did a fairly good job when he had to. He glanced at his watch. "I'll send round a boy to Mr. Greene's."

"And you'll contact the police as well." Ned spoke in his best lordly manner.

Patrick and Donwell exchanged a look.

"We try not to involve the police, sir," Donwell said. He cleared his throat—and seemed on the verge of asking who exactly he was.

Patrick jumped in with an explanation. "It would make us look pretty damned stupid if the whole thing was DePayne's imagination. We better get going. See you, Donwell."

He ushered Ned out the door into the long shadows of the afternoon.

"You don't want the police to get credit for Miller's capture, do you," Ned said as they strode toward a line of carriages. "But if he escapes because no one contacted the police…"

He didn't finish his thought, so Patrick did. "If he's guilty and gets away, I'll quit my job. But see, the thing is, the cops don't like being shown up as fools. It'll take some arguing to point out that they overlooked their suspect's servant, and I don't want to take the time to convince them."

He gave the address to the driver, then climbed into the hansom with Ned.

It was one of the smaller models of hansom, closed in because of the threat of rain, but Patrick liked the close space because he could talk quietly without the driver or any pedestrians overhearing. He confessed the rest of the story to Ned. "You know I was a cop a few years ago. I didn't tell you how I didn't leave the force on good terms. I peached on my fellow officers."

"You what?"

"I informed on 'em. I worked with a state office that was supposed to rid the city of corruption. The office didn't have the funds or enough power. In the end, the attempt to clean up the department didn't do much good. It's mortifying to remember how fast word got out I was one of the rats, and that ended my career."

"You have no reason to be embarrassed."

"I felt like a fool, that's why. Not quite Don Quixote tilting at windmills, but close enough."

"I don't understand why you should feel that way. You made a sincere attempt to improve the work you care about. You were doing your duty, and despite the fact that it cost you your job, I'd say you were a hero, not a fool."

Patrick's heart swelled at the affection and indignation on Ned's face. "Thank you. When you say it like that, I'm less annoyed with myself."

"Good. It's time I helped you face your past the way you made me face mine."

"You were never a fool about anything, Ned. Not really." Patrick wished he could pull him into an embrace. He slid closer on the leather seat so they touched from hip to thigh, and Ned's heat seemed to soak through his whole left side and spread through him.

As the carriage passed under the shadow of the busy street car barn with its huge mansard towers and the raised tracks, Patrick came back to himself. "We're almost there. Try to look like a tourist. I'll be your friendly native guide showing you about New York. That way if we gawk at the buildings, no one will think we're oddities." He pulled a rumpled map from his inside pocket. "This will help."

The Colored Home and Hospital looked like any other hospital in the city. The nurses walking up the steps wore the white aprons and headdresses of any nurse. The only difference was the color of their skin.

Patrick had heard plans to build a massive new apartment complex, but in the meantime, the buildings surrounding the hospital were the usual mix of stores, most with apartments above.

Patrick stood in front of the hospital facing away from it. He made a slow circle, estimating the numbers of apartments with a view of the hospital entrance. He put his hands on his hips. "This won't be easy. Miller must have been what passed for brains with those three since he hasn't been caught. We'll go door to door and ask shopkeepers."

"And we might ask a postman, should we find one." Ned hesitated. "Won't the shops will be closing soon?"

"And what's your point?"

"We'd get more done if we didn't work together."

Patrick really, really hated letting Ned out of his sight. "Fine, but we'll stick close. Got that? Neither of us wandering off on his own."

Ned gave a curt nod, and they worked their way down the apartments to the end of the block. Then they threaded their way past several carriages and a cart to cross the street. Ned talked to a man at a newspaper stand, while Patrick talked to a woman with a nearly empty pushcart.

Patrick was just walking to the tobacconists when he heard the newsstand man, a burly fellow with a checkered cap, tell Ned in ringing tones, "I don't know nothing about the hair 'cause he always got on a hat, but he's pale as butter and has no chin. He got an accent like yours. English, am I right?"

He put out his hand. Ned looked at his face and then hand, confused, but Patrick knew what the man wanted. He dropped some coins onto his palm.

The man pointed one grubby finger at a tailor's shop two doors down. "Lives there."

"Anything else?"

The man said no. Patrick thanked him and dropped another few coins onto his outstretched palm.

Ned had already started toward the building, and Patrick raced to catch up. He grabbed Ned's arm. "You weren't thinking of going there alone, were you?" Patrick snarled.

Ned shook off his grip. "I promise you I'm not an incompetent fool. I was only going to ask to look at the names. Why are you so worried?"

Patrick shoved his hands into his pockets. "Dammit, I like knowing you're safe."

"I shan't have that reassurance about you, will I?"

Patrick didn't have an answer for that, other than cursing or stomping his feet.

"No one is safe, not on the street, not in his home," Ned said softly. "I know that better than anyone."

He pulled open the door next to the tailor's shop. Patrick froze when he heard the newsstand man's carrying voice. "Those guys, there," he said. "Them."

Chapter Fifteen

Patrick suddenly leapt down the front steps and broke into a run.

"Patrick?" Ned let go of the heavy front door. He trotted back down to follow, but Patrick ran too quickly. A tall figure rounded the corner, and Patrick pelted after him.

The newsstand man leaned on his elbows at the front of his small booth, watching Patrick tearing down the pavement. As Ned passed the stand, the man called to him, "That's him. The guy you were asking about."

Edmund slowed. "Why on earth did you tell him we were looking for him?"

The man shrugged and shook some coins in his hand, probably the same ones Patrick had given him. "Guy's been paying me to keep an eye out for cops. No reason I can't do both, I say."

A sharp crack rang out. "Summon the police," Edmund called to the man and the tobacconist who'd come out of his shop. Because he'd long ago learned how much the public enjoyed murder, he shouted, "That man is responsible for the gruesome murders on Lafayette Street." Then he ran as fast as he could. Behind him, he heard shrill whistles and cries of "Police!"

Ned almost passed the narrow alleyway where two figures struggled on the ground. Patrick lay on his back. He and the other man grabbed at each other's hands. No, Patrick was trying to get control of the gun the other man held.

Ned dashed into the alley, keeping his attention on the gun's barrel. When it pointed in his direction, he kept running, veering slightly to the side.

The two fighters were so involved in trying to get control of the gun or gouge each other's eyes out, they didn't notice Edmund. He grabbed a brick, which crumbled in his hand.

He spotted bits of a broken china bowl—probably a chamber pot, but he only cared that one large piece had a sharp and pointed edge.

The gun went off, and Edmund dropped to his knees instinctively, swallowing his shout for Patrick—they still didn't seem to notice him. For a few heartbeats, he watched to see if the bullet had struck either combatant, but neither slowed in the struggle.

They rolled and scraped across the ground. The bowler hat fell off the other man's head, revealing a nearly bald pate with fringe of dark brown hair—unnaturally dark brown.

Another twist of bodies. Miller dropped the gun but used his elbow to smash Patrick's head down on the cobblestones. Patrick stopped moving. Miller reached for the gun, but Edmund was there. He slammed his booted foot onto Miller's fingers.

"Stop," Edmund shouted, but Miller only screamed an obscenity and reached for the weapon again with his bloody hand.

Edmund kicked the gun away, then dropped down next to Miller. "Stop, would you," he screamed. Miller rolled closer to the gun.

"Stop!" He'd been thrown into one of those dreams where he'd scream and no one would listen. Edmund rose from his crouch.

Miller growled and turned toward him. Their eyes met, and Edmund flinched at the pure insane fury.

Miller said something under his breath and climbed to his feet. He took a limping step toward Edmund. "Don't come nearer," Edmund said. "Kenneth Miller, stop moving."

Miller stopped and blinked. "We've met?" He sounded like a man halted on the street by an acquaintance whose name he can't recall. A perfectly normal man.

The words burst from Edmund. "You killed my family. You, Weller, and maybe that pathetic Gregory Sloan. You killed my family."

"Little Lawton. All growed up? It's that long ago." Miller pursed his lips. "Your family was so pretty."

"Until you met up with them." Edmund would not let the rage chilling his veins control him. "You hurt your own sister."

"That was for her own good." Miller sounded outraged too.

Though he limped now, Miller moved quickly—but Edmund moved faster. Miller might have escaped, but not after Edmund slashed at his face and neck with the sharp pottery shard. The hard edge cut Edmund's hand a little, but he didn't care. He struck out again and again.

Miller fell to his knees, put his hands to his neck, and began to scream, a hoarse animal cry.

Ned dropped the pottery fragment. He scrambled around Miller to Patrick, who'd rolled onto his hands and knees.

Someone else yelled, "Stop!" Heavy boots thudded down the alley. The police had arrived.

They waited for a police wagon to take them to the station. Edmund's hand that had held the pottery shard had stopped bleeding, and Patrick waved off the doctor who'd been fetched from the Colored Hospital.

"Very well, you should go see a white doctor about your thick skull," the doctor said with frosty politeness. He had a thick New York accent.

"I don't object to your race," Patrick said. "It's your profession I don't like. I don't need a doctor."

"Keep getting into street brawls, and you better learn to love us." The doctor turned and strode back to his hospital, his white coat flapping.

Edmund felt sick as he looked at Patrick's face, still smeared with blood. The sight only reminded him of the danger Patrick had escaped. At least no visions from the long-dead past rose; apparently the present nightmare was enough to keep Edmund's busy brain occupied.

The man he loved had nearly died. The thought made Edmund so angry, he wanted to throttle Patrick. "Now I understand why you worried about my presence during the hunt," he snarled at Patrick. "I think I hate your job."

"Thank you for saving my life," Patrick said.

They spoke softly so the policeman standing near them couldn't hear.

They sat on the steps of a building, waiting for a police wagon. Miller had been taken to a hospital—and not the one across the street.

As they waited, a large, well-polished carriage rolled up. A fat man in impeccable evening wear exited, adjusting his top hat. He had several chins and a waxed mustache.

"Kelly!" he shouted. Another man emerged, Edmund recognized Mr. Foster, the man who'd accompanied them to the jail. Had that meeting really taken place only that morning?

Two more men in white tie and top hats gathered on the sidewalk. Each well-dressed man congratulated Patrick and shook his hand and patted him on the back, despite the fact that his clothes were covered with muck and garbage from the alley.

"Sir, may I introduce you to Mr. Edmund Sloan?" Patrick could show good manners after all.

Edmund shook hands with the gleaming fat man and then several others. His bandaged hand burned when they grasped it. He didn't mind the pain. The cut he'd given himself holding the pottery shard kept him focused on the fact that he'd attacked the attacker.

Once the police had been mollified, Mr. Greene decided to keep the impromptu celebration going.

"We'll go to an oyster house. Can't very well take you tattered boys to Delmonico's," Mr. Greene said.

The restaurant was hardly shabby, and there was a cloakroom where Edmund and Patrick washed their hands and faces and even brushed the worst of the dirt off their clothes.

Edmund stood at the bar with the others, his foot resting on the brass rail. He drank. He couldn't eat a bite, but he also didn't want to leave, not without Patrick. He watched them toss back oysters and glasses of beer, talking and laughing and smoking all the while.

One beer down, and Edmund's panic ebbed. Yet the horror lurked still. How amazing that this sort of existence was normal for these men... First a prison and then a scene of violence? No, not normal for them, only for Patrick, a man of action. The others, in their clean evening clothes, lived vicariously through him.

"And you, Mr. Sloan. This can't be the sort of visit you were expecting?" Mr. Greene said, not for the first time. He'd been fetched from a party, where he must have already consumed plenty of alcohol. "But New York has proved plenty exciting, eh?"

"I'd rather not see a gun pointed at me again."

Patrick, on his other side, seemed to lean against him just a little. "You don't know how sorry I am you had to cope with that," he murmured. "But without you, I'd be a good deal sorrier, or maybe not, since I'd be dead."

Edmund allowed his thigh to press against Patrick. He'd grown used to the desire that would strike him when they touched, but tonight it rose higher than ever, another sign of his body's primitive urges.

Maybe his savagery still showed, because another man asked, "But did it feel good to slash the bastard who'd done your family?"

Too good. Too much like the animals those three men had been. "Quite," he said icily and even through the fog of drink the men got the message: he didn't want talk about what he'd done to Miller. Not with these men, at any rate—maybe with Patrick, later, in the dark. His body liked that idea.

"Miller will survive to stand trial, and what do you bet he's capable of coherent thoughts, unlike that other DePayne monster. He'll give a good account of how we beat the New York and London Police," Mr. Greene said. Again. He'd gloated over that fact at least a few times.

A runner appeared, shouting Mr. Greene's name. It was a messenger sent by Donwell. Mr. Greene tipped him and handed the note to Mr. Foster.

"Don't have my glasses. Read it and tell us what's going on," Greene ordered.

Mr. Foster held the note close to a lamp burning near the huge silver-plated tray of oyster shells. After a minute, he said, "Donwell reports Miller is awake and better still, talking. Says here Miller claims he met Weller at the family estate when he was hired as servant to...to, um." He looked at Edmund, then continued, "To look after the man now known as DePayne. He says Weller was the one who thought of breaking into the Lawton house for money."

"Did he say why they did such awful things to the bodies of those poor people?" The gentleman who asked didn't even glance at Edmund's direction, so he probably didn't know Edmund's connection to the sordid past. Very good.

After another brief look at Edmund, Foster said, "No, they asked about the gruesome aspects of the crimes here and in England, but he had nothing to say on the matter. Miller did claim the Lawton nanny had no idea they were the perpetrators. That's why they blind-folded her and gave her chloroform."

"He would say she's innocent. She's his sister." Patrick tipped an oyster into his mouth, swallowed, and said, "Still, I don't think she knew the truth about her brother, or she wouldn't have let me into her house. And she did like the Lawtons. *All* of them." He gazed at Edmund as he spoke.

Edmund's throat had closed up. He put down his drink and stared at Patrick's hand resting on the polished bar near him. Those knuckles and the strong wrist seemed a good distraction from Edmund's usual frailty, because the sickness passed and he could swallow.

He finished his second beer and suddenly needed to walk, run, or fuck. His body needed to move.

"Thank you for your consideration this evening," he told Mr. Greene. "I'm glad we didn't have to spend hours at the police station. Mr. Foster, you'll come with me to make a statement? Good. Tomorrow at two."

He shook hands again and walked out of the bar. He'd return to the hotel. The cool evening breeze ruffled his hair, and he didn't want to put his hat on.

"Ned?" Patrick was out of breath behind him. "Did you mean to leave me behind?"

Had he meant to? He wasn't sure. He didn't seem to be thinking, only moving—operating on an animal level. Do animals hold on to their history? he thought. This is what happens when you disentangle yourself from the clutch of the past and swim to shore.

"No, I thought you had to stay with your employer."

"I'll see him tomorrow." Patrick raised a hand and whistled. A hack trundled over to them.

Once they settled into the darkness of the carriage, Patrick spoke again. "If you want me to go, to stop bothering you, I'd understand."

"No. All I want…" Edmund laughed like an idiot. His needs were so very simple for once. "I want to take a proper bath and change out of these clothes." *Perhaps burn them*, he didn't add.

"You swear you're all right?"

"Better than I ever expected."

"Do you mind if I go with you to your hotel? Just to make sure you're not shaken up?"

"I'm fine." Suddenly, Edmund felt better than fine. He was alive, free, and, more than that, ready to celebrate that truth—but not in a carriage. He nudged Patrick in the ribs. "Is that all you wanted to do?"

"Since you're asking, I'd hoped to bring you back to my place to keep an eye on you."

"And?" Edmund tapped his leg, then let his hand rest on Patrick's thigh.

"Well. I'd make sure you're all right, of course."

"I don't require you to take care of me, Mr. Kelly. I've outgrown that need. But listen. Whatever else happens from now on, I want you there," he told Patrick. "And about the immediate future—surely you have some ideas? Because I have quite a few for you. Assuming your head doesn't ache."

"Oh." The loquacious Patrick seemed speechless for once.

"Good. Every one of my plans begins with bathing. I wonder if we'd both fit in the hotel's tub. At the same time."

Patrick gave a sound that was something like a growl mixed with a moan. Pure lust that created a surge of anticipation in Edmund.

He pretended to misunderstand. "You're snarling? Oh dear. I don't mean to insult you or your apartment. Your home has its charms, but…"

Patrick's low laugh interrupted him. "Garbage. My place is a pit compared to your hotel, not to mention that mansion of yours back in England."

"It is not a pit." Edmund felt indignant. "I have spent a great deal of time there lately, waiting for you to arrive home. I love that apartment perhaps even more than my own home in London. I shall treasure that fine location for the rest of my life, I believe." He winced at his own sentimental response and Patrick's hoot of laughter.

"Aw, you must be joking with me. It's tiny, it doesn't have hot water, and the super is a lazy bastard."

"The stupor admired my clothes and allowed me to have a key, so I like thc man."

Patrick chuckled again. "Stupor fits, but I believe you mean the super."

"Yes, that's the gentleman in question. You ask me what's so special about your apartment? That's simple." He put his hands behind his head. "You. It's where I'd find you. I'm reminded of the great philosopher Gaius Plinius Secundus's saying: *ubi cor, ibi domus*."

Patrick moved closer and whispered in his ear. "You forget that I took almost as much Latin as you did. And I agree. Home is where the heart is."

The End

Look for these titles by Summer Devon

Solitary Shifter series:
Taming the Bander
Revealing the Beast
Releasing the Shifter

Single title
The Private Secretary
The Gentleman and the Lamplighter
Sibling Rivals
Goodbye Phillip
Tail of the Dog
Goodbye Phillip
Must Loathe Norcross
The Hanged Man's Hero
Hot Under the Collar
The Hanged Man's Hero

Victorian Gay Detective
His American Detective
His Irish Detective

Titles Written with Bonnie Dee:
Seducing Stephen
The Gentleman and the Rogue
The Nobleman and the Spy
Sin and the Preacher's Son
The Psychic and the Sleuth
The Gentleman's Keeper
The Gentleman's Madness
Mending Him
The Bohemian and the Banker
The Shepherd and Solicitor
The Professor and the Smuggler

Victorian Holiday Hearts series:
Simon and the Christmas Spirit
Will and the Valentine Saint
Mike and the Spring Awakening
Delaney and the Autumn Masque

Titles Written as Kate Rothwell (m/f romance)
Somebody Wonderful
Somebody to Love
Someone to Cherish
Thank You, Mrs. M
Seducing Miss Dunaway (free novella)

Protecting Miss Samuels
Powder of Sin
Her Mad Baron
Love Between the Lines
Mademoiselle Makes a Match
The Earl, a Girl, and a Promise

About the Author

Summer Devon is the alter ego of Kate Rothwell. Kate/Summer lives in Connecticut, USA, and also writes books, usually gaslight historicals, as Kate.

For more information about Summer and Kate, go to
http://katerothwell.com
http://summerdevon.com.

Summer can also be found at
https://www.facebook.com/S.DevonAuthor

Printed in Great Britain
by Amazon

42081495R00172